The Flying Inn

The Flying Inn
G.K. Chesterton

MINT EDITIONS

The Flying Inn was first published in 1914.

This edition published by Mint Editions 2021.

ISBN 9781513280530 | E-ISBN 9781513285559

Published by Mint Editions®

 MINT
EDITIONS

minteditionbooks.com

Publishing Director: Jennifer Newens
Design & Production: Rachel Lopez Metzger
Project Manager: Micaela Clark
Typesetting: Westchester Publishing Services

Contents

I

A SERMON ON INNS

The sea was a pale elfin green and the afternoon had already felt the fairy touch of evening as a young woman with dark hair, dressed in a crinkly copper-coloured sort of dress of the artistic order, was walking rather listlessly along the parade of Pebblewick-on-Sea, trailing a parasol and looking out upon the sea's horizon. She had a reason for looking instinctively out at the sea-line; a reason that many young women have had in the history of the world. But there was no sail in sight.

On the beach below the parade were a succession of small crowds, surrounding the usual orators of the seaside; whether niggers or socialists, whether clowns or clergymen. Here would stand a man doing something or other with paper boxes; and the holiday makers would watch him for hours in the hope of some time knowing what it was that he was doing with them. Next to him would be a man in a top hat with a very big Bible and a very small wife, who stood silently beside him, while he fought with his clenched fist against the heresy of Milnian Sublapsarianism so wide-spread in fashionable watering-places. It was not easy to follow him, he was so very much excited; but every now and then the words "our Sublapsarian friends" would recur with a kind of wailing sneer. Next was a young man talking of nobody knew what (least of all himself), but apparently relying for public favour mainly on having a ring of carrots round his hat. He had more money lying in front of him than the others. Next were niggers. Next was a children's service conducted by a man with a long neck who beat time with a little wooden spade. Farther along there was an atheist, in a towering rage, who pointed every now and then at the children's service and spoke of Nature's fairest things being corrupted with the secrets of the Spanish Inquisition—by the man with the little spade, of course. The atheist (who wore a red rosette) was very withering to his own audience as well. "Hypocrites!" he would say; and then they would throw him money. "Dupes and dastards!" and then they would throw him more money. But between the atheist and the children's service was a little owlish man in a red fez, weakly waving a green gamp umbrella. His face was brown and wrinkled like a walnut, his nose was of the sort we associate with Judæa, his beard was the sort of black wedge we associate rather with Persia. The young woman had never seen him before; he was a new exhibit in the now familiar museum of cranks and quacks. The young woman was one of those people in whom a real sense of humour is always at issue with a certain temperamental tendency to boredom or melancholia; and she lingered a moment, and leaned on the rail to listen.

It was fully four minutes before she could understand a word the man was saying; he spoke English with so extraordinary an accent that she supposed at first that he was talking in his own oriental tongue. All the noises of that articulation were odd; the most marked was an extreme prolongation of the short "u" into "oo"; as in "poo-oot" for "put." Gradually the girl got used to the dialect, and began to understand the words; though some time elapsed even then before she could form any conjecture of their subject matter. Eventually it appeared to her that he had some fad about English civilisation having been founded by the Turks; or, perhaps by the Saracens after their victory in the Crusades. He also seemed to think that Englishmen would soon return to this way of thinking; and seemed to be urging the spread of teetotalism as an evidence of it. The girl was the only person listening to him.

"Loo-ook," he said, wagging a curled brown finger, "loo-ook at your own inns" (which he pronounced as "ince"). "Your inns of which you write in your boo-ooks! Those inns were not poo-oot up in the beginning to sell ze alcoholic Christian drink. They were put up to sell ze non-alcoholic Islamic drinks. You can see this in the names of your inns. They are eastern names, Asiatic names. You have a famous public house to which your omnibuses go on the pilgrimage. It is called the Elephant and Castle. That is not an English name. It is an Asiatic name. You will say there are castles in England, and I will agree with you. There is the Windsor Castle. But where," he cried sternly, shaking his green umbrella at the girl in an angry oratorical triumph, "where is the Windsor Elephant? I have searched all Windsor Park. No elephants."

The girl with the dark hair smiled, and began to think that this man was better than any of the others. In accordance with the strange system of concurrent religious endowment which prevails at watering-places, she dropped a two shilling piece into the round copper tray beside him. With honourable and disinterested eagerness, the old gentleman in the red fez took no notice of this, but went on warmly, if obscurely, with his argument.

"Then you have a place of drink in this town which you call The Bool!"

"We generally call it The Bull," said the interested young lady, with a very melodious voice.

"You have a place of drink, which you call The Bool," he reiterated in a sort of abstract fury, "and surely you see that this is all vary ridiculous!"

"No, no!" said the girl, softly, and in deprecation.

"Why should there be a Bull?" he cried, prolonging the word in his own way. "Why should there be a Bull in connection with a festive locality? Who thinks about a Bull in gardens of delight? What need is there of a Bull when we watch the tulip-tinted maidens dance or pour the sparkling sherbert? You yourselves, my friends?" And he looked around radiantly, as if addressing an enormous mob. "You yourselves have a proverb, 'It is not calculated to promote prosperity to have a Bull in a china shop.' Equally, my friends, it would not be calculated to promote prosperity to have a Bull in a wine shop. All this is clear."

He stuck his umbrella upright in the sand and struck one finger against another, like a man getting to business at last.

"It iss as clear as the sun at noon," he said solemnly. "It iss as clear as the sun at noon that this word Bull, which is devoid of restful and pleasurable associations, is but the corruption of another word, which possesses restful and pleasurable associations. The word is not Bull; it is the Bul-Bul!" His voice rose suddenly like a trumpet and he spread abroad his hands like the fans of a tropic palm-tree.

After this great effect he was a little more subdued and leaned gravely on his umbrella. "You will find the same trace of Asiatic nomenclature in the names of all your English inns," he went on. "Nay, you will find it, I am almost certain, in all your terms in any way connected with your revelries and your reposes. Why, my good friends, the very name of that insidious spirit by which you make strong your drinks is an Arabic word: alcohol. It is obvious, is it not, that this is the Arabic article 'Al,' as in Alhambra, as in Algebra; and we need not pause here to pursue its many appearances in connection with your festive institutions, as in your Alsop's beer, your Ally Sloper, and your partly joyous institution of the Albert Memorial. Above all, in your greatest feasting day—your Christmas day—which you so erroneously suppose to be connected with your religion, what do you say then? Do you say the names of the Christian Nations? Do you say, 'I will have a little France. I will have a little Ireland. I will have a little Scotland. I will have a little Spain?' No—o." And the noise of the negative seemed to waggle as does the bleating of a sheep. "You say, 'I will have a little Turkey,' which is your name for the Country of the Servant of the Prophet!"

And once more he stretched out his arms sublimely to the east and west and appealed to earth and heaven. The young lady, looking at the sea-green horizon with a smile, clapped her grey gloved hands softly together as if at a peroration. But the little old man with the fez was far from exhausted yet.

"In reply to this you will object—" he began.

"O no, no," breathed the young lady in a sort of dreamy rapture. "I don't object. I don't object the littlest bit!"

"In reply to this you will object—" proceeded her preceptor, "that some inns are actually named after the symbols of your national superstitions. You will hasten to point out to me that the Golden Cross is situated opposite Charing Cross, and you will expatiate at length on King's Cross, Gerrard's Cross and the many crosses that are to be found in or near London. But you must not forget," and here he wagged his green umbrella roguishly at the girl, as if he was going to poke her with it, "none of you, my friends, must forget what a large number of Crescents there are in London! Denmark Crescent; Mornington Crescent! St. Mark's Crescent! St. George's Crescent! Grosvenor Crescent! Regent's Park Crescent! Nay, Royal Crescent! And why should we forget Pelham Crescent? Why, indeed? Everywhere, I say, homage paid to the holy symbol of the religion of the Prophet! Compare with this network and pattern of crescents, this city almost consisting of crescents, the meagre array of crosses, which remain to attest the ephemeral superstition to which you were, for one weak moment, inclined."

The crowds on the beach were rapidly thinning as tea-time drew nearer. The west grew clearer and clearer with the evening, till the sunshine seemed to have got behind the pale green sea and be shining through, as through a wall of thin green glass. The very transparency of sky and sea might have to this girl, for whom the sea was the romance and the tragedy, the hint of a sort of radiant hopelessness. The flood made of a million emeralds was ebbing as slowly as the sun was sinking: but the river of human nonsense flowed on for ever.

"I will not for one moment maintain," said the old gentleman, "that there are no difficulties in my case; or that all the examples are as obviously true as those that I have just demonstrated. No-o. It is obvious, let us say, that the 'Saracen's Head' is a corruption of the historic truth 'The Saracen is Ahead'—I am far from saying it is equally obvious that the 'Green Dragon' was originally 'the Agreeing Dragoman'; though I hope to prove in my book that it is so. I will only say here that it is su-urely more probable that one poo-ooting himself forward to attract the wayfarer in the desert, would compare himself to a friendly and persuadable guide or courier, rather than to a voracious monster. Sometimes the true origin is very hard to trace; as in the inn that commemorates our great Moslem Warrior, Amir Ali Ben Bhoze, whom you have so quaintly abbreviated into Admiral Benbow. Sometimes it is even more difficult for the seeker after truth. There is a place of drink near to here called 'The Old Ship'—"

The eyes of the girl remained on the ring of the horizon as rigid as the ring itself; but her whole face had coloured and altered. The sands were almost emptied by now: the atheist was as non-existent as his God; and those who had hoped to know what was being done to the paper boxes had gone away to their tea without knowing it. But the young woman still leaned on the railing. Her face was suddenly alive; and it looked as if her body could not move.

"It shood be admitted—" bleated the old man with the green umbrella, "that there is no literally self-evident trace of the Asiatic nomenclature in the words 'the old ship.' But even here the see-eeker after Truth can poot himself in touch with facts. I questioned the proprietor of 'The Old Ship' who is, according to such notes as I have kept, a Mr. Pumph."

The girl's lip trembled.

"Poor old Hump!" she said. "Why, I'd forgotten about him. He must be very nearly as worried as I am! I hope this man won't be too silly about this! I'd rather it weren't about this!"

"And Mr. Pumph to-old me the inn was named by a vary intimate friend of his, an Irishman who had been a Captain in the Britannic Royal Navy, but had resigned his po-ost in anger at the treatment of Ireland. Though quitting the service, he retained joost enough of the superstition of your western sailors, to wish his friend's inn to be named after his old ship. But as the name of the ship was 'The United Kingdom—'"

His female pupil, if she could not exactly be said to be sitting at his feet, was undoubtedly leaning out very eagerly above his head. Amid the solitude of the sands she called out in a loud and clear voice, "Can you tell me the Captain's name?"

The old gentleman jumped, blinked and stared like a startled owl. Having been talking for hours as if he had an audience of thousands, he seemed suddenly very much embarrassed to find that he had even an audience of one. By this time they seemed to be almost the only human creatures along the shore; almost the only living creatures, except the seagulls. The sun, in dropping finally, seemed to have broken as a blood orange might break; and lines of blood-red light were spilt along the split, low, level skies. This abrupt and belated brilliance took all the colour out of the man's red cap and green umbrella; but his dark figure, distinct against the sea and the sunset, remained the same, save that it was more agitated than before.

"The name," he said, "the Captain's name. I—I understood it was Dalroy. But what I wish to indicate, what I wish to expound, is that here again the seeker after truth can find the connection of his ideas. It was explained to me by Mr. Pumph that he was rearranging the place of festivity, in no inconsiderable proportion because of the anticipated return of the Captain in question, who had, as it appeared, taken service in some not very large Navy, but had left it and was coming home. Now, mark all of you, my friends," he said to the seagulls "that even here the chain of logic holds."

He said it to the seagulls because the young lady, after staring at him with starry eyes for a moment and leaning heavily on the railing, had turned her back and disappeared rapidly into the twilight. After her hasty steps had fallen silent there was no other noise than the faint but powerful purring of the now distant sea, the occasional shriek of a sea-bird, and the continuous sound of a soliloquy.

"Mark, all of you," continued the man flourishing his green umbrella so furiously that it almost flew open like a green flag unfurled, and then striking it deep in the sand, in the sand in which his fighting fathers had so often struck their tents, "mark all of you this marvellous fact! That when, being for a time, for a time, astonished—embarrassed— brought up as you would say short—by the absence of any absolute evidence of Eastern influence in the phrase 'the old ship,' I inquired from what country the Captain was returning, Mr. Pumph said to me in solemnity, 'From Turkey.' From Turkey! From the nearest country of the Religion! I know men say it is not our country; that no man knows where we come from, of what is our country. What does it matter where we come from if we carry a message from Paradise? With a great galloping of horses we carry it, and have no time to stop in places. But

G.K. CHESTERTON

what we bring is the only creed that has regarded what you will call in your great words the virginity of a man's reason, that has put no man higher than a prophet, and has respected the solitude of God."

And again he spread his arms out, as if addressing a mass meeting of millions, all alone on the dark seashore.

II

The End of Olive Island

The great sea-dragon of the changing colours that wriggles round the world like a chameleon, was pale green as it washed on Pebblewick, but strong blue where it broke on the Ionian Isles. One of the innumerable islets, hardly more than a flat white rock in the azure expanse, was celebrated as the Isle of Olives; not because it was rich in such vegetation, but because, by some freak of soil or climate, two or three little olives grew there to an unparalleled height. Even in the full heat of the South it is very unusual for an olive tree to grow any taller than a small pear tree; but the three olives that stood up as signals on this sterile place might well be mistaken, except for the shape, for moderate sized pines or larches of the north. It was also connected with some ancient Greek legend about Pallas the patroness of the olive; for all that sea was alive with the first fairyland of Hellas; and from the platform of marble under the olive trees could be seen the grey outline of Ithaca.

On the island and under the trees was a table set in the open air and covered with papers and inkstands. At the table were sitting four men, two in uniform and two in plain black clothes. Aides-de-camps, equerries and such persons stood in a group in the background; and behind them a string of two or three silent battle-ships lay along the sea. For peace was being given to Europe.

There had just come to an end the long agony of one of the many unsuccessful efforts to break the strength of Turkey and save the small Christian tribes. There had been many other such meetings in the later phases of the matter as, one after another, the smaller nations gave up the struggle, or the greater nations came in to coerce them. But the interested parties had now dwindled to these four. For the Powers of Europe being entirely agreed on the necessity for peace on a Turkish basis, were content to leave the last negotiations to England and Germany, who could be trusted to enforce it; there was a representative of the Sultan, of course; and there was a representative of the only enemy of the Sultan who had not hitherto come to terms.

For one tiny power had alone carried on the war month after month, and with a tenacity and temporary success that was a new nine-days marvel every morning. An obscure and scarcely recognized prince calling himself the King of Ithaca had filled the Eastern Mediterranean with exploits that were not unworthy of the audacious parallel that the name of his island suggested. Poets could not help asking if it were Odysseus come again; patriotic Greeks, even if they themselves had been forced to lay down their arms, could not help feeling curious as to what Greek race or name was boasted by the new and heroic royal house. It was, therefore, with some amusement that the world at last discovered that the descendant of Ulysses was a cheeky Irish adventurer named Patrick Dalroy; who had once been in the English Navy, had got into a quarrel through his Fenian sympathies and resigned his commission. Since then he had seen many adventures in many uniforms; and always got himself or some one else into hot water with an extraordinary mixture of cynicism and quixotry. In his fantastic little kingdom, of course, he had been his own General, his own Admiral, his own Foreign Secretary and his own Ambassador; but he was always careful to follow the wishes of his people in the essentials of peace and war; and it was at their direction that he had come to lay down his sword at last. Besides his professional skill, he was chiefly famous for his enormous bodily strength and stature. It is the custom in newspapers nowadays to say that mere barbaric muscular power is valueless in modern military actions, but this view may be as much exaggerated as its opposite. In such wars as these of the Near East, where whole populations are slightly armed and personal assault is common, a leader who can defend his head often has a real advantage; and it is not true, even in a general way, that strength is of no use. This was admitted by Lord Ivywood, the English Minister, who was pointing out in detail to King Patrick the hopeless superiority of the light pattern of Turkish field gun; and the King of Ithaca, remarking that he was quite convinced, said he would take it with him, and ran away with it under his arm. It would be conceded by the greatest of the Turkish warriors, the terrifying Oman Pasha, equally famous for his courage in war and his cruelty in peace; but who carried on his brow a scar from Patrick's sword, taken after three hours' mortal combat—and taken without spite or shame, be it said, for the Turk is always at his best in that game. Nor would the quality be doubted by Mr. Hart, a financial friend of the German Minister, whom Patrick Dalroy, after asking him which of his front windows he would prefer to be thrown into, threw into his bedroom window on the first floor with so considerate an exactitude that he alighted on the bed, where he was in a position to receive any medical attention. But, when all is said, one muscular Irish gentleman on an island cannot fight all Europe for ever, and he came, with a kind of gloomy good humour, to offer the terms now dictated to him by his adopted country. He could not even knock all the diplomatists down (for which he possessed both the power and the inclination), for he realised, with the juster part of his mind, that they were only obeying orders, as he was. So he sat heavily and sleepily at the little table, in the green and white uniform of the Navy of Ithaca (invented by himself); a big bull of a man, monstrously young for his size, with a bull neck and two blue bull's eyes for eyes, and red hair rising so steadily off his scalp that it looked as if his head had caught fire: as some said it had.

The most dominant person present was the great Oman Pasha himself, with his strong face starved by the asceticism of war, his hair and mustache seeming rather blasted with lightning than blanched with age; a red fez on his head, and between the red fez and mustache, a scar at which the King of Ithaca did not look. His eyes had an awful lack of expression.

Lord Ivywood, the English Minister, was probably the handsomest man in England, save that he was almost colourless both in hair and complexion. Against that blue marble sea he might almost have been one of its old marble statues that are faultless in line but show nothing but shades of grey or white. It seemed a mere matter of the luck of lighting whether his hair looked dull silver or pale brown; and his splendid mask never changed in colour or expression. He was one of the last of the old Parliamentary orators; and yet he was probably a comparatively young man; he could make anything he had to mention blossom into verbal beauty; yet his face remained dead while his lips were alive. He had little old-fashioned ways, as out of old Parliaments; for instance, he would always stand up, as in a senate, to speak to those three other men, alone on a rock in the ocean.

In all this he perhaps appeared more personal in contrast to the man sitting next to him, who never spoke at all but whose face seemed to speak for him. He was Dr. Gluck, the German Minister, whose face had nothing German about it; neither the German vision nor the German sleep. His face was as vivid as a highly coloured photograph and altered like a cinema: but his scarlet lips never moved in speech. His almond eyes seemed to shine with all the shifting fires of the opal; his small, curled black mustache seemed sometimes almost to hoist itself afresh, like a live, black snake; but there came from him no sound. He put a paper in front of Lord Ivywood. Lord Ivywood took a pair of eyeglasses to read it, and looked ten years older by the act.

It was merely a statement of agenda; of the few last things to be settled at this last conference. The first item ran:

"The Ithacan Ambassador asks that the girls taken to harems after the capture of Pylos be restored to their families. This cannot be granted." Lord Ivywood rose. The mere beauty of his voice startled everyone who had not heard it before.

"Your Excellencies and gentlemen," he said, "a statement to whose policy I by no means assent, but to whose historic status I could not conceivably aspire, has familiarised you with a phrase about peace with honour. But when we have to celebrate a peace between such historic soldiers as Oman Pasha and His Majesty the King of Ithaca, I think we may say that it is peace with glory."

He paused for half an instant; yet even the silence of sea and rock seemed full of multitudinous applause, so perfectly had the words been spoken.

"I think there is but one thought among us, whatever our many just objections through these long and harassing months of negotiations—I think there is but one thought now. That the peace may be as full as the war—that the peace may be as fearless as the war."

Once more he paused an instant; and felt a phantom clapping, as it were, not from the hands but the heads of the men. He went on.

"If we are to leave off fighting, we may surely leave off haggling. A statute of limitations or, if you will, an amnesty, is surely proper when so sublime a peace seals so sublime a struggle. And if there be anything in which an old diplomatist may advise you, I would most strongly say this: that there should be no new disturbance of whatever amicable or domestic ties have been formed during this disturbed time. I will admit I am sufficiently old-fashioned to think any interference with the interior life of the family a precedent of no little peril. Nor will I be so illiberal as not to extend to the ancient customs of Islam what I would extend to the ancient customs of Christianity. A suggestion has been brought before us that we should enter into a renewed war of recrimination as to whether certain women have left their homes with or without their own consent. I can conceive no controversy more perilous to begin or more impossible to conclude. I will venture to say that I express all your thoughts, when I say that, whatever wrongs may have been wrought on either side, the homes, the marriages, the family arrangements of this great Ottoman Empire, shall remain as they are today."

No one moved except Patrick Dalroy, who put his hand on his sword-hilt for a moment and looked at them all with bursting eyes; then his hand fell and he laughed out loud and sudden.

Lord Ivywood took no notice, but picked up the agenda paper again, and again fitted on the glasses that made him look older. He read the second item—needless to say, not aloud. The German Minister with the far from German face, had written this note for him:

"Both Coote and the Bernsteins insist there must be Chinese for the marble. Greeks cannot be trusted in the quarries just now."

"But while," continued Lord Ivywood, "we desire these fundamental institutions, such as the Moslem family, to remain as they are even at this moment, we do not assent to social stagnation. Nor do we say for one moment that the great tradition of Islam is capable alone of sustaining the necessities of the Near East. But I would seriously ask your Excellencies, why should we be so vain as to suppose that the only cure for the Near East is of necessity the Near West? If new ideas are needed, if new blood is needed, would it not be more natural to appeal to those most living, those most laborious civilisations which form the vast reserve of the Orient? Asia in Europe, if my friend Oman Pasha will allow me the criticism, has hitherto been Asia in arms. May we not yet see Asia in Europe and yet Asia in peace? These at least are the reasons which lead me to consent to a scheme of colonisation."

Patrick Dalroy sprang erect, pulling himself out of his seat by clutching at an olive-branch above his head. He steadied himself by putting one hand on the trunk of the tree, and simply stared at them all. There fell on him the huge helplessness of mere physical power. He could throw them into the sea; but what good would that do? More men on the wrong side would be accredited to the diplomatic campaign; and the only man on the right side would be discredited for anything. He shook the branching olive tree above him in his fury. But he did not for one moment disturb Lord Ivywood, who had just read the third item on his private agenda ("Oman Pasha insists on the destruction of the vineyards") and was by this time engaged in a peroration which afterwards became famous and may be found in many rhetorical text books and primers. He was well into the middle of it before Dalroy's rage and wonder allowed him to follow the words.

G.K. CHESTERTON

". . . do we indeed owe nothing," the diplomatist was saying "to that gesture of high refusal in which so many centuries ago the great Arabian mystic put the wine-cup from his lips? Do we owe nothing to the long vigil of a valiant race, the long fast by which they have testified against the venomous beauty of the Vine? Ours is an age when men come more and more to see that the creeds hold treasures for each other, that each religion has a secret for its neighbour, that faith unto faith uttereth speech, and church unto church showeth knowledge. If it be true, and I claim again the indulgence of Oman Pasha when I say I think it is true, that we of the West have brought some light to Islam in the matter of the preciousness of peace and of civil order, may we not say that Islam in answer shall give us peace in a thousand homes, and encourage us to cut down that curse that has done so much to thwart and madden the virtues of Western Christendom. Already in my own country the orgies that made horrible the nights of the noblest families are no more. Already the legislature takes more and more sweeping action to deliver the populace from the bondage of the all-destroying drug. Surely the prophet of Mecca is reaping his harvest; the cession of the disputed vineyards to the greatest of his champions is of all acts the most appropriate to this day; to this happy day that may yet deliver the East from the curse of war and the West from the curse of wine. The gallant prince who meets us here at last, to offer an olive branch even more glorious than his sword, may well have our sympathy if he himself views the cession with some sentimental regret; but I have little doubt that he also will live to rejoice in it at last. And I would remind you that it is not the vine alone that has been the sign of the glory of the South. There is another sacred tree unstained by loose and violent memories, guiltless of the blood of Pentheus or of Orpheus and the broken lyre. We shall pass from this place in a little while as all things pass and perish:

> *Far called, our navies melt away.*
> *On dune and headland sinks the fire,*
> *And all our pomp of yesterday*
> *Is one with Nineveh and Tyre.*

But so long as sun can shine and soil can nourish, happier men and women after us shall look on this lovely islet and it shall tell its own story; for they shall see these three holy olive trees lifted in everlasting benediction, over the humble spot out of which came the peace of the world."

The other two men were staring at Patrick Dalroy; his hand had tightened on the tree, and a giant billow of effort went over his broad breast. A small stone jerked itself out of the ground at the foot of the tree as if it were a grasshopper jumping; and then the coiled roots of the olive tree rose very slowly out of the earth like the limbs of a dragon lifting itself from sleep.

"I offer an olive branch," said the King of Ithaca, totteringly leaning the loose tree so that its vast shadow, much larger than itself, fell across the whole council. "An olive branch," he gasped, "more glorious than my sword. Also heavier."

Then he made another effort and tossed it into the sea below.

The German, who was no German, had put up his arm in apprehension when the shadow fell across him. Now he got up and edged away from the table; seeing that the wild Irishman was tearing up the second tree. This one came out more easily; and before he flung it after the first, he stood with it a moment; looking like a man juggling with a tower.

Lord Ivywood showed more firmness; but he rose in tremendous remonstrance. Only the Turkish Pasha still sat with blank eyes, immovable. Dalroy rent out the last tree and hurled it, leaving the island bare.

"There!" said Dalroy, when the third and last olive had splashed in the tide. "Now I will go. I have seen something today that is worse than death: and the name of it is Peace."

Oman Pasha rose and held out his hand.

"You are right," he said in French, "and I hope we meet again in the only life that is a good life. Where are you going now?"

"I am going," said Dalroy, dreamily, "to 'The Old Ship.'"

"Do you mean?" asked the Turk, "that you are going back to the warships of the English King?"

"No," answered the other, "I am going back to 'The Old Ship' that is behind the apple trees by Pebblewick; where the Ule flows among the trees. I fear I shall never see you there."

After an instant's hesitation he wrung the red hand of the great tyrant and walked to his boat without a glance at the diplomatists.

III

The Sign of "The Old Ship"

U pon few of the children of men has the surname of Pump fallen, and of these few have been maddened into naming a child Humphrey in addition to it. To such extremity, however, had the parents of the innkeeper at "The Old Ship" proceeded, that their son might come at last to be called "Hump" by his dearest friends, and "Pumph" by an aged Turk with a green umbrella. All this, or all he knew of it, he endured with a sour smile; for he was of a stoical temper.

Mr. Humphrey Pump stood outside his inn, which stood almost on the seashore, screened only by one line of apple trees, dwarfed, twisted and salted by the sea air; but in front of it was a highly banked bowling green, and behind it the land sank abruptly; so that one very steep sweeping road vanished into the depth and mystery of taller trees. Mr. Pump was standing immediately under his trim sign, which stood erect in the turf; a wooden pole painted white and suspending a square white board, also painted white but further decorated with a highly grotesque blue ship, such as a child might draw, but into which Mr. Pump's patriotism had insinuated a disproportionately large red St. George's cross.

Mr. Humphrey Pump was a man of middle size, with very broad shoulders, wearing a sort of shooting suit with gaiters. Indeed, he was engaged at the moment in cleaning and reloading a double-barrelled gun, a short but powerful weapon which he had invented, or at least improved, himself; and which, though eccentric enough as compared with latest scientific arms, was neither clumsy nor necessarily out of date. For Pump was one of those handy men who seem to have a hundred hands like Briareus; he made nearly everything for himself and everything in his house was slightly different from the same thing in anyone else's house. He was also as cunning as Pan or a poacher in everything affecting every bird or dish, every leaf or berry in the woods. His mind was a rich soil of subconscious memories and traditions; and he had a curious kind of gossip so allusive as to almost amount to reticence; for he always took it for granted that everyone knew his county and its tales as intimately as he did; so he would mention the most mysterious and amazing things without relaxing a muscle on his face, which seemed to be made of knotted wood. His dark brown hair ended in two rudimentary side whiskers, giving him a slightly horsey look, but in the old-fashioned sportsman's style. His smile was rather wry and crabbed; but his brown eyes were kindly and soft. He was very English.

As a rule his movements, though quick, were cool; but on this occasion he put down the gun on the table outside the inn in a rather hurried manner and came forward dusting his hands in an unusual degree of animation and even defiance. Beyond the goblin green apple trees and against the sea had appeared the tall, slight figure of a girl, in a dress about the colour of copper and a large shady hat. Under the hat her face was grave and beautiful though rather swarthy. She shook hands with Mr. Pump; then he very ceremoniously put a chair for her and called her "Lady Joan."

"I thought I would like a look at the old place," she said. "We have had some happy times here when we were boys and girls. I suppose you hardly see any of your old friends now."

"Very little," answered Pump, rubbing his short whisker reflectively. "Lord Ivywood's become quite a Methody parson, you know, since he took the place; he's pulling down beer-shops right and left. And Mr. Charles was sent to Australia for lying down flat at the funeral. Pretty stiff I call it; but the old lady was a terror."

"Do you ever hear," asked Lady Joan Brett, carelessly, "of that Irishman, Captain Dalroy?"

"Yes, more often than from the rest," answered the innkeeper. "He seems to have done wonders in this Greek business. Ah! He was a sad loss to the Navy!"

"They insulted his country," said the girl, looking at the sea with a heightened colour. "After all, Ireland was his country; and he had a right to resent it being spoken of like that."

"And when they found he'd painted him green," went on Mr. Pump.

"Painted him what?" asked Lady Joan.

"Painted Captain Dawson green," continued Mr. Pump in colourless tones. "Captain Dawson said green was the colour of Irish traitors, so Dalroy painted him green. It was a great temptation, no doubt, with this fence being painted at the time and the pail of stuff there; but, of course, it had a very prejudicial effect on his professional career."

"What an extraordinary story!" said the staring Lady Joan, breaking into a rather joyless laugh. "It must go down among your county legends. I never heard that version before. Why, it might be the origin of the 'Green Man' over there by the town."

"Oh, no," said Pump, simply, "that's been there since before Waterloo times. Poor old Noyle had it until they put him away. You remember old Noyle, Lady Joan. Still alive, I hear, and still writing love-letters to Queen Victoria. Only of course they aren't posted now."

"Have you heard from your Irish friend lately?" asked the girl, keeping a steady eye on the sky-line.

"Yes, I had a letter last week," answered the innkeeper. "It seems not impossible that he may return to England. He's been acting for one of these Greek places, and the negotiations seem to be concluded. It's a queer thing that his lordship himself was the English minister in charge of them."

"You mean Lord Ivywood," said Lady Joan, rather coldly. "Yes, he has a great career before him, evidently."

"I wish he hadn't got his knife into us so much," chuckled Pump. "I don't believe there'll be an inn left in England. But the Ivywoods were always cranky. It's only fair to him to remember his grandfather."

"I think it's very ungallant on your part," said Lady Joan, with a mournful smile, "to ask a lady to remember his grandfather."

"You know what I mean, Lady Joan," said her host, good humouredly. "And I never was hard on the case myself; we all have our little ways. I shouldn't like it done to my pig; but I don't see why a man shouldn't have his own pig in his own pew with him if he likes it. It wasn't a free seat. It was the family pew."

Lady Joan broke out laughing again. "What horrible things you do seem to have heard of," she said. "Well, I must be going, Mr. Hump—I mean Mr. Pump—I used to call you Hump. . . oh, Hump, do you think any of us will ever be happy again?"

"I suppose it rests with Providence," he said, looking at the sea.

"Oh, do say Providence again!" cried the girl. "It's as good as 'Masterman Ready.'"

With which inconsequent words she betook herself again to the path by the apple trees and walked back by the sea front to Pebblewick.

The inn of "The Old Ship" lay a little beyond the old fishing village of Pebblewick; and that again was separated by an empty half-mile or so from the new watering-place of Pebblewick-on-Sea. But the dark-haired lady walked steadily along the sea-front, on a sort of parade which had been stretched out to east and west in the insane optimism of watering-places, and, as she approached the more crowded part, looked more and more carefully at the groups on the beach. Most of them were much the same as she had seen them more than a month before. The seekers after truth (as the man in the fez would say) who assembled daily to find out what the man was doing with the paper-boxes, had not found out yet; neither had they wearied of their intellectual pilgrimage. Pennies were still thrown to the thundering atheist in acknowledgment of his incessant abuse; and this was all the more mysterious because the crowd was obviously indifferent, and the atheist was obviously sincere. The man with the long neck who led Low Church hymns with a little wooden spade had indeed disappeared; for children's services of this kind are generally a moving feast; but the man whose only claim consisted of carrots round his hat was still there; and seemed to have even more money than before. But Lady Joan could see no sign of the little old man in the fez. She could only suppose that he had failed entirely; and, being in a bitter mood, she told herself bitterly that he had sunk out of sight precisely because there was in his rubbish a touch of unearthly and insane clear-headedness of which all these vulgar idiots were incapable. She did not confess to herself consciously that what had made both the man in the fez and the man at the inn interesting was the subject of which they had spoken.

As she walked on rather wearily along the parade she caught sight of a girl in black with faint fair hair and a tremulous, intelligent face which she was sure she had seen before. Pulling together all her aristocratic training for the remembering of middle class people, she managed to remember that this was a Miss Browning who had done typewriting work for her a year or two before; and immediately went forward to greet her, partly out of genuine good nature and partly as a relief from her own rather dreary thoughts. Her tone was so seriously frank and friendly that the lady in black summoned the social courage to say:

"I've so often wanted to introduce you to my sister who's much cleverer than I am, though she does live at home; which I suppose is very old-fashioned. She knows all sorts of intellectual people. She is talking to one of them now; this Prophet of the Moon that everyone's talking about. Do let me introduce you."

Lady Joan Brett had met many prophets of the moon and of other things. But she had the spontaneous courtesy which redeems the vices of her class, and she followed Miss Browning to a seat on the parade. She greeted Miss Browning's sister with glowing politeness; and this may really be counted to her credit; for she had great difficulty in looking at Miss Browning's sister at all. For on the seat beside her, still in a red fez but in a brilliantly new black frock coat and every appearance of prosperity, sat the old gentleman who had lectured on the sands about the inns of England.

"He lectured at our Ethical Society," whispered Miss Browning, "on the word Alcohol. Just on the word Alcohol. He was perfectly thrilling. All about Arabia and Algebra, you know, and how everything comes from the East. You really would be interested."

"I am interested," said Lady Joan.

"Poot it to yourselfs," the man in the fez was saying to Miss Browning's sister, "joost what sort of meaning the names of your ince can have if they do not commemorate the unlimitable influence of Islam. There is a vary populous Inn in London, one of the most distinguished, one of the most of the Centre, and it is called the Horseshoe? Now, my friendss, why should anyone commemorate a horse-shoe? It iss but an appendage to a creature more interesting than itself. I have already demonstrated to you that the very fact that you have in your town a place of drink called the Bool—"

"I should like to ask—" began Lady Joan, suddenly.

"A place of drink called the Bool," went on the man in the fez, deaf to all distractions, "and I have urged that the Bool is a disturbing thought, while the BulBul is a reassuring thought. But even you my friends, would not name a place after a ring in a Bool's nose and not after the Bool? Why then name an equivalent place after the shoo, the mere shoo, upon a horse's hoof, and not after the noble horse? Surely it is clear, surely it is evident that the term 'horse-shoe' is a cryptic term, an esoteric term, a term made during the days when the ancient Moslem faith of this English country was oppressed by the passing superstition of the Galileans. That bent shape, that duplex curving shape, which you call horse-shoe, is it not clearly the Crescent?" and he cast his arms wide as he had done on the sands, "the Crescent of the Prophet of the only God?"

"I should like to ask," began Lady Joan, again, "how you would explain the name of the inn called 'The Green Man,' just behind that row of houses."

"Exactly! exactly!" cried the Prophet of the Moon, in almost insane excitement. "The seeker after truth could not at all probably find a more perfect example of these principles. My friendss, how could there be a green man? You are acquainted with green grass, with green leaves, with green cheese, with green chartreuse. I ask if any one of you, however wide her social circle, has ever been acquainted with a green man. Surely, surely, it is evident, my friendss, that this is an imperfect version, an abbreviated version, of the original words. What can be clearer than that the original expression, was 'the green-turban'd man,' in allusion to the well-known uniform of the descendants of the Prophet? 'Turban'd' surely is just the sort of word, exactly the sort of foreign and unfamiliar word, that might easily be slurred over and ultimately suppressed."

"There is a legend in these parts," said Lady Joan, steadily, "that a great hero, hearing the colour that was sacred to his holy island insulted, really poured it over his enemy for a reply."

"A legend! a fable!" cried the man in the fez, with another radiant and rational expansion of the hands. "Is it not evident that no such thing can have really happened?"

"Oh, yes—it really happened," said the young lady, softly. "There is not much to comfort one in this world; but there are some things. Oh, it really happened."

And taking a graceful farewell of the group, she resumed her rather listless walk along the parade.

IV

The Inn Finds Wings

Mr. Humphrey Pump stood in front of his inn once more, the cleaned and loaded gun still lay on the table, and the white sign of The Ship still swung in the slight sea breeze over his head; but his leatherish features were knotted over a new problem. He held two letters in his hand, letters of a very different sort, but letters that pointed to the same difficult problem. The first ran:

Dear Hump—

"I'm so bothered that I simply must call you by the old name again. You understand I've got to keep in with my people. Lord Ivywood is a sort of cousin of mine, and for that and some other reasons, my poor old mother would just die if I offended him. You know her heart is weak; you know everything there is to know in this county. Well, I only write to warn you that something is going to be done against your dear old inn. I don't know what this Country's coming to. Only a month or two ago I saw a shabby old pantaloon on the beach with a green gamp, talking the craziest stuff you ever heard in your life. Three weeks ago I heard he was lecturing at Ethical Societies—whatever they are—for a handsome salary. Well, when I was last at Ivywood—I must go because Mamma likes it—there was the living lunatic again, in evening dress, and talked about by people who really *know*. I mean who know better.

"Lord Ivywood is entirely under his influence and thinks him the greatest prophet the world has ever seen. And Lord Ivywood is not a fool; one can't help admiring him. Mamma, I think, wants me to do more than admire him. I am telling you everything, Hump, because I think perhaps this is the last honest letter I shall ever write in the world. And I warn you seriously that Lord Ivywood is *sincere*, which is perfectly terrible. He will be the biggest English statesman, and he does really mean to ruin—the old ships. If ever you see me here again taking part in such work, I hope you may forgive me.

"Somebody we mentioned, whom I shall never see again, I leave to your friendship. It is the second best thing I can give, and I am not sure it may not be better than the first would have been. Goodbye.

J. B.

This letter seemed to distress Mr. Pump rather than puzzle him. It ran as follows:

Sir—

"The Committee of the Imperial Commission of Liquor Control is directed to draw your attention to the fact that you have disregarded the Committee's communications under section 5A of the Act for the Regulation of Places of Public Entertainment; and that you are now under Section 47C of the Act amending the Act for the Regulation of Places of Public Entertainment aforesaid. The charges on which prosecution will be founded are as follows:

(1) Violation of sub-section 23*f* of the Act, which enacts that no pictorial signs shall be exhibited before premises of less than the ratable value of £2000 per annum.
(2) Violation of sub-section 113*d* of the Act, which enacts that no liquor containing alcohol shall be sold in any inn, hotel, tavern or public-house, except when demanded under a medical certificate from one of the doctors licensed by the State Medical Council, or in the specially excepted cases of Claridge's Hotel and the Criterion Bar, where urgency has already been proved.

"As you have failed to acknowledge previous communications on this subject, this is to warn you that legal steps will be taken immediately,

We are yours truly,
Ivywood, President
J. Leveson, Secretary

Mr. Humphrey Pump sat down at the table outside his inn and whistled in a way which, combined with his little whiskers made him for the moment seem literally like an ostler. Then, the very real wit and learning he had returned slowly into his face and with his warm, brown eyes he considered the cold, grey sea. There was not much to be got out of the sea. Humphrey Pump might drown himself in the sea; which would be better for Humphrey Pump than being finally separated from "The Old Ship." England might be sunk under the sea; which would be better for England than never again having such places as "The Old Ship." But these were not serious remedies nor rationally attainable; and Pump could only feel that the sea had simply warped him as it had warped his apple trees. The sea was a dreary business altogether. There was only one figure walking on the sands. It was only when the figure drew nearer and nearer and grew to more than human size, that he sprang to his feet with a cry. Also the level light of morning lit the man's hair, and it was red.

The late King of Ithaca came casually and slowly up the slope of the beach that led to "The Old Ship." He had landed in a boat from a battleship that could still be seen near the horizon, and he still wore the astounding uniform of apple-green and silver which he had himself invented as that of a navy that had never existed very much, and which now did not exist at all. He had a straight naval sword at his side; for the terms of his capitulation had never required him to surrender it; and inside the uniform and beside the sword there was what there always had been, a big and rather bewildered man with rough red hair, whose misfortune was that he had good brains, but that his bodily strength and bodily passions were a little too strong for his brains.

He had flung his crashing weight on the chair outside the inn before the innkeeper could find words to express his astounded pleasure in seeing him. His first words were "have you got any rum?"

Then, as if feeling that his attitude needed explanation, he added, "I suppose I shall never be a sailor again after tonight. So I must have rum."

Humphrey Pump had a talent for friendship, and understood his old friend. He went into the inn without a word; and came back idly pushing or rolling with an alternate foot (as if he were playing football with two footballs at once) two objects that rolled very easily. One was a big keg or barrel of rum and the other a great solid drum of a cheese.

Among his thousand other technical tricks he had a way of tapping a cask without a tap, or anything that could impair its revolutionary or revolving qualities. He was feeling in his pocket for the instrument with which he solved such questions, when his Irish friend suddenly sat bolt upright, as one startled out of sleep, and spoke with his strongest and most unusual brogue.

"Oh thank ye, Hump, a thousand times; and I don't think I really want something to drink at arl. Now I know I can have it, I don't seem to want it at arl. But hwhat I do want—" and he suddenly dashed his big fist on the little table so that one of its legs leapt and nearly snapped— "hwhat I do want is some sort of account of what's happening in this England of yours that shan't be just obviously rubbish."

"Ah," said Pump, fingering the two letters thoughtfully. "And what do you mean by rubbish?"

"I carl it rubbish" cried Patrick Dalroy, "when ye put the Koran into the Bible and not the Apocrypha; and I carl it rubbish when a mad parson's allowed to propose to put a crescent on St. Paul's Cathedral. I know the Turks are our allies now, but they often were before, and I never heard that Palmerston or Colin Campbell had any truck with such trash."

"Lord Ivywood is very enthusiastic, I know," said Pump, with a restrained amusement. "He was saying only the other day at the Flower Show here that the time had come for a full unity between Christianity and Islam."

"Something called Chrislam perhaps," said the Irishman, with a moody eye. He was gazing across the grey and purple woodlands that stretched below them at the back of the inn; and into which the steep, white road swept downwards and disappeared. The steep road looked like the beginning of an adventure; and he was an adventurer.

"But you exaggerate, you know," went on Pump, polishing his gun, "about the crescent on St. Paul's. It wasn't exactly that. What Dr. Moole suggested, I think, was some sort of double emblem, you know, combining cross and crescent."

"And called the Crescent," muttered Dalroy.

"And you can't call Dr. Moole a parson either," went on Mr. Humphrey Pump, polishing industriously. "Why, they say he's a sort of atheist, or what they call an agnostic, like Squire Brunton who used to bite elm trees by Marley. The grand folks have these fashions, Captain, but they've never lasted long that I know of."

"I think it's serious this time," said his friend, shaking his big red head. "This is the last inn on this coast, and will soon be the last inn in England. Do you remember the 'Saracen's Head' in Plumsea, along the shore there?"

"I know," assented the innkeeper. "My aunt was there when he hanged his mother; but it's a charming place."

"I passed there just now; and it has been destroyed," said Dalroy.

"Destroyed by fire?" asked Pump, pausing in his gun-scrubbing.

"No," said Dalroy, "destroyed by lemonade. They've taken away its license or whatever you call it. I made a song about it, which I'll sing to you now!" And with an astounding air of suddenly revived spirits, he roared in a voice like thunder the following verses, to a simple but spirited tune of his own invention:

> *"The Saracen's Head looks down the lane,*
> *Where we shall never drink wine again;*
> *For the wicked old Women who feel well-bred*
> *Have turned to a tea-shop the Saracen's Head.*
>
> *"The Saracen's Head out of Araby came,*
> *King Richard riding in arms like flame,*
> *And where he established his folk to be fed*
> *He set up his spear—and the Saracen's Head.*
>
> *"But the Saracen's Head outlived the Kings,*
> *It thought and it thought of most horrible things;*
> *Of Health and of Soap and of Standard Bread,*
> *And of Saracen drinks at the Saracen's Head."*

"Hullo!" cried Pump, with another low whistle. "Why here comes his lordship. And I suppose that young man in the goggles is a Committee or something."

"Let him come," said Dalroy, and continued in a yet more earthquake bellow:

> *"So the Saracen's Head fulfils its name,*
> *They drink no wine—a ridiculous game—*
> *And I shall wonder until I'm dead,*
> *How it ever came into the Saracen's Head."*

As the last echo of this lyrical roar rolled away among the apple-trees, and down the steep, white road into the woods, Captain Dalroy leaned back in his chair and nodded good humouredly to Lord Ivywood, who was standing on the lawn with his usual cold air, but with slightly compressed lips. Behind him was a dark young man with double eyeglasses and a number of printed papers in his hand; presumably J. Leveson, Secretary. In the road outside stood a group of three which struck Pump as strangely incongruous, like a group in a three act farce. The first was a police inspector in uniform; the second was a workman in a leather apron, more or less like a carpenter, and the third was an old man in a scarlet Turkish fez, but otherwise dressed in very fashionable English clothes in which he did not seem very comfortable. He was explaining something about the inn to the policeman and the carpenter, who appeared to be restraining their amusement.

"Fine song that, my lord," said Dalroy, with cheerful egotism. "I'll sing you another," and he cleared his throat.

"Mr. Pump," said Lord Ivywood, in his bell-like and beautiful voice, "I thought I would come in person, if only to make it clear that every indulgence has been shown you. The mere date of this inn brings it within the statute of 1909; it was erected when my great grandfather was Lord of the Manor here, though I believe it then bore a different name, and—"

"Ah, my lord," broke in Pump with a sigh, "I'd rather deal with your great grandfather, I would, though he married a hundred negresses instead of one, than see a gentleman of your family taking away a poor man's livelihood."

"The act is specially designed in the interests of the relief of poverty," proceeded Lord Ivywood, in an unruffled manner, "and its final advantages will accrue to all citizens alike." He turned for an instant to the dark secretary, saying, "You have that second report?" and received a folded paper in answer.

"It is here fully explained," said Lord Ivywood, putting on his elderly eyeglasses, "that the purpose of the Act is largely to protect the savings of the more humble and necessitous classes. I find in paragraph three, 'we strongly advise that the deleterious element of alcohol be made illegal save in such few places as the Government may specially exempt for Parliamentary or other public reasons, and that the provocative and demoralising display on inn signs be strictly forbidden except in the cases thus specially exempted: the absence of such temptations will, in

G.K. CHESTERTON

our opinion, do much to improve the precarious financial conditions of the working class.' That disposes, I think, of any such suggestion as Mr. Pump's, that our inevitable acts of social reform are in any sense oppressive. To Mr. Pump's prejudice it may appear for the moment to bear hardly upon him; but" (and here Lord Ivywood's voice took one of its moving oratorical turns), "what better proof could we desire of the insidiousness of the sleepy poison we denounce, what better evidence could we offer of the civic corruption that we seek to cure, than the very fact that good and worthy men of established repute in the county can, by living in such places as these, become so stagnant and sodden and unsocial, whether through the fumes of wine or through meditations as maudlin about the past, that they consider the case solely as their own case, and laugh at the long agony of the poor."

Captain Dalroy had been studying Ivywood with a very bright blue eye; and he spoke now much more quietly than he generally did.

"Excuse me one moment, my lord," he said. "But there was one point in your important explanation which I am not sure I have got right. Do I understand you to say that, though sign-boards are to be generally abolished, yet where, if anywhere, they are retained, the right to sell fermented liquor will be retained also? In other words, though an Englishman may at last find only one inn-sign left in England, yet if the place has an inn-sign, it will also have your gracious permission to be really an inn?"

Lord Ivywood had an admirable command of temper, which had helped him much in his career as a statesman. He did not waste time in wrangling about the Captain's *locus standi* in the matter. He replied quite simply,

"Yes, Your statement of the facts is correct."

"Whenever I find an inn-sign permitted by the police, I may go in and ask for a glass of beer—also permitted by the police."

"If you find any such, yes," answered Ivywood, quite temperately. "But we hope soon to have removed them altogether."

Captain Patrick Dalroy rose enormously from his seat with a sort of stretch and yawn.

"Well, Hump," he said to his friend, "the best thing, it seems to me, is to take the important things with us."

With two sight-staggering kicks he sent the keg of rum and the round cheese flying over the fence, in such a direction that they bounded on the descending road and rolled more and more rapidly down toward the dark woods into which the path disappeared. Then he gripped the pole of the inn-sign, shook it twice and plucked it out of the turf like a tuft of grass.

It had all happened before anyone could move, but as he strode out into the road the policeman ran forward. Dalroy smote him flat across face and chest with the wooden sign-board, so as to send him flying into the ditch on the other side of the road. Then turning on the man in the fez he poked him with the end of the pole so sharply in his new white waistcoat and watch-chain as to cause him to sit down suddenly in the road, looking very serious and thoughtful.

The dark secretary made a movement of rescue, but Humphrey Pump, with a cry, caught up his gun from the table and pointed it at him, which so alarmed J. Leveson, Secretary, as to cause him almost to double up with his emotions. The next moment Pump, with his gun under his arm, was scampering down the hill after the Captain, who was scampering after the barrel and the cheese.

Before the policeman had struggled out of the ditch, they had all disappeared into the darkness of the forest. Lord Ivywood who had remained firm through the scene, without a sign of fear or impatience (or, I will add, amusement), held up his hand and stopped the policeman in his pursuit.

"We should only make ourselves and the law ridiculous," he said, "by pursuing those ludicrous rowdies now. They can't escape or do any real harm in the state of modern communications. What is far more important, gentlemen, is to destroy their stores and their base. Under the Act of 1911 we have a right to confiscate and destroy any property in an inn where the law has been violated."

And he stood for hours on the lawn, watching the smashing of bottles and the breaking up of casks and feeding on fanatical pleasure: the pleasure his strange, cold, courageous nature could not get from food or wine or woman.

V

The Astonishment of the Agent

Lord Ivywood shared the mental weakness of most men who have fed on books; he ignored, not the value but the very existence of other forms of information. Thus Humphrey Pump was perfectly aware that Lord Ivywood considered him an ignorant man who carried a volume of Pickwick and could not be got to read any other book. But Lord Ivywood was quite unaware that Humphrey never looked at him without thinking that he could be most successfully hidden in a wood of small beeches, as his grey-brown hair and sallow, ashen face exactly reproduced the three predominant tints of such a sylvan twilight. Mr. Pump, I fear, had sometimes partaken of partridge or pheasant, in his early youth, under circumstances in which Lord Ivywood was not only unconscious of the hospitality he was dispensing, but would have sworn that it was physically impossible for anyone to elude the vigilance of his efficient system of game-keeping. But it is very unwise in one who counts himself superior to physical things to talk about physical impossibility.

Lord Ivywood was in error, therefore, when he said that the fugitives could not possibly escape in modern England. You can do a great many things in modern England if you have noticed; some things, in fact, which others know by pictures or current speech; if you know, for instance, that most roadside hedges are taller and denser than they look, and that even the largest man lying just behind them, takes up far less room than you would suppose; if you know that many natural sounds are much more like each other than the enlightened ear can believe, as in the case of wind in leaves and of the sea; if you know that it is easier to walk in socks than in boots, if you know how to take hold of the ground; if you know that the proportion of dogs who will bite a man under any circumstances is rather less than the proportion of men who will murder you in a railway carriage; if you know that you need not be drowned even in a river, unless the tide is very strong, and unless you practise putting yourself into the special attitudes of a suicide; if you know that country stations have objectless, extra waiting rooms that nobody ever goes into; and if you know that county folk will forget you if you speak to them, but talk about you all day if you don't.

By the exercise of these and other arts and sciences Humphrey Pump was able to guide his friend across country, mostly in the character of trespasser and occasionally in that of something like housebreaker, and eventually, with sign, keg, cheese and all to step out of a black pinewood onto a white road in a part of the county where they would not be sought for the present.

Opposite them was a cornfield and on their right, in the shades of the pine trees, a cottage, a very tumbledown cottage that seemed to have collapsed under its own thatch. The red-haired Irishman's face wore a curious smile. He stuck the inn-sign erect in the road and went and hammered on the door.

It was opened tremulously by an old man with a face so wrinkled that the wrinkles seemed more distinctly graven than the features themselves, which seemed lost in the labyrinth of them. He might have crawled out of the hole in a gnarled tree and he might have been a thousand years old.

He did not seem to notice the sign-board, which stood rather to the left of the door; and what life remained in his eyes seemed to awake in wonder at Dalroy's stature and strange uniform and the sword at his side. "I beg your pardon," said the Captain, courteously. "I fear my uniform startles you. It is Lord Ivywood's livery. All his servants are to dress like this. In fact, I understand the tenants also and even yourself, perhaps. . . excuse my sword. Lord Ivywood is very particular that every man should have a sword. You know his beautiful, eloquent way of putting his views. 'How can we profess,' he was saying to me yesterday, while I was brushing his trousers. 'How can we profess that all men are brothers while we refuse to them the symbol of manhood; or with what assurance can we claim it as a movement of modern emancipation to deny the citizen that which has in all ages marked the difference between the free man and the slave. Nor need we anticipate any such barbaric abuses as my honourable friend who is cleaning the knives has prophesied, for this gift is a sublime act of confidence in your universal passion for the severe splendours of Peace; and he that has the right to strike is he who has learnt to spare.'"

Talking all this nonsense with extreme rapidity and vast oratorical flourishes of the hand, Captain Dalroy proceeded to trundle both the big cheese and the cask of rum into the house of the astonished cottager: Mr. Pump following with a grim placidity and his gun under his arm.

"Lord Ivywood," said Dalroy, setting the rum cask with a bump on the plain deal table, "wishes to take wine with you. Or, more strictly speaking, rum. Don't you run away, my friend, with any of these stories about Lord Ivywood being opposed to drink. Three-bottle Ivywood, we call him in the kitchen. But it must be rum; nothing but rum for the Ivywoods. 'Wine may be a mocker,' he was saying the other day (and I particularly noted the phrasing, which seemed to be very happy even for his lordship; he was standing at the top of the steps, and I stopped cleaning them to make a note of it), 'wine may be a mocker; strong drink may be raging, but nowhere in the sacred pages will you find one word of censure of the sweeter spirit sacred to them that go down to the sea in ships; no tongue of priest and prophet was ever lifted to break the sacred silence of Holy Writ about Rum.' He then explained to me," went on Dalroy, signing to Pump to tap the cask according to his own technical secret, "that the great tip for avoiding any bad results that a bottle or two of rum might have on young and inexperienced people was to eat cheese with it, particularly this kind of cheese that I have here. I've forgotten its name."

"Cheddar," said Pump, quite gravely.

"But mind you!" continued the Captain almost ferociously, shaking his big finger in warning at the aged man. "Mind you 'no *bread* with the cheese. All the devastating ruin wrought by cheese and the once happy homes of this country, has been due to the reckless and insane experiment of eating bread with it.' You'll get no bread from me, my friend. Indeed, Lord Ivywood has given directions that the allusion to this ignorant and depraved habit shall be eliminated from the Lord's Prayer. Have a drink."

He had already poured out a little of the spirit into two thick tumblers and a broken teacup, which he had induced the aged man to produce; and now solemnly pledged him.

"Thank ye kindly, sir," said the old man, using his cracked voice for the first time. Then he drank; and his old face changed as if it were an old horn lantern in which the flame began to rise.

"Ar," he said. "My son he be a sailor."

"I wish him a happy voyage," said the Captain. "And I'll sing you a song about the first sailor there ever was in the world; and who (as Lord Ivywood acutely observes) lived before the time of rum."

He sat down on a wooden chair and lifted his loud voice once more, beating on the table with the broken tea-cup.

"Old Noah, he had an ostrich farm, and fowls on the greatest scale;
He ate his egg with a ladle in an egg-cup big as a pail,
And the soup he took was Elephant Soup and the fish he took was Whale;
But they all were small to the cellar he took when he set out to sail;
And Noah, he often said to his wife when he sat down to dine,
'I don't care where the water goes if it doesn't get into the wine.'

"The cataract of the cliff of heaven fell blinding off the brink,
As if it would wash the stars away as suds go down a sink,
The seven heavens came roaring down for the throats of hell to drink,
And Noah, he cocked his eye and said, 'It looks like rain, I think,
The water has drowned the Matterhorn as deep as a Mendip mine,
But I don't care where the water goes if it doesn't get into the wine.'

"But Noah he sinned, and we have sinned; on tipsy feet we trod,
Till a great big black teetotaller was sent to us for a rod,
And you can't get wine at a P.S.A. or chapel or Eisteddfod;
For the Curse of Water has come again because of the wrath of God,
And water is on the Bishop's board and the Higher Thinker's shrine,
But I don't care where the water goes if it doesn't get into the wine."

"Lord Ivywood's favorite song," concluded Mr. Patrick Dalroy, drinking. "Sing us a song yourself."

Rather to the surprise of the two humourists, the old gentleman actually began in a quavering voice to chant,

"King George that lives in London Town,
I hope they will defend his crown,
And Bonyparte be quite put down
On Christmas Day in the morning.

"Old Squire is gone to the Meet today
All in his—"

It is perhaps fortunate for the rapidity of this narrative that the old gentleman's favourite song, which consists of forty-seven verses, was interrupted by a curious incident. The door of the cottage opened and a sheepish-looking man in corduroys stood silently in the room for a few seconds and then said, without preface or further explanation,

"Four ale."

"I beg your pardon?" inquired the polite Captain.

"Four ale," said the man with solidity; then catching sight of Humphrey seemed to find a few more words in his vocabulary.

"Morning, Mr. Pump. Didn't know as how you'd moved 'The Old Ship.'"

Mr. Pump, with a twist of a smile, pointed to the old man whose song had been interrupted.

"Mr. Marne's seeing after it now, Mr. Gowl," said Pump with the strict etiquette of the country side. "But he's got nothing but this rum in stock as yet."

"Better'nowt," said the laconic Mr. Gowl; and put down some money in front of the aged Marne, who eyed it wonderingly. As he was turning with a farewell and wiping his mouth with the back of his hand, the door once more moved, letting in white sunlight and a man in a red neckerchief.

"Morning, Mr. Marne; Morning, Mr. Pump; Morning, Mr. Gowl," said the man in the red neckerchief.

"Morning, Mr. Coote," said the other three, one after another.

"Have some rum, Mr. Coote?" asked Humphrey Pump, genially. "That's all Mr. Marne's got just now."

Mr. Coote also had a little rum; and also laid a little money under the rather vague gaze of the venerable cottager. Mr. Coote was just proceeding to explain that these were bad times, but if you saw a sign you were all right still; a lawyer up at Grunton Abbot had told him so; when the company was increased and greatly excited by the arrival of a boisterous and popular tinker, who ordered glasses all round and said he had his donkey and cart outside. A prolonged, rich and confused conversation about the donkey and cart then ensued, in which the most varied views were taken of their merits; and it gradually began to dawn on Dalroy that the tinker was trying to sell them.

An idea, suited to the romantic opportunism of his present absurd career, suddenly swept over his mind, and he rushed out to look at the cart and donkey. The next moment he was back again, asking the tinker what his price was, and almost in the same breath offering a much bigger price than the tinker would have dreamed of asking. This was considered, however, as a lunacy specially allowed to gentlemen; the tinker had some more rum on the strength of the payment, and then Dalroy, offering his excuses, sealed up the cask and took it and the cheese to be stowed in the bottom of the cart. The money, however, he still left lying in shining silver and copper before the silver beard of old Marne.

No one acquainted with the quaint and often wordless camaraderie of the English poor will require to be told that they all went out and stared at him as he loaded the cart and saw to the harness of the donkey—all except the old cottager, who sat as if hypnotised by the sight of the money. While they were standing there they saw coming down the white, hot road, where it curled over the hill, a figure that gave them no pleasure, even when it was a mere marching black spot in the distance. It was a Mr. Bullrose, the agent of Lord Ivywood's estates.

Mr. Bullrose was a short, square man with a broad, square head with ridges of close, black curls on it, with a heavy, froglike face and starting, suspicious eyes; a man with a good silk hat but a square business jacket. Mr. Bullrose was not a nice man. The agent on that sort of estate hardly ever is a nice man. The landlord often is; and even Lord Ivywood had an arctic magnanimity of his own, which made most people want, if possible, to see him personally. But Mr. Bullrose was petty. Every really practical tyrant must be petty.

He evidently failed to understand the commotion in front of Mr. Marne's partly collapsed cottage, but he felt there must be something wrong about it. He wanted to get rid of the cottage altogether, and had not, of course, the faintest intention of giving the cottager any compensation for it. He hoped the old man would die; but in any case he could easily clear him out if it became suddenly necessary, for he could not possibly pay the rent for this week. The rent was not very much; but it was immeasurably too much for the old man who had no conceivable way of borrowing or earning it. That is where the chivalry of our aristocratic land system comes in.

"Good-bye, my friends," the enormous man in the fantastic uniform was saying, "all roads lead to rum, as Lord Ivywood said in one of his gayer moments, and we hope to be back soon, establishing a first class hotel here, of which prospectuses will soon be sent out."

The heavy froglike face of Mr. Bullrose, the agent, grew uglier with astonishment; and the eyes stood out more like a snail's than a frog's. The indefensible allusion to Lord Ivywood would in any case have caused a choleric intervention, if it had not been swallowed up in the earthquake suggestion of an unlicensed hotel on the estate. This again would have effected the explosion, if that and everything else had not been struck still and rigid by the sight of a solid, wooden sign-post already erected outside old Marne's miserable cottage.

"I've got him now," muttered Mr. Bullrose. "He can't possibly pay; and out he shall go." And he walked swiftly towards the door of the cottage, almost at the same moment that Dalroy went to the donkey's head, as if to lead it off along the road.

"Look here, my man," burst out Bullrose, the instant he was inside the cottage. "You've cooked yourself this time. His lordship has been a great deal too indulgent with you; but this is going to be the end of it. The insolence of what you've done outside, especially when you know his lordship's wishes in such things, has just put the lid on." He stopped a moment and sneered. "So unless you happen to have the exact rent down to a farthing or two about you, out you go. We're sick of your sort."

In a very awkward and fumbling manner, the old man pushed a heap of coins across the table. Mr. Bullrose sat down suddenly on the wooden chair with his silk hat on, and began counting them furiously. He counted them once; he counted them twice; and he counted them again. Then he stared at them more steadily than the cottager had done.

"Where did you get this money?" he asked in a thick, gross voice. "Did you steal it?"

"I ain't very spry for stealin'," said the old man in quavering comedy.

Bullrose looked at him and then at the money; and remembered with fury that Ivywood was a just though cold magistrate on the bench.

"Well, anyhow," he cried, in a hot, heady way, "we've got enough against you to turn you out of this. Haven't you broken the law, my man, to say nothing of the regulations for tenants, in sticking up that fancy sign of yours outside the cottage? Eh?"

The tenant was silent.

"Eh?" reiterated the agent.

"Ar," replied the tenant.

"Have you or have you not a sign-board outside this house?" shouted Bullrose, hammering the table.

The tenant looked at him for a long time with a patient and venerable face, and then said: "Mubbe, yes. Mubbe, no."

"I'll mubbe you," cried Mr. Bullrose, springing up and sticking his silk hat on the back of his head. "I don't know whether you people are too drunk to see anything, but I saw the thing with my own eyes out in the road. Come out, and deny it if you dare!"

"Ar," said Mr. Marne, dubiously.

He tottered after the agent, who flung open the door with a businesslike fury and stood outside on the threshold. He stood there quite a long time, and he did not speak. Deep in the hardened mud of his materialistic mind there had stirred two things that were its ancient enemies; the old fairy tale in which every thing can be believed; the new scepticism in which nothing can be believed—not even one's own eyes. There was no sign, nor sign of a sign, in the landscape.

On the withered face of the old man Marne there was a faint renewal of that laughter that has slept since the Middle Ages.

VI

The Hole in Heaven

That delicate ruby light which is one of the rarest but one of the most exquisite of evening effects warmed the land, sky and seas as if the whole world were washed in wine; and dyed almost scarlet the strong red head of Patrick Dalroy as he stood on the waste of furze and bracken, where he and his friends had halted. One of his friends was re-examining a short gun, rather like a double-barrelled carbine, the other was eating thistles.

Dalroy himself was idle and ruminant, with his hands in his pockets and his eye on the horizon. Landwards the hills, plains and woods lay bathed in the rose-red light; but it changed somewhat to purple, to cloud and something like storm over the distant violet strip of sea. It was towards the sea that he was staring.

Suddenly he woke up; and seemed almost to rub his eyes, or at any rate, to rub his red eyebrow.

"Why, we're on the road back of Pebblewick," he said. "That's the damned little tin chapel by the beach."

"I know," answered his friend and guide. "We've done the old hare trick; doubled, you know. Nine times out of ten it's the best. Parson Whitelady used to do it when they were after him for dog-stealing. I've pretty much followed his trail; you can't do better than stick to the best examples. They tell you in London that Dick Turpin rode to York. Well, I know he didn't; for my old grandfather up at Cobble's End knew the Turpins intimately—threw one of them into the river on a Christmas day; but I think I can guess what he did do and how the tale got about. If Dick was wise, he went flying up the old North Road, shouting 'York! York!' or what not, before people recognised him; then if he did the thing properly, he might half an hour afterwards walk down the Strand with a pipe in his mouth. They say old Boney said, 'Go where you aren't expected,' and I suppose as a soldier he was right. But for a gentleman dodging the police like yourself, it isn't exactly the right way of putting it. I should say, 'Go where you ought to be expected'— and you'll generally find your fellow creatures don't do what they ought about expecting any more than about anything else."

"Well, this bit between here and the sea," said the Captain, in a brown study, "I know it so well—so well that—that I rather wish I'd never seen it again. Do you know," he asked, suddenly pointing to a patch and pit of sand that showed white in the dusky heath a hundred yards away, "do you know what makes that spot so famous in history?"

"Yes," answered Mr. Pump, "that's where old Mother Grouch shot the Methodist."

"You are in error," said the Captain. "Such an incident as you describe would in no case call for special comment or regret. No, that spot is famous because a very badly brought up girl once lost a ribbon off a plait of black hair and somebody helped her to find it."

"Has the other person been well brought up?" asked Pump, with a faint smile.

"No," said Dalroy, staring at the sea. "He has been brought down." Then, rousing himself again, he made a gesture toward a further part of the heath. "Do you know the remarkable history of that old wall, the one beyond the last gorge over there?"

"No," replied the other, "unless you mean Dead Man's Circus, and that happened further along."

"I do not mean Dead Man's Circus," said the Captain. "The remarkable history of that wall is that somebody's shadow once fell on it; and that shadow was more desirable than the substance of all other living things. It is *this*," he cried, almost violently, resuming his flippant tone, "it is this circumstance, Hump, and not the trivial and everyday incident of a dead man going to a circus to which you have presumed to compare it, it is *this* historical event which Lord Ivywood is about to commemorate by rebuilding the wall with solid gold and Greek marbles stolen by the Turks from the grave of Socrates, enclosing a column of solid gold four hundred feet high and surmounted by a colossal equestrian statue of a bankrupt Irishman riding backwards on a donkey."

He lifted one of his long legs over the animal, as if about to pose for the group; then swung back on both feet again, and again looked at the purple limit of the sea.

"Do you know, Hump," he said, "I think modern people have somehow got their minds all wrong about human life. They seem to expect what Nature has never promised; and then try to ruin all that Nature has really given. At all those atheist chapels of Ivywood's they're always talking of Peace, Perfect Peace, and Utter Peace, and Universal Joy and souls that beat as one. But they don't look any more cheerful than anyone else; and the next thing they do is to start smashing a thousand good jokes and good stories and good songs and good friendships by pulling down 'The Old Ship.'" He gave a glance at the loose signpost lying on the heath beside him, almost as if to reassure himself that it was not stolen. "Now it seems to me," he went on, "that this is asking for too much and getting too little. I don't know whether God means a man to have happiness in that All in All and Utterly Utter sense of happiness. But God does mean a man to have a little Fun; and I mean to go on having it. If I mustn't satisfy my heart, I can gratify my humour. The cynical fellows who think themselves so damned clever have a sort of saying, 'Be good and you will be happy; but you will not have a jolly time.' The cynical fellows are quite wrong, as they generally are. They have got hold of the exact opposite of the truth. God knows I don't set up to be good; but even a rascal sometimes has to fight the world in the same way as a saint. I think I have fought the world; *et militavi non sine*—what's the Latin for having a lark? I can't pretend to Peace and Joy, and all the rest of it, particularly in this original briar-patch. I haven't been happy, Hump, but I have had a jolly time."

The sunset stillness settled down again, save for the cropping of the donkey in the undergrowth; and Pump said nothing sympathetically; and it was Dalroy once more who took up his parable.

"So I think there's too much of this playing on our emotions, Hump; as this place is certainly playing the cat and banjo with mine. Damn it all, there are other things to do with the rest of one's life! I don't like all this fuss about feeling things—it only makes people miserable. In my present frame of mind I'm in favour of doing things. All of which, Hump," he said with a sudden lift of the voice that always went in him with a rushing, irrational return of merely animal spirits—"All of which I have put into a Song Against Songs, that I will now sing you."

"I shouldn't sing it here," said Humphrey Pump, picking up his gun and putting it under his arm. "You look large in this open place; and you sound large. But I'll take you to the Hole in Heaven you've been talking about so much, and hide you as I used to hide you from that tutor—I couldn't catch his name—man who could only get drunk on Greek wine at Squire Wimpole's."

"Hump!" cried the Captain, "I abdicate the throne of Ithaca. You are far wiser than Ulysses. Here I have had my heart torn with temptations to ten thousand things between suicide and abduction, and all by the mere sight of that hole in the heath, where we used to have picnics.

And all that time I'd forgotten we used to call it the Hole in Heaven. And, by God, what a good name—in both senses."

"I thought you'd have remembered it, Captain," said the innkeeper, "from the joke young Mr. Matthews made."

"In the heat of some savage hand to hand struggle in Albania," said Mr. Dalroy, sadly, passing his palm across his brow, "I must have forgotten for one fatal instant the joke young Mr. Matthews made."

"It wasn't very good," said Mr. Pump, simply. "Ah, his aunt was the one for things like that. She went too far with old Gudgeon, though."

With these words he jumped and seemed to be swallowed up by the earth. But they had merely strolled the few yards needed to bring them to the edge of the sand-pit on the heath of which they had been speaking. And it is one of the truths concealed by Heaven from Lord Ivywood, and revealed by Heaven to Mr. Pump, that a hiding-place can be covered when you are close to it; and yet be open and visible from some spot of vantage far off. From the side by which they approached it, the sudden hollow of sand, a kind of collapsed chamber in the heath, seemed covered with a natural curve of fern and furze, and flashed out of sight like a fairy.

"It's all right," he called out from under a floor or roof of leaves. "You'll remember it all when you get here. This is the place to sing your song, Captain. Lord bless me, Captain, don't I remember your singing that Irish song you made up at college—bellowing it like a bull of Bashan—all about hearts and sleeves or some such things—and her ladyship and the tutor never heard a breath, because that bank of sand breaks everything. It's worth knowing all this, you know. It's a pity it's not part of a young gentleman's education. Now you shall sing me the song in favour of having no feelings, or whatever you call it."

Dalroy was staring about him at the cavern of his old picnics, so forgotten and so startlingly familiar. He seemed to have lost all thought of singing anything, and simply to be groping in the dark house of his own boyhood. There was a slight trickle from a natural spring in sandstone just under the ferns, and he remembered they used to try to boil the water in a kettle. He remembered a quarrel about who had upset the kettle which, in the morbidity of first love, had given him for days the tortures of the damned. When the energetic Pump broke once more through the rather thorny roof, on an impulse to accumulate their other eccentric possessions, Patrick remembered about a thorn in a finger, that made his heart stop with something that was pain and perfect music. When Pump returned with the rum-keg and the cheese and rolled them with a kick down the shelving sandy side of the hole, he remembered, with almost wrathful laughter, that in the old days he had rolled down that slope himself, and thought it a rather fine thing to do. He felt then as if he were rolling down a smooth side of the Matterhorn. He observed now that the height was rather less than that of the second storey of one of the stunted cottages he had noted on his return. He suddenly understood he had grown bigger; bigger in a bodily sense. He had doubts about any other.

"The Hole in Heaven!" he said. "What a good name! What a good poet I was in those days! The Hole in Heaven. But does it let one in, or let one out?"

In the last level shafts of the fallen sun the fantastic shadow of the long-eared quadruped, whom Pump had now tethered to a new and nearer pasture, fell across the last sunlit scrap of sand. Dalroy looked at the long exaggerated shadow of the ass; and laughed that short explosive laugh he had uttered when the doors of the harems had been closed after the Turkish war. He was normally a man much too loquacious; but he never explained those laughs.

Humphrey Pump plunged down again into the sunken nest, and began to broach the cask of rum in his own secret style, saying—

"We can get something else somehow tomorrow. For tonight we can eat cheese and drink rum, especially as there's water on tap, so to speak. And now, Captain, sing us the Song Against Songs."

Patrick Dalroy drank a little rum out of a small medicine glass which the generally unaccountable Mr. Pump unaccountably produced from his waistcoat pocket; but Patrick's colour had risen, his brow was almost as red as his hair; and he was evidently reluctant.

"I don't see why I should sing all the songs," he said. "Why the divil don't you sing a song yourself? And now I come to think of it," he cried, with an accumulating brogue, not, perhaps, wholly unaffected by the rum, which he had not, in fact, drunk for years, "and now I come to think of it, what about that song of yours? All me youth's coming back in this blest and cursed place; and I remember that song of yours, that never existed nor ever will. Don't ye remember now, Humphrey Pump, that night when I sang ye no less than seventeen songs of me own composition?"

"I remember it very well," answered the Englishman, with restraint.

"And don't ye remember," went on the exhilarated Irishman, with solemnity, "that unless ye could produce a poetic lyric of your own, written and sung by yourself, I threatened to. . ."

"To sing again," said the impenetrable Pump. "Yes, I know."

He calmly proceeded to take out of his pockets, which were, alas, more like those of a poacher than an innkeeper, a folded and faded piece of paper.

"I wrote it when you asked me," he said simply. "I have never tried to sing it. But I'll sing it myself, when you've sung your song, against anybody singing at all."

"All right," cried the somewhat excited Captain, "to hear a song from you—why, I'll sing anything. This is the Song Against Songs, Hump."

And again he let his voice out like a bellow against the evening silence.

"The song of the sorrow of Melisande is a weary song and a dreary song,
The glory of Mariana's grange had got into great decay,
The song of the Raven Never More has never been called a cheery song,
And the brightest things in Baudelaire are anything else but gay.
But who will write us a riding song,
Or a hunting song or a drinking song,
Fit for them that arose and rode,
When day and the wine were red?
But bring me a quart of claret out,
And I will write you a clinking song,
A song of war and a song of wine,
And a song to wake the dead.

"The song of the fury of Fragolette is a florid song and a torrid song,
The song of the sorrow of Tara is sung to a harp unstrung,
The song of the cheerful Shropshire Kid I consider a perfectly horrid song,
And the song of the happy Futurist is a song that can't be sung.
But who will write us a riding song,
Or a fighting song or a drinking song,
Fit for the fathers of you and me,
That knew how to think and thrive?
But the song of Beauty and Art and Love
Is simply an utterly stinking song,
To double you up and drag you down.
And damn your soul alive."

"Take some more rum," concluded the Irish officer, affably, "and let's hear your song at last."

With the gravity inseparable from the deep conventionality of country people, Mr. Pump unfolded the paper on which he had recorded the only antagonistic emotion that was strong enough in him to screw his infinite English tolerance to the pitch of song. He read out the title very carefully and in full.

"Song Against Grocers, by Humphrey Pump, sole proprietor of 'The Old Ship,' Pebblewick. Good Accommodation for Man and Beast. Celebrated as the House at which both Queen Charlotte and Jonathan Wilde put up on different occasions; and where the Ice-cream man was mistaken for Bonaparte. This song is written against Grocers."

> "God made the wicked Grocer,
> For a mystery and a sign,
> That men might shun the awful shops,
> And go to inns to dine;
> Where the bacon's on the rafter
> And the wine is in the wood,
> And God that made good laughter
> Has seen that they are good.
>
> "The evil-hearted Grocer
> Would call his mother 'Ma'am,'
> And bow at her and bob at her,
> Her aged soul to damn;
> And rub his horrid hands and ask,
> What article was next;
> Though mortis in articulo,
> Should be her proper text.
>
> "His props are not his children
> But pert lads underpaid,
> Who call out 'Cash!' and bang about,
> To work his wicked trade;
> He keeps a lady in a cage,
> Most cruelly all day,
> And makes her count and calls her 'Miss,'
> Until she fades away.

"The righteous minds of inn-keepers
Induce them now and then
To crack a bottle with a friend,
Or treat unmoneyed men;
But who hath seen the Grocer
Treat housemaids to his teas,
Or crack a bottle of fish-sauce,
Or stand a man a cheese?

"He sells us sands of Araby
As sugar for cash down,
He sweeps his shop and sells the dust,
The purest salt in town;
He crams with cans of poisoned meat
Poor subjects of the King,
And when they die by thousands
Why, he laughs like anything.

"The Wicked Grocer groces
In spirits and in wine,
Not frankly and in fellowship,
As men in inns do dine;
But packed with soap and sardines
And carried off by grooms,
For to be snatched by Duchesses,
And drunk in dressing-rooms.

"The hell-instructed Grocer
Has a temple made of tin,
And the ruin of good inn-keepers
Is loudly urged therein;
But now the sands are running out
From sugar of a sort,
The Grocer trembles; for his time
Just like his weight is short."

Captain Dalroy was getting considerably heated with his nautical liquor, and his appreciation of Pump's song was not merely noisy but active. He leapt to his feet and waved his glass. "Ye ought to be

Poet Laureate, Hump—ye're right, ye're right; we'll stand all this no longer!"

He dashed wildly up the sand slope and pointed with the sign-post towards the darkening shore, where the low shed of corrugated iron stood almost isolated.

"There's your tin temple!" he said. "Let's burn it!"

They were some way along the coast from the large watering-place of Pebblewick and between the gathering twilight and the rolling country it could not be clearly seen. Nothing was now in sight but the corrugated iron hall by the beach and three half-built red brick villas.

Dalroy appeared to regard the hall and the empty houses with great malevolence.

"Look at it!" he said. "Babylon!"

He brandished the inn-sign in the air like a banner, and began to stride towards the place, showering curses.

"In forty days," he cried, "shall Pebblewick be destroyed. Dogs shall lap the blood of J. Leveson, Secretary, and Unicorns—"

"Come back Pat," cried Humphrey, "you've had too much rum."

"Lions shall howl in its high places," vociferated the Captain.

"Donkeys will howl, anyhow," said Pump. "But I suppose the other donkey must follow."

And loading and untethering the quadruped, he began to lead him along.

VII

THE SOCIETY OF SIMPLE SOULS

Under sunset, at once softer and more sombre, under which the leaden sea took on a Lenten purple, a tint appropriate to tragedy, Lady Joan Brett was once more drifting moodily along the sea-front. The evening had been rainy and lowering; the watering-place season was nearly over; and she was almost alone on the shore; but she had fallen into the habit of restlessly pacing the place, and it seemed to satisfy some subconscious hunger in her rather mixed psychology. Through all her brooding her animal senses always remained abnormally active: she could *smell* the sea when it had ebbed almost to the horizon, and in the same way she heard, through every whisper of waves or wind, the swish or flutter of another woman's skirt behind her. There is, she felt, something unmistakable about the movements of a lady who is generally very dignified and rather slow, and who happens to be in a hurry.

She turned to look at the lady who was thus hastening to overtake her; lifted her eyebrows a little and held out her hand. The interruption was known to her as Lady Enid Wimpole, cousin of Lord Ivywood; a tall and graceful lady who unbalanced her own elegance by a fashionable costume that was at once funereal and fantastic; her fair hair was pale but plentiful; her face was not only handsome and fastidious in the aquiline style, but when considered seriously was sensitive, modest, and even pathetic, but her wan blue eyes seemed slightly prominent, with that expression of cold eagerness that is seen in the eyes of ladies who ask questions at public meetings.

Joan Brett was herself, as she had said, a connection of the Ivywood family; but Lady Enid was Ivywood's first cousin, and for all practical purposes his sister. For she kept house for him and his mother, who was now so incredibly old that she only survived to satisfy conventional opinion in the character of a speechless and useless *chaperon*. And Ivywood was not the sort who would be likely to call out any activity in an old lady exercising that office. Nor, for that matter, was Lady Enid Wimpole; there seemed to shine on her face the same kind of inhuman, absent-minded common sense that shone on her cousin's.

"Oh, I'm so glad I've caught you up," she said to Joan. "Lady Ivywood wants you *so* much to come to us for the week-end or so, while Philip is still there. He always admired your sonnet on Cyprus so much, and he wants to talk to you about this policy of his in Turkey. Of course he's awfully busy, but I shall be seeing him tonight after the meeting."

"No living creature," said Lady Joan, with a smile, "ever saw him except before or after a meeting."

"Are you a Simple Soul?" asked Lady Enid, carelessly.

"Am I a simple soul?" asked Joan, drawing her black brows together. "Merciful Heavens, no! What can you mean?"

"Their meeting's on tonight at the small Universal Hall, and Philip's taking the chair," explained the other lady. "He's very annoyed that he has to leave early to get up to the House, but Mr. Leveson can take the chair for the last bit. They've got Misysra Ammon."

"Got Mrs. Who?" asked Joan, in honest doubt.

"You make game of everything," said Lady Enid, in cheerless amiability. "It's the man everyone's talking about—*you* know as well as I do. It's really his influence that has *made* the Simple Souls."

"Oh!" said Lady Joan Brett.

Then after a long silence, she added: "Who are the Simple Souls? I should be interested in them, if I could meet any." And she turned her dark, brooding face on the darkening purple sea.

"Do you mean to say, my dear," asked Lady Enid Wimpole, "that you haven't met any of them yet?"

"No," said Joan, looking at the last dark line of sea. "I never met but one simple soul in my life."

"But you must come to the meeting!" cried Lady Enid, with frosty and sparkling gaity. "You must come at once! Philip is certain to be eloquent on a subject like this, and of course Misysra Ammon is *always* so wonderful."

Without any very distinct idea of where she was going or why she was going there, Joan allowed herself to be piloted to a low lead or tin shed, beyond the last straggling hotels, out of the echoing shell of which she could prematurely hear a voice that she thought she recognised. When she came in Lord Ivywood was on his feet, in exquisite evening dress, but with a light overcoat thrown over the seat behind him. Beside him, in less tasteful but more obvious evening dress, was the little old man she had heard on the beach.

No one else was on the platform, but just under it, rather to Joan's surprise, sat Miss Browning, her old typewriting friend in her old black dress, industriously taking down Lord Ivywood's words in shorthand. A yard or two off, even more to her surprise, sat Miss Browning's more domestic sister, also taking down the same words in shorthand.

"That is Misysra Ammon," whispered Lady Enid, earnestly, pointing a delicate finger at the little old man beside the chairman.

"I know him," said Joan. "Where's the umbrella?"

". . . at least evident," Lord Ivywood was saying, "that one of those ancestral impossibilities is no longer impossible. The East and the West are one. The East is no longer East nor the West West; for a small isthmus has been broken, and the Atlantic and Pacific are a single sea. No man assuredly has done more of this mighty work of unity than the brilliant and distinguished philosopher to whom you will have the pleasure of listening tonight; and I profoundly wish that affairs more practical, for I will not call them more important, did not prevent my remaining to enjoy his eloquence, as I have so often enjoyed it before. Mr. Leveson has kindly consented to take my place, and I can do no more than express my deep sympathy with the aims and ideals which will be developed before you tonight. I have long been increasingly convinced that underneath a certain mask of stiffness which the Mahomedan religion has worn through certain centuries, as a somewhat similar mask has been worn by the religion of the Jews, Islam has in it the potentialities of being the most progressive of all religions; so that a century or two to come we may see the cause of peace, of science and of reform everywhere supported by Islam as it is everywhere supported by Israel. Not in vain, I think, is the symbol of that faith the Crescent, the growing thing. While other creeds carry emblems implying more or less of finality, for this great creed of hope its very imperfection is its pride, and men shall walk fearlessly in new and wonderful paths, following the increasing curve which contains and holds up before them the eternal promises of the orb."

It was characteristic of Lord Ivywood that, though he was really in a hurry, he sat down slowly and gravely amid the outburst of applause. The quiet resumption of the speaker's seat, like the applause itself, was an artistic part of the peroration. When the last clap or stamp had subsided, he sprang up alertly, his light great-coat over his arm, shook hands with the lecturer, bowed to the audience and slid quickly out of the hall. Mr. Leveson, the swarthy young man with the drooping double-eyeglass rather bashfully to the front, took the empty seat on the platform, and in a few words presented the eminent Turkish mystic Misysra Ammon, sometimes called the Prophet of the Moon.

Lady Joan found the Prophet's English accent somewhat improved by good society, but he still elongated the letter "u" in the same bleating manner, and his remarks had exactly the same rabidly wrong-headed ingenuity as his lecture upon English inns. It appeared that he was speaking on the higher Polygamy; but he began with a sort of general defence of the Moslem civilisation, especially against the charge of sterility and worldly ineffectiveness.

"It iss joost in the practical tings," he was saying, "it iss joost in the practical tings, if you could come to consider them in a manner quite equal, that our methods are better than your methods. My ancestors invented the curved swords, because one cuts better with a curved sword. Your ancestors possessed the straight swords out of some romantic fancy of being what you call straight; or, I will take a more plain example, of which I have myself experience. When I first had the honour of meeting Lord Ivywood, I was unused to your various ceremonies and had a little difficulty, joost a little difficulty, in entering Mr. Claridge's hotel, where his lordship had invited me. A servant of the hotel was standing joost beside me on the doorstep. I stoo-ooped down to take off my boo-oots, and he asked me what I was dooing. I said to him: 'My friend, I am taking off my boo-oots.'"

A smothered sound came from Lady Joan Brett, but the lecturer did not notice it and went on with a beautiful simplicity.

"I told him that in my country, when showing respect for any spot, we do not take off our hats; we take off our boo-oots. And because I would keep on my hat and take off my boo-oots, he suggested to me that I had been afflicted by Allah, in the head. Now was not that foony?"

"Very," said Lady Joan, inside her handkerchief, for she was choking with laughter. Something like a faint smile passed over the earnest faces of the two or three most intelligent of the Simple Souls, but for the most part the Souls seemed very simple indeed, helpless looking people with limp hair and gowns like green curtains, and their dry faces were as dry as ever.

"But I explained to him. I explained to him for a long time, for a carefully occupied time, that it was more practical, more business-like, more altogether for utility, to take off the boo-oots than to remove the hat. 'Let us,' I said to him 'consider what many complaints are made against the footwear, what few complaints against the headwear.

You complain if in your drawing-rooms is the marching about of muddy boo-oots. Are any of your drawing-rooms marked thus with the marching about of muddy hats? How very many of your husbands kick you with the boo-oot! Yet how few of your husbands on any occasion butt you with the hat?'"

He looked round with a radiant seriousness, which made Lady Joan almost as speechless for sympathy as she was for amusement. With all that was most sound in his too complicated soul she realized the presence of a man really convinced.

"The man on the doorstep, he would not listen to me," went on Misysra Ammon, pathetically. "He said there would be a crowd if I stood on the doorstep, holding in my hand my boo-oots. Well, I do not know why, in your country you always send the young males to be the first of your crowds. They certainly were making a number of noises, the young males."

Lady Joan Brett stood up suddenly and displayed enormous interest in the rest of the audience in the back parts of the hall. She felt that if she looked for one moment more at the serious face with the Jewish nose and the Persian beard, she would publicly disgrace herself; or, what was quite as bad (for she was the generous sort of aristocrat) publicly insult the lecturer. She had a feeling that the sight of all the Simple Souls in bulk might have a soothing effect. It had. It had what might have been mistaken for a depressing effect. Lady Joan resumed her seat with a controlled countenance.

"Now, why," asked the Eastern philosopher, "do I tell so simple a little story of your London streets—a thing happening any day? The little mistake had no preju-udicial effect. Lord Ivywood came out, at the end. He made no attempt to explain the true view of so important matters to Mr. Claridge's servant, though Mr. Claridge's servant remained on the doorstep. But he commanded Mr. Claridge's servant to restore to me one of my boo-oots, which had fallen down the front steps, while I was explaining this harmlessness of the hat in the home. So all was, for me, very well. But why do I tell such little tales?"

He spread out his hands again, in his fanlike eastern style. Then he clapped them together, so suddenly that Joan jumped, and looked instinctively for the entrance of five hundred negro slaves, laden with jewels. But it was only his emphatic gesture of eloquence. He went on with an excited thickening of the accent.

"Because, my friends, this is the best example I could give of the wrong and slanderous character of the charge that we fail in our domesticities.

That we fail especially in our treatment of the womenkind. I appeal to any lady, to any Christian lady. Is not the boo-oot more devastating, more dreaded in the home than the hat? The boot jumps, he bound, he run about, he break things, he leave on the carpet the earths of the garden. The hat, he remain quiet on his hat-peg. Look at him on his hat-peg; how quiet and good he remain! Why not let him remain quiet also on his head?"

Lady Joan applauded warmly, as did several other ladies, and the sage went on, encouraged.

"Can you not therefore trust, dear ladies, this great religion to understand you concerning other things, as it understands you regarding boo-oots? What is the common objection our worthy enemies make against our polygamy? That it is disdainful of the womanhood. But how can this be so, my friends, when it allows the womanhood to be present in so large numbers? When in your House of Commons you put a hundred English members and joost one little Welsh member, you do not say 'The Welshman is on top; he is our Sultan; may he live for ever!' If your jury contained eleven great large ladies and one leetle man you would not say 'this is unfair to the great large ladies.' Why should you shrink, then, ladies, from this great polygamical experiment which Lord Ivywood himself—"

Joan's dark eyes were still fixed on the wrinkled, patient face of the lecturer, but every word of the rest of the lecture was lost to her. Under her glowing Spanish tint she had turned pale with extraordinary emotions, but she did not stir a hair.

The door of the hall stood open, and occasional sounds came even from that deserted end of the town. Two men seemed to be passing along the distant parade; one of them was singing. It was common enough for workmen to sing going home at night, and the voice, though a loud one, would have been too far off for Joan to hear the words. Only Joan happened to know the words. She could almost see them before her, written in a round swaggering hand on the pink page of an old school-girl album at home. She knew the words and the voice.

> "I come from Castlepatrick and my heart is on my sleeve,
> And any sword or pistol boy can hit ut with me leave,
> It shines there for an epaulette, as golden as a flame,
> As naked as me ancestors, as noble as me name.
> For I come from Castlepatrick and my heart is on my sleeve,
> But a lady stole it from me on St. Gallowglass's Eve."

Startlingly and with strong pain there sprang up before Joan's eyes a patch of broken heath with a very deep hollow of white sand, blinding in the sun. No words, no name, only the place.

"The folks that live in Liverpool, their heart is in their boots;
They go to Hell like lambs, they do, because the hooter hoots.
Where men may not be dancin', though the wheels may dance all day;
And men may not be smokin', but only chimneys may.
But I come from Castlepatrick and my heart is on my sleeve,
But a lady stole it from me on St. Poleyander's Eve.

"The folks that live in black Belfast, their heart is in their mouth;
They see us making murders in the meadows of the South;
They think a plough's a rack they do, and cattle-calls are creeds,
And they think we're burnin' witches when we're only burnin' weeds.
But I come from Castlepatrick, and me heart is on me sleeve;
But a lady stole it from me on St. Barnabas's Eve."

The voice had stopped suddenly, but the last lines were so much more distinct that it was certain the singer had come nearer, and was not marching away.

It was only after all this, and through a sort of cloud, that Lady Joan heard the indomitable Oriental bringing his whole eloquent address to a conclusion.

". . . And if you do not refu-use the sun that returns and rises in the East with every morning, you will not refu-use either this great social experiment, this great polygamical method which also arose out of the East, and always returns. For this is that Higher Polygamy which always comes, like the sun itself, out of the orient, but is only at its noontide splendour when the sun is high in heaven."

She was but vaguely conscious of Mr. Leveson, the man with the dark face and the eyeglasses, acknowledging the entrancing lecture in suitable terms, and calling on any of the Simple Souls who might have questions to ask, to ask them. It was only when the Simple Souls had displayed their simplicity with the usual parade of well-bred reluctance and fussy self-effacement, that anyone addressed the chair. And it was only after somebody had been addressing the chair for some time that Joan gradually awoke to the fact that the address was somewhat unusual.

VIII

Vox Populi Vox Dei

I am sure," Mr. Leveson, the Secretary, had said, with a somewhat constrained smile, "that after the eloquent and epoch-making speech to which we have listened there will be some questions asked, and we hope to have a debate afterwards. I am sure somebody will ask a question." Then he looked interrogatively at one weary looking gentleman in the fourth row and said, "Mr. Hinch?"

Mr. Hinch shook his head with a pallid passion of refusal, wonderful to watch, and said, "I couldn't! I really couldn't!"

"We should be very pleased," said Mr. Leveson, "if any lady would ask a question."

In the silence that followed it was somehow psychologically borne in on the whole audience that one particular great large lady (as the lecturer would say) sitting at the end of the second row was expected to ask a question. Her own wax-work immobility was witness both to the expectation and its disappointment. "Are there any other questions?" asked Mr. Leveson—as if there had been any yet. He seemed to speak with a slight air of relief.

There was a sort of stir at the back of the hall and half way down one side of it. Choked whispers could be heard of "Now then, Garge!"— "Go it Garge! Is there any questions! Gor!"

Mr. Leveson looked up with an alertness somewhat akin to alarm. He realised for the first time that a few quite common men in coarse, unclean clothes, had somehow strolled in through the open door. They were not true rustics, but the semi-rustic labourers that linger about the limits of the large watering-places. There was no "Mr." among them. There was a general tendency to call everybody George.

Mr. Leveson saw the situation and yielded to it. He modelled himself on Lord Ivywood and did much what he would have done in all cases, but with a timidity Lord Ivywood would not have shown. And the same social training that made him ashamed to be with such men, made him ashamed to own his shame. The same modern spirit that taught him to loathe such rags, also taught him to lie about his loathing.

"I am sure we should be very glad," he said, nervously, "if any friends from outside care to join in our inquiry. Of course, we're all Democrats," and he looked round at the grand ladies with a ghastly smile, "and believe in the Voice of the People and so on. If our friend at the back of the hall will put his question briefly, we need not insist, I think, on his putting it in writing?"

There were renewed hoarse encouragements to George (that rightly christened champion) and he wavered forward on legs tied in the middle with string. He did not appear to have had any seat since his arrival, and made his remarks standing half way down what we may call the central aisle.

"Well, I want to ask the proprietor," he began.

"Questions," said Mr. Leveson, swiftly seizing a chance for that construction of debate which is the main business of a modern chairman, "must be asked of the chair, if they are points of order. If they concern the address, they should be asked of the lecturer."

"Well, I ask the lecturer," said the patient Garge, "whether it ain't right that when you 'ave the thing outside you should 'ave the thing inside." (Hoarse applause at the back.)

Mr. Leveson was evidently puzzled and already suspicious that something was quite wrong. But the enthusiasm of the Prophet of the Moon sprang up instantly at any sort of question and swept the Chairman along with it.

"But it iss the essence of our who-ole message," he cried, spreading out his arms to embrace the world, "that the outer manifestation should be one with the inner manifestation. My friendss, it iss this very tru-uth our friend has stated, that iss responsible for our apparent lack of symbolism in Islam! We appear to neglect the symbol because we insist on the satisfactory symbol. My friend in the middle will walk round all our mosques and say loudly, 'Where is the statue of Allah?' But can my friend in the middle really execute a complete and generally approved statue of Allah?"

Misysra Ammon sat down greatly satisfied with his answer, but it was doubted by many whether he had conveyed the satisfaction to his friend in the middle. That seeker after truth wiped his mouth with the back of his hand with an unsatisfied air and said:

"No offence, sir. But ain't it the Law, sir, that if you 'ave that outside we're all right? I came in 'ere as natural as could be. But Gorlumme, I never see a place like this afore." (Hoarse laughter behind.)

"No apology is needed, my friend," cried the Eastern sage, eagerly, "I can conceive you are not perhaps du-uly conversant with such schools of truth. But the Law is All. The Law is Allah. The inmost u-unity of—"

"Well, ain't it the Law?" repeated the dogged George, and every time he mentioned the Law the poor men who are its chief victims applauded loudly. "I'm not one to make a fuss. I never was one to make a fuss. I'm a law-abidin' man, I am. (More applause.) Ain't it the Law that if so be such is your sign and such is your profession, you ought to serve us?"

"I fear I not quite follow," cried the eager Turk. "I ought?"

"To serve us," shouted a throng of thick voices from the back of the hall, which was already much more crowded than before.

"Serve you!" cried Misysra, leaping up like a spring released, "The Holy Prophet came from Heaven to serve you! The virtue and valour of a thousand years, my friends, has had no hunger but to serve you! We are of all faiths, the most the faith of service. Our highest prophet is no more than the servant of God, as I am, as you all are. Even for our symbol we choose a satellite, and honour the Moon because it only serves the Earth, and does not pretend to be the Sun."

"I'm sure," cried Mr. Leveson, jumping up with a tactful grin, "that the lecturer has answered this last point in a most eloquent and effective way, and the motor cars are waiting for some of the ladies who have come from some distance, and I really think the proceedings—"

All the artistic ladies were already getting on their wraps, with faces varying from bewilderment to blank terror. Only Lady Joan lingered, trembling with unexplained excitement. The hitherto speechless Hinch had slid up to the Chairman's seat and whispered to him:

"You must get all the ladies away. I can't imagine what's up, but something's up."

"Well?" repeated the patient George. "So be it's the Law, where is it?"

"Ladies and Gentlemen," said Mr. Leveson, in his most ingratiating manner, "I think we have had a most delightful evening, and—"

"No, we ain't," cried a new and nastier voice from a corner of the room. "Where is it?"

"That's what we got a right to know," said the law-abiding George. "Where is it?"

"Where is what?" cried the nearly demented secretary in the chair. "What do you want?"

The law-abiding Mr. George made a half turn and a gesture towards the man in the corner and said:

"What's yours, Jim?"

"I'll 'ave a drop of Scotch," said the man in the corner.

Lady Enid Wimpole, who had lingered a little in loyalty to Joan, the only other lady still left, caught both her wrists and cried in a thrilling whisper,

"Oh, we must go to the car, dear! They're using the most awful language!"

AWAY ON THE WETTEST EDGE of the sands by the sea the prints of two wheels and four hoofs were being slowly washed away by a slowly rising tide; which was, indeed, the only motive of the man Humphrey Pump, leading the donkey cart, in leading it almost ankle deep in water.

"I hope you're sober again now," he said with some seriousness to his companion, a huge man walking heavily and even humbly with a straight sword swinging to and fro at his hip—"for honestly it was a mug's game to go and stick up the old sign before that tin place. I haven't often spoken to you like this, Captain, but I don't believe any other man in the county could get you out of the hole as I can. But to go down there and frighten the ladies—why there's been nothing so silly here since Bishop's Folly. You could hear the ladies screaming before we left."

"I heard worse than that long before we left," said the large man, without lifting his head. "I heard one of them laugh. . . Christ, do you think I shouldn't hear her laugh?"

There was a silence. "I didn't mean to speak sharp," said Humphrey Pump with that incorruptible kindliness which was the root of his Englishry, and may yet save the soul of the English. "But it's the truth I was pretty well bothered about how to get out of this business. You're braver than I am, you see, and I own I was frightened about both of us. If I hadn't known my way to the lost tunnel, I should be fairly frightened still."

"Known your way to what?" asked the Captain, lifting his red head for the first time.

"Oh, you know all about No More Ivywood's lost tunnel," said Pump, carelessly. "Why, we all used to look for it when we were boys. Only I happened to find it."

"Have mercy on an exile," said Dalroy, humbly. "I don't know which hurt him most, the things he forgets or the things he remembers."

Mr. Pump was silent for a little while and then said, more seriously than usual, "Well, the people from London say you must put up placards and statues and subscriptions and epitaphs and the Lord knows what, to the people who've found some new trick and made it come off. But only a man that knows his own land for forty miles round, knows what a lot of people, and clever people too, there were who found new tricks, and had to hide them because they didn't come off. There was Dr. Boone, up by Gill-in-Hugby, who held out against Dr. Collison and the vaccination. His treatment saved sixty patients who had got small-pox; and Dr. Collison's killed ninety-two patients who hadn't got anything. But Boone had to keep it dark; naturally, because all his lady patients grew mustaches. It was a result of the treatment. But it wasn't a result he wishes to dwell on. Then there was old Dean Arthur, who discovered balloons if ever a man did. He discovered them long before they were discovered. But people were suspicious about such things just then— there was a revival of the witch business in spite of all the parsons—and he had to sign a paper saying where he'd got the notion. Well, it stands to reason, you wouldn't like to sign a paper saying you'd got it from the village idiot when you were both blowing soap-bubbles; and that's all he could have signed, for he was an honest gentleman, the poor old Dean. Then there was Jack Arlingham and the diving bell—but you remember all about that. Well, it was just the same with the man that made this tunnel—one of the mad Ivywoods. There's many a man, Captain, that has a statue in the great London squares for helping to make the railway-trains. There's many a man has his name in Westminster Abbey for doing something in discovering steamboats. Poor old Ivywood discovered both at once; and had to be put under control. He had a notion that a railway train might be made to rush right into the sea and turn into a steamboat; and it seemed all right, according as he worked it out. But his family were so ashamed of the thing, that they didn't like the tunnel even mentioned. I don't think anybody knows where it is but me and Bunchy Robinson. We shall be there in a minute or two. They've thrown the rocks about at this end; and let the thick plantation grow at the other, but I've got a race horse through before now, to save it from Colonel Chepstow's little games, and I think I can manage this donkey. Honestly, I think it's the only place we'll be safe in after what we've left behind us at Pebblewick. But it's the best place in the world, there's no doubt, for lying low and starting afresh. Here we are. You think you can't get behind that rock, but you can. In fact, you have."

Dalroy found himself, with some bewilderment, round the corner of a rock and in a long bore or barrel of blackness that ended in a very dim spot of green. Hearing the hoofs of the ass and the feet of his friend behind him, he turned his head, but could see nothing but the pitch darkness of a closed coal cellar. He turned again to the dim green speck, and marching forward was glad to see it grow larger and brighter, like a big emerald, till he came out on a throng of trees, mostly thin, but growing so thickly and so close to the cavernous entrance of the tunnel that it was quite clear the place was meant to be choked up by forests and forgotten. The light that came glimmering through the trees was so broken and tremulous that it was hard to tell whether it was daybreak or moonrise.

"I know there's water here," said Pump. "They couldn't keep it out of the stone-work when they made the tunnel, and old Ivywood hit the hydraulic engineer with a spirit level. With the bit of covert here and the sea behind us we ought to be able to get food of one kind or another, when the cheese has given out, and donkeys can eat anything. By the way," he added with some embarrassment, "you don't mind my saying it, Captain, but I think we'd better keep that rum for rare occasions. It's the best rum in England, and may be the last, if these mad games are going on. It'll do us good to feel it's there, so we can have it when we want it. The cask's still nearly full."

Dalroy put out his hand and shook the other's. "Hump," he said, seriously, "you're right. It's a sacred trust for Humanity; and we'll only drink it ourselves to celebrate great victories. In token of which I will take a glass now, to celebrate our glorious victory over Leveson and his tin tabernacle."

He drained one glass and then sat down on the cask, as if to put temptation behind him. His blue ruminant bull's eye seemed to plunge deeper and deeper into the emerald twilight of the trees in front of him, and it was long before he spoke again.

At last he observed, "I think you said, Hump, that a friend of yours—a gentleman named Bunchy Robinson, I think—was also a *habitué* here."

"Yes, he knew the way," answered Pump, leading the donkey to the most suitable patch of pasturage.

"May we, do you think, have the pleasure of a visit from Mr. Robinson?" inquired the Captain.

"Not unless they're jolly careless up in Blackstone Gaol," replied Pump. And he moved the cheese well into the arch of the tunnel. Dalroy still sat with his square chin on his hand, staring at the mystery of the little wood.

G.K. CHESTERTON

"You seem absent-minded, Captain," remarked Humphrey.

"The deepest thoughts are all commonplaces," said Dalroy. "That is why I believe in Democracy, which is more than you do, you foul blood-stained old British Tory. And the deepest commonplace of all is that Vanitas Vanitatem, which is not pessimism but is really the opposite of pessimism. It is man's futility that makes us feel he must be a god. And I think of this tunnel, and how the poor old lunatic walked about on this grass, watching it being built, the soul in him on fire with the future. And he saw the whole world changed and the seas thronged with his new shipping; and now," and Dalroy's voice changed and broke, "now there is good pasture for the donkey and it is very quiet here."

"Yes," said Pump, in some way that conveyed his knowledge that the Captain was thinking of other things also. The Captain went on dreamily:

"And I think about another Lord Ivywood recorded in history who also had a great vision. For it is a great vision after all, and though the man is a prig, he is brave. He also wants to drive a tunnel—between East and West—to make the Indian Empire more British; to effect what he calls the orientation of England, and I call the ruin of Christendom. And I am wondering just now whether the clear intellect and courageous will of a madman will be strong enough to burst and drive that tunnel, as everything seems to show at this moment that it will. Or whether there be indeed enough life and growth in your England to leave it at last as this is left, buried in English forests and wasted by an English sea."

The silence fell between them again, and again there was only the slight sound the animal made in eating. As Dalroy had said, it was very quiet there.

But it was not quiet in Pebblewick that night; when the Riot Act was read, and all the people who had seen the sign-board outside fought all the people who hadn't seen the sign-board outside; or when babies and scientists next morning, seeking for shells and other common objects of the sea-shore, found that their study included fragments of the outer clothing of Leveson and scraps of corrugated iron.

IX

The Higher Criticism and Mr. Hibbs

Pebblewick boasted an enterprising evening paper of its own, called "The Pebblewick Globe," and it was the great vaunt of the editor's life that he had got out an edition announcing the mystery of the vanishing sign-board, almost simultaneously with its vanishing. In the rows that followed sandwich men found no little protection from the blows indiscriminately given them behind and before, in the large wooden boards they carried inscribed:

The Vanishing Pub
Pebblewick's Fairy Tale
Special

And the paper contained a categorical and mainly correct account of what had happened, or what seemed to have happened, to the eyes of the amazed Garge and his crowd of sympathisers. "George Burn, carpenter of this town, with Samuel Gripes, drayman in the service of Messrs. Jay and Gubbins, brewers, together with a number of other well-known residents, passed by the new building erected on the West Beach for various forms of entertainment and popularly called the small Universal Hall. Seeing outside it one of the old inn-signs now so rare, they drew the quite proper inference that the place retained the license to sell alcoholic liquors, which so many other places in this neighborhood have recently lost. The persons inside, however, appear to have denied all knowledge of the fact, and when the party (after some regrettable scenes in which no life was lost) came out on the beach again, it was found that the inn-sign had been destroyed or stolen. All parties were quite sober, and had indeed obtained no opportunity to be anything else. The mystery is underlying inquiry."

But this comparatively realistic record was local and spontaneous, and owed not a little to the accidental honesty of the editor. Moreover, evening papers are often more honest than morning papers, because they are written by ill-paid and hardworked underlings in a great hurry, and there is no time for more timid people to correct them. By the time the morning papers came out next day a faint but perceptible change had passed over the story of the vanishing sign-board. In the daily paper which had the largest circulation and the most influence in that part of the world, the problem was committed to a gentleman known by what seemed to the non-journalistic world the singular name of Hibbs However. It had been affixed to him in jest in connection with the almost complicated caution with which all his public criticisms were qualified at every turn; so that everything came to depend upon the conjunctions; upon "but" and "yet" and "though" and similar words. As his salary grew larger (for editors and proprietors like that sort of thing) and his old friends fewer (for the most generous of friends cannot but feel faintly acid at a success which has in it nothing of the infectious flavour of glory) he grew more and more to value himself as a diplomatist; a man who always said the right thing. But he was not without his intellectual nemesis; for at last he became so very diplomatic as to be darkly and densely unintelligible. People who knew him had no difficulty in believing that what he had said was the right thing, the tactful thing, the thing that should save the situation; but they had great difficulty in discovering what it was. In his early days he had had a great talent for one of the worst tricks of modern journalism, the trick of dismissing the important part of a question as if it could wait, and appearing to get to business on the unimportant part of it. Thus, he would say, "Whatever we may think of the rights and wrongs of the vivisection of pauper children, we shall all agree that it should only be done, in any event, by fully qualified practitioners." But in the later and darker days of his diplomacy, he seemed rather to dismiss the important part of a subject, and get to grips with some totally different subject, following some timid and elusive train of associations of his own. In his late bad manner, as they say of painters, he was just as likely to say, "Whatever we may think of the rights and wrongs of the vivisection of pauper children, no progressive mind can doubt that the influence of the Vatican is on the decline." His nickname had stuck to him in honour of a paragraph he was alleged to have written when the American President was wounded by a bullet fired by a lunatic in New Orleans, and which was said to have run, "The President passed a good night and his condition is greatly improved. The assassin is not, however, a German, as was at first supposed." Men stared at that mysterious conjunction till they wanted to go mad and to shoot somebody themselves.

Hibbs However was a long, lank man, with straight, yellowish hair and a manner that was externally soft and mild but secretly supercilious. He had been, when at Cambridge, a friend of Leveson, and they had both prided themselves on being moderate politicians. But if you have had your hat smashed over your nose by one who has very recently described himself as a "law-abidin' man," and if you have had to run for your life with one coat-tail, and encouraged to further bodily activity by having irregular pieces of a corrugated iron roof thrown after you by men more energetic than yourself, you will find you emerge with emotions which are not solely those of a moderate politician. Hibbs However had already composed a leaderette on the Pebblewick incident, which rather pointed to the truth of the story, so far as his articles ever pointed to anything. His motives for veering vaguely in this direction were, as usual, complex. He knew the millionaire who owned the paper had a hobby of Spiritualism, and something might always come out of not suppressing a marvellous story. He knew that two at least of the prosperous artisans or small tradesmen who had attested the tale were staunch supporters of The Party. He knew that Lord Ivywood must be mildly but not effectually checked; for Lord Ivywood was of The Other Party. And there could be no milder or less effectual way of checking him than by allowing the paper to lend at least a temporary credit to a well-supported story that came from outside, and certainly had not been (like so many stories) created in the office. Amid all these considerations had Hibbs However steered his way to a more or less confirmatory article, when the sudden apparition of J. Leveson, Secretary, in the sub-editor's room with a burst collar and broken eye-glasses, led Mr. Hibbs into a long, private conversation with him and a comparative reversal of his plans. But of course he did not write a new article; he was not of that divine order who make all things new. He chopped and changed his original article in such a way that it was something quite beyond the most bewildering article he had written in the past; and is still prized by those highly cultured persons who collect the worst literature of the world.

It began, indeed, with the comparatively familiar formula, "Whether we take the more lax or the more advanced view of the old disputed problem of the morality or immorality of the wooden sign-board as such, we shall all agree that the scenes enacted at Pebblewick were very discreditable, to most, though not all, concerned." After that, tact degenerated into a riot of irrelevance. It was a wonderful article. The reader could get from it a faint glimpse of Mr. Hibbs's opinion on almost every other subject except the subject of the article. The first half of the next sentence made it quite clear that Mr. Hibbs (had he been present) would not have lent his active assistance to the Massacre of St. Bartholomew or the Massacres of September. But the second half of the sentence suggested with equal clearness that, since these two acts were no longer, as it were, in contemplation, and all attempts to prevent them would probably arrive a little late, he felt the warmest friendship for the French nation. He merely insisted that his friendship should never be mentioned except in the French language. It must be called an "entente" in the language taught to tourists by waiters. It must on no account be called an "understanding," in a language understanded of the people. From the first half of the sentence following it might safely be inferred that Mr. Hibbs had read Milton, or at least the passage about sons of Belial; from the second half that he knew nothing about bad wine, let alone good. The next sentence began with the corruption of the Roman Empire and contrived to end with Dr. Clifford. Then there was a weak plea for Eugenics; and a warm plea against Conscription, which was not True Eugenics. That was all; and it was headed "The Riot at Pebblewick."

Yet some injustice would be done to Hibbs However if we concealed the fact that this chaotic leader was followed by quite a considerable mass of public correspondence. The people who write to newspapers are, it may be supposed, a small, eccentric body, like most of those that sway a modern state. But at least, unlike the lawyers, or the financiers, or the members of Parliament, or the men of science, they are people of all kinds scattered all over the country, of all classes, counties, ages, sects, sexes, and stages of insanity. The letters that followed Hibbs's article are still worth looking up in the dusty old files of his paper.

A dear old lady in the densest part of the Midlands wrote to suggest that there might really have been an old ship wrecked on the shore, during the proceedings. "Mr. Leveson may have omitted to notice it, or, at that late hour of the evening, it may have been mistaken for a sign-board, especially by a person of defective sight. My own sight has been failing for some time; but I am still a diligent reader of your paper." If Mr. Hibbs's diplomacy had left one nerve in his soul undrugged, he would have laughed, or burst into tears, or got drunk, or gone into a monastery over a letter like that. As it was, he measured it with a pencil, and decided that it was just too long to get into the column.

Then there was a letter from a theorist, and a theorist of the worst sort. There is no great harm in the theorist who makes up a new theory to fit a new event. But the theorist who starts with a false theory and then sees everything as making it come true is the most dangerous enemy of human reason. The letter began like a bullet let loose by the trigger. "Is not the whole question met by Ex. iv. 3? I enclose pamphlets in which I have proved the point quite plainly, and which none of the Bishops or the so-called Free Church Ministers have attempted to answer. The connection between the rod or pole and the snake so clearly indicated in Scripture is no less clear in this case. It is well known that those who follow after strong drink often announce themselves as having seen a snake. Is it not clear that those unhappy revellers beheld it in its transformed state as a pole; see also Deut. xviii. 2. If our so-called religious leaders," etc. The letter went on for thirty-three pages and Hibbs was perhaps justified in this case in thinking the letter rather too long.

Then there was the scientific correspondent who said—Might it not be due to the acoustic qualities of the hall? He had never believed in the corrugated iron hall. The very word "hall" itself (he added playfully) was often so sharpened and shortened by the abrupt echoes of those repeated metallic curves, that it had every appearance of being the word "hell," and had caused many theological entanglements, and some police prosecutions. In the light of these facts, he wished to draw the editor's attention to some very curious details about this supposed presence or absence of an inn-sign. It would be noted that many of the witnesses, and especially the most respectable of them, constantly refer to something that is supposed to be outside. The word "outside" occurs at least five times in the depositions of the complaining persons. Surely by all scientific analogy we may infer that the unusual phrase "inn-sign" is an acoustic error for "inside." The word "inside" would so naturally occur in any discussion either about the building or the individual, when the debate was of a hygienic character. This letter was signed "Medical Student," and the less intelligent parts of it were selected for publication in the paper.

Then there was a really humorous man, who wrote and said there was nothing at all inexplicable or unusual about the case. He himself (he said) had often seen a sign-board outside a pub when he went into it, and been quite unable to see it when he came out. This letter (the only one that had any quality of literature) was sternly set aside by Mr. Hibbs.

Then came a cultured gentleman with a light touch, who merely made a suggestion. Had anyone read H. G. Wells's story about the kink in space? He contrived, indescribably, to suggest that no one had even heard of it except himself; or, perhaps, of Mr. Wells either. The story indicated that men's feet might be in one part of the world and their eyes in another. He offered the suggestion for what it was worth. The particular pile of letters on which Hibbs However threw it, showed only too clearly what it was worth.

Then there was a man, of course, who called it all a plot of frenzied foreigners against Britain's shore. But as he did not make it quite clear whether the chief wickedness of these aliens had lain in sticking the sign up or in pulling it down, his remarks (the remainder of which referred exclusively to the conversational misconduct of an Italian ice-cream man, whose side of the case seemed insufficiently represented) carried the less weight.

And then, last but the reverse of least, there plunged in all the people who think they can solve a problem they cannot understand by abolishing everything that has contributed to it. We all know these people. If a barber has cut his customer's throat because the girl has changed her partner for a dance or donkey ride on Hampstead Heath, there are always people to protest against the mere institutions that led up to it. This would not have happened if barbers were abolished, or if cutlery were abolished, or if the objection felt by girls to imperfectly grown beards were abolished, or if the girls were abolished, or if heaths and open spaces were abolished, or if dancing were abolished, or if donkeys were abolished. But donkeys, I fear, will never be abolished.

There were plenty of such donkeys in the common land of this particular controversy. Some made it an argument against democracy, because poor Garge was a carpenter. Some made it an argument against Alien Immigration, because Misysra Ammon was a Turk. Some proposed that ladies should no longer be admitted to any lectures anywhere, because they had constituted a slight and temporary difficulty at this one, without the faintest fault of their own. Some urged that all holiday resorts should be abolished; some urged that all holidays should be abolished. Some vaguely denounced the sea-side; some, still more vaguely, proposed to remove the sea. All said that if this or that, stones or sea-weed or strange visitors or bad weather or bathing machines were swept away with a strong hand, this which had happened would not have happened. They only had one slight weakness, all of them; that they did not seem to have the faintest notion of what *had* happened. And in this they were not inexcusable. Nobody did know what had happened; nobody knows it to this day, of course, or it would be unnecessary to write this story. No one can suppose this story is written from any motive save that of telling the plain, humdrum truth.

That queer confused cunning which was the only definable quality possessed by Hibbs However had certainly scored a victory so far, for the tone of the weekly papers followed him, with more intelligence and less trepidation; but they followed him. It seemed more and more clear that some kind of light and sceptical explanation was to be given of the whole business, and that the whole business was to be dropped.

The story of the sign-board and the ethical chapel of corrugated iron was discussed and somewhat disparaged in all the more serious and especially in the religious weeklies, though the Low Church papers seemed to reserve their distaste chiefly for the sign-board; and the High Church papers chiefly for the Chapel. All agreed that the combination was incongruous, and most treated it as fabulous. The only intellectual organs which seemed to think it might have happened were the Spiritualist papers, and their interpretation had not that solidity which would have satisfied Mr. George.

It was not until almost a year after that it was felt in philosophical circles that the last word had been said on the matter. An estimate of the incident and of its bearing on natural and supernatural history occurred in Professor Widge's celebrated "Historicity of the Petro-Piscatorial Phenomena"; which so profoundly affected modern thought when it came out in parts in the *Hibbert Journal*. Everyone remembers Professor Widge's main contention, that the modern critic must apply to the thaumaturgics of the Lake of Tiberias the same principle of criticism which Dr. Bunk and others have so successfully applied to the thaumaturgics of the Cana narrative: "Authorities as final as Pink and Toscher," wrote the Professor, "have now shown with an emphasis that no emancipated mind is entitled to question, that the Aqua-Vinic thaumaturgy at Cana is wholly inconsistent with the psychology of the 'master of the feast,' as modern research has analysed it; and indeed with the whole Judæo-Aramaic psychology at that stage of its development, as well as being painfully incongruous with the elevated ideals of the ethical teacher in question. But as we rise to higher levels of moral achievement, it will probably be found necessary to apply the Canaic principle to other and later events in the narrative. This principle has, of course, been mainly expounded by Huscher in the sense that the whole episode is unhistorical, while the alternative theory, that the wine was non-alcoholic and was naturally infused into the water, can claim on its side the impressive name of Minns. It is clear that if we apply the same alternative to the so-called Miraculous Draught of Fishes we must either hold with Gilp, that the fishes were stuffed representations of fishes artificially placed in the lake (see the Rev. Y. Wyse's "Christo-Vegetarianism as a World-System," where this position is forcibly set forth), or we must, on the Huscherian hypothesis, deprive the Piscatorial narrative of all claim to historicity whatever.

"The difficulty felt by the most daring critics (even Pooke) in adopting this entirely destructive attitude, is the alleged improbability of so detailed a narrative being founded on so slight a phrase as the anti-historical critics refer it to. It is urged by Pooke, with characteristic relentless reasoning, that according to Huscher's theory a metaphorical but at least noticeable remark, such as, 'I will make you fishers of men,' was expanded into a realistic chronicle of events which contains no mention, even in the passages evidently interpolated, of any men actually found in the nets when they were hauled up out of the sea; or, more properly, lagoon.

"It must appear presumptuous or even bad taste for anyone in the modern world to differ on any subject from Pooke; but I would venture to suggest that the very academic splendour and unique standing of the venerable professor (whose ninety-seventh birthday was so beautifully celebrated in Chicago last year), may have forbidden him all but intuitive knowledge of how errors arise among the vulgar. I crave pardon for mentioning a modern case known to myself (not indeed by personal presence, but by careful study of all the reports) which presents a curious parallel to such ancient expansions of a text into an incident, in accordance with Huscher's law.

"It occurred at Pebblewick, in the south of England. The town had long been in a state of dangerous religious excitement. The great religious genius who has since so much altered our whole attitude to the religions of the world, Misysra Ammon, had been lecturing on the sands to thousands of enthusiastic hearers. Their meetings were often interrupted, both by children's services run on the most ruthless lines of orthodoxy and by the League of the Red Rosette, the formidable atheist and anarchist organization. As if this were not enough to swell the whirlpool of fanaticism, the old popular controversy between the

Milnian and the Complete Sublapsarians broke out again on the fated beach. It is natural to conjecture that in the thickening atmosphere of theology in Pebblewick, some controversialist quoted the text 'An evil and adulterous generation *seek for a sign*. But no sign shall be given it save the sign of the prophet Jonas.'

"A mind like that of Pooke will find it hard to credit, but it seems certain that the effect of this text on the ignorant peasantry of southern England was actually to make them go about looking for a sign, in the sense of those old tavern signs now so happily disappearing. The 'sign of the Prophet Jonas,' they somehow translated in their stunted minds into a sign-board of the ship out of which Jonah was thrown. They went about literally looking for 'The Sign of the Ship,' and there are some cases of their suffering Smail's Hallucination and actually seeing it. The whole incident is a curious parallel to the Gospel narrative and a triumphant vindication of Huscher's law."

Lord Ivywood paid a public compliment to Professor Widge, saying that he had rolled back from his country what might have been an ocean of superstitions. But, indeed, poor Hibbs had struck the first and stunning blow that scattered the brains of all men.

X

THE CHARACTER OF QUOODLE

There lay about in Lord Ivywood's numerous gardens, terraces, outhouses, stable yards and similar places, a dog that came to be called by the name of Quoodle. Lord Ivywood did not call him Quoodle. Lord Ivywood was almost physically incapable of articulating such sounds. Lord Ivywood did not care for dogs. He cared for the Cause of dogs, of course; and he cared still more for his own intellectual self-respect and consistency. He would never have permitted a dog in his house to be physically ill-treated; nor, for that matter, a rat; nor, for that matter, even a man. But if Quoodle was not physically ill-treated, he was at least socially neglected, and Quoodle did not like it. For dogs care for companionship more than for kindness itself.

Lord Ivywood would probably have sold the dog, but he consulted experts (as he did on everything he didn't understand and many things that he did), and the impression he gathered from them was that the dog, technically considered, would fetch very little; mostly, it seemed, because of the mixture of qualities that it possessed. It was a sort of mongrel bull-terrier, but with rather too much of the bull-dog; and this fact seemed to weaken its price as much as it strengthened its jaw. His Lordship also gained a hazy impression that the dog might have been valuable as a watch-dog if it had not been able to follow game like a pointer; and that even in the latter walk of life it would always be discredited by an unfortunate talent for swimming as well as a retriever. But Lord Ivywood's impressions may very well have been slightly confused, as he was probably thinking about the Black stone of Mecca, or some such subject at the moment. The victim of this entanglement of virtues, therefore, still lay about in the sunlight of Ivywood, exhibiting no general result of that entanglement except the most appalling ugliness.

Now Lady Joan Brett did appreciate dogs. It was the whole of her type and a great deal of her tragedy that all that was natural in her was still alive under all that was artificial; and she could smell hawthorn or the sea as far off as a dog can smell his dinner. Like most aristocrats she would carry cynicism almost to the suburbs of the city of Satan; she was quite as irreligious as Lord Ivywood, or rather more. She could be quite equally frigid or supercilious when she felt inclined. And in the great social talent of being tired, she could beat him any day of the week. But the difference remained in spite of her sophistries and ambitions; that her elemental communications were not cut, and his were. For her the sunrise was still the rising of a sun, and not the turning on of a light by a convenient cosmic servant. For her the Spring was really the Season in the country, and not merely the Season in town. For her cocks and hens were natural appendages to an English house; and not (as Lord Ivywood had proved to her from an encyclopædia) animals of Indian origin, recently imported by Alexander the Great. And so for her a dog was a dog, and not one of the higher animals, nor one of the lower animals, nor something that had the sacredness of life, nor something that ought to be muzzled, nor something that ought not to be vivisected. She knew that in every practical sense proper provision would be made for the dog; as, indeed, provision was made for the yellow dogs in Constantinople by Abdul Hamid, whose life Lord Ivywood was writing for the *Progressive Potentates* series. Nor was she in the least sentimental about the dog or anxious to turn him into a pet. It simply came natural to her in passing to rub all his hair the wrong way and call him something which she instantly forgot.

The man who was mowing the garden lawn looked up for a moment, for he had never seen the dog behave in exactly that way before. Quoodle arose, shook himself, and trotted on in front of the lady, leading her up an iron side staircase, of which, as it happened, she had never made use before. It was then, most probably, that she first took any special notice of him; and her pleasure, like that which she took in the sublime prophet from Turkey, was of a humorous character. For the complex quadruped had retained the bow legs of the bull-dog; and, seen from behind, reminded her ridiculously of a swaggering little Major waddling down to his Club.

The dog and the iron stairway between them led her into a series of long rooms, one opening into the other. They formed part of what she had known in earlier days as the disused Wing of Ivywood House, which had been neglected or shut up, probably because it bore some defacements from the fancies of the mad ancestor, the memory of whom the present Lord Ivywood did not think helpful to his own political career. But it seemed to Joan that there were indications of a recent attempt to rehabilitate the place. There was a pail of whitewash in one of the empty rooms, a step-ladder in another, here and there a curtain rod, and at last, in the fourth room a curtain. It hung all alone on the old woodwork, but it was a very gorgeous curtain, being a kind of orange-gold relieved with wavy bars of crimson, which somehow seemed to suggest the very spirit and presence of serpents, though they had neither eyes nor mouths among them.

In the next of the endless series of rooms she came upon a kind of ottoman, striped with green and silver standing alone on the bare floor. She sat down on it from a mixed motive of fatigue and of impudence, for she dimly remembered a story which she had always thought one of the funniest in the world, about a lady only partly initiated in Theosophy who had been in the habit of resting on a similar object, only to discover afterward that it was a Mahatma, covered with his eastern garment and prostrate and rigid in ecstasy. She had no hopes of sitting on a Mahatma herself, but the very thought of it made her laugh, because it would make Lord Ivywood look such a fool. She was not sure whether she liked or disliked Lord Ivywood, but she felt quite certain that it would gratify her to make him look a fool. The moment she had sat down on the ottoman, the dog, who had been trotting beside her, sat down also, and on the edge of her skirt.

After a minute or two she rose (and the dog rose), and she looked yet farther down that long perspective of large rooms, in which men like Phillip Ivywood forget that they are only men. The next was more ornate and the next yet more so; it was plain that the scheme of decoration that was in progress had been started at the other end. She could now see that the long lane ended in rooms that from afar off looked like the end of a kaleidoscope, rooms like nests made only from humming birds or palaces built of fixed fireworks. Out of this furnace of fragmentary colours she saw Ivywood advancing toward her, with his black suit and his white face accented by the contrast. His lips were moving, for he was talking to himself, as many orators do. He did not seem to see her, and she had to strangle a subconscious and utterly senseless cry, "He is blind!"

The next moment he was welcoming her intrusion with the well-bred surprise and rather worldly simplicity suitable to such a case, and Joan fancied she understood why his face had seemed a little bleaker and blinder than usual. It was by contrast. He was carrying clutched to his forefinger, as his ancestors might have carried a falcon clutched to the wrist, a small bright coloured semi-tropical bird, the expression of whose head, neck and eye was the very opposite of his own. Joan thought she had never seen a living creature with a head so lively and insulting. Its provocative eye and pointed crest seemed to be offering to fight fifty game-cocks. It was no wonder (she told herself) that by the side of this gaudy gutter-snipe with feathers Ivywood's faint-coloured hair and frigid face looked like the hair and face of a corpse walking.

"You'll never know what this is," said Ivywood, in his most charming manner. "You've heard of him a hundred times and never had a notion of what he was. This is the Bulbul."

"I never knew," replied Joan. "I am afraid I never cared. I always thought it was something like a nightingale."

"Ah, yes," answered Ivywood, "but this is the real Bulbul peculiar to the East, *Pycnonotus Hæmorrhous*. You are thinking of *Daulias Golzii*."

"I suppose I am," replied Lady Joan with a faint smile. "It is an obsession. When shall I not be thinking of Daulias Galsworthy? Was it Galsworthy?" Then feeling quite touched by the soft austerity of her companion's face, she caressed the gaudy and pugnacious bird with one finger and said, "It's a dear little thing."

The quadruped intimately called Quoodle did not approve of all this at all. Like most dogs, he liked to be with human beings when they were silent, and he extended a magnificent toleration to them as long as they were talking to each other. But conversational attention paid to any other animal at all remote from a mongrel bull-terrier wounded Mr. Quoodle in his most sensitive and gentlemanly feelings. He emitted a faint growl. Joan, with all the instincts that were in her, bent down and pulled his hair about once more, and felt the instant necessity of diverting the general admiration from *Pycnonotus Hæmorrhous*. She turned it to the decoration at the end of the refurnished wing; for they had already come to the last of the long suite of rooms, which ended in some unfinished but exquisite panelling in white and coloured woods, inlaid in the oriental manner. At one corner the whole corridor ended by curving into a round turret chamber overlooking the landscape; and which Joan, who had known the house in childhood, was sure was an innovation. On the other hand a black gap, still left in the lower left-hand corner of the oriental woodwork, suddenly reminded her of something she had forgotten.

"Surely," she said (after much mere æsthetic ecstasy), "there used to be a staircase there, leading to the old kitchen garden, or the old chapel or something."

Ivywood nodded gravely. "Yes," he said, "it did lead to the ruins of a Mediæval Chapel, as you say. The truth is it led to several things that I cannot altogether consider a credit to the family in these days. All that scandal and joking about the unsuccessful tunnel (your mother may have told you of it), well, it did us no good in the County, I'm afraid; so as it's a mere scrap of land bordering on the sea, I've fenced it off and let it grow wild. But I'm boarding up the end of the room here for quite another reason. I want you to come and see it."

He led her into the round corner turret in which the new architecture ended, and Joan, with her thirst for the beautiful, could not stifle a certain thrill of beatitude at the prospect. Five open windows of a light and exquisite Saracenic outline looked out over the bronze and copper and purple of the Autumn parks and forests to the peacock colours of the sea. There was neither house nor living thing in sight, and, familiar as she had been with that coast, she knew she was looking out from a new angle of vision on a new landscape of Ivywood.

"You can write sonnets?" said Ivywood with something more like emotion in his voice than she had ever heard in it. "What comes first into your mind with these open windows?"

"I know what you mean," said Joan after a silence. "The same hath oft. . ."

"Yes," he said. "That is how I felt. . . of perilous seas in fairy lands forlorn."

There was another silence and the dog sniffed round and round the circular turret chamber.

"I want it to be like that," said Ivywood in a low and singularly moved intonation. "I want this to be the end of the house. I want this to be the end of the world. Don't you feel that is the real beauty of all this eastern art; that it is coloured like the edges of things, like the little clouds of morning and the islands of the blest? Do you know," and he lowered his voice yet more, "it has the power over me of making me feel as if I were myself absent and distant; some oriental traveller who was lost and for whom men were looking. When I see that greenish lemon yellow enamel there let into the white, I feel that I am standing thousands of leagues from where I stand."

"You are right," said Joan, looking at him with some wonder, "I have felt like that myself."

"This art," went on Ivywood as in a dream, "does indeed take the wings the morning and abide in the uttermost parts of the sea. They say it contains no form of life, but surely we can read its alphabet as easily as the red hieroglyphics of sunrise and sunset which are on the fringes of the robe of God."

"I never heard you talk like that before," said the lady, and again stroked the vivid violet feathers of the small eastern bird.

Mr. Quoodle could stand it no longer. He had evidently formed a very low opinion of the turret chamber and of oriental art generally, but seeing Joan's attention once more transferred to his rival, he trotted out into the longer room, and finding the gap in the woodwork which was soon to be boarded up, but which still opened on an old dark staircase, he went "galumphing" down the stairs.

Lord Ivywood gently placed the bird on the girl's own finger, and went to one of the open windows, leaning out a little.

"Look here," he said, "doesn't this express what we both feel? Isn't this the sort of fairy-tale house that ought to hang on the last wall of the world?"

And he motioned her to the window-sill, just outside which hung the bird's empty cage, beautifully wrought in brass or some of the yellow metals.

"Why that is the best of all!" cried Lady Joan. "It makes one feel as if it really were the Arabian Nights. As if this were a tower of the gigantic Genii with turrets up to the moon; and this were an enchanted Prince caged in a golden palace suspended by the evening star."

Something stirred in her dim but teeming subconsciousness, something like a chill or change like that by which we half know that weather has altered, or distant and unnoticed music suddenly ceased.

"Where is the dog?" she asked suddenly.

Ivywood turned with a mild, grey eye.

"Was there a dog here?" he asked.

"Yes," said Lady Joan Brett, and gave him back the bird, which he restored carefully to its cage.

The dog after whom she inquired had in truth trundled down a dark, winding staircase and turned into the daylight, into a part of the garden he had never seen before; nor, indeed, had anybody else for some time past. It was altogether tangled and overgrown with weeds, and the only trace of human handiwork, the wreck of an old Gothic Chapel, stood waist high in numberless nettles and soiled with crawling fungoids. Most of these merely discoloured the grey crumbling stone with shades of bronze or brown; but some of them, particularly on the side farthest from the house, were of orange or purple tints almost bright enough for Lord Ivywood's oriental decoration. Some fanciful eyes that fell on the place afterward found something like an allegory in those graven and broken saints or archangels feeding such fiery and ephemeral parasites as those toadstools like blood or gold. But Mr. Quoodle had never set himself up as an allegorist, and he merely trotted deeper and deeper into the grey-green English jungle. He grumbled very much at the thistles and nettles, much as a city man will grumble at the jostling of a crowd. But he continued to press forward, with his nose near the ground, as if he had already smelt something that interested him. And, indeed, he had smelt something in which a dog, except on special occasions, is much more interested than he is in dogs. Breaking through a last barrier of high and hoary purple thistles he came out on a semicircle of somewhat clearer ground, dotted with slender trees, and having, by way of back scene, the brown brick arch of an old tunnel. The tunnel was boarded up with a very irregular fence or mask made of motley wooden lathes, and looked, somehow, rather like a pantomime cottage. In front of this a sturdy man in very shabby shooting clothes was standing attending to a battered old frying-pan which he held over a rather irregular flame which, small as it was, smelt strongly of burnt rum. In the frying-pan, and also on the top of a cask or barrel that served for a table hard by, were a number of the grey, brown, and even orange fungi which were plastered over the stone angels and dragons of the fallen chapel.

"Hullo, old man," said the person in the shooting jacket with tranquillity and without looking up from his cooking. "Come to pay us a visit? Come along then." He flashed one glance at the dog and returned to the frying pan. "If your tail were two inches shorter, you'd be worth a hundred pounds. Had any breakfast?"

The dog trotted across to him and began nosing and sniffing round his dilapidated leather gaiters. The man did not interrupt his cookery, on which his eyes were fixed and both his hands were busy; but he crooked his knee and foot so as to caress the quadruped in a nerve under the angle of the jaw, the stimulation of which (as some men of science have held) is for a dog what a good cigar is for a man. At the same moment a huge voice like on ogre's came from within the masked tunnel, calling out, "And who are ye talking to?"

A very crooked kind of window in the upper part of the pantomime cottage burst open and an enormous head, with erect, startling, and almost scarlet hair and blue eyes as big as a bullfrog's, was thrust out above the scene.

"Hump," cried the ogre. "Me moral counsels have been thrown away. In the last week I've sung you fourteen and a half songs of me own composition; instead of which you go about stealing dogs. You're following in the path of Parson Whats-his-name in every way, I'm afraid."

"No," said the man with the frying pan, impartially, "Parson Whitelady struck a very good path for doubling on Pebblewick, that I was glad to follow. But I think he was quite silly to steal dogs. He was young and brought up pious. I know too much about dogs to steal one."

"Well," asked the large red-haired man, "and how do you get a dog like that?"

"I let him steal me," said the person stirring the pan. And indeed the dog was sitting erect and even arrogant at his feet, as if he was a watch-dog at a high salary, and had been there before the building of the tunnel.

XI

Vegetarianism in the Drawing-Room

The Company that assembled to listen to the Prophet of the Moon, on the next occasion of his delivering any formal address, was much more select than the comparatively mixed and middle-class society of the Simple Souls. Miss Browning and her sister, Mrs. Mackintosh, were indeed present; for Lord Ivywood had practically engaged them both as private secretaries, and kept them pretty busy, too. There was also Mr. Leveson, because Lord Ivywood believed in his organizing power; and also Mr. Hibbs, because Mr. Leveson believed in his political judgment, whenever he could discover what it was. Mr. Leveson had straight, dark hair, and looked nervous. Mr. Hibbs had straight, fair hair, and also looked nervous. But the rest of the company were more of Ivywood's own world, or the world of high finance with which it mixes both here and on the continent. Lord Ivywood welcomed, with something approaching to warmth, a distinguished foreign diplomatist, who was, indeed, none other than that silent German representative who had sat beside him in that last conference on the Island of the Olives. Dr. Gluck was no longer in his quiet, black suit, but wore an ornate, diplomatic uniform with a sword and Prussian, Austrian or Turkish Orders; for he was going on from Ivywood to a function at Court. But his curl of red lips, his screw of black mustache, and his unanswering almond eyes had no more changed than the face of a wax figure in a barber's shop window.

The Prophet had also effected an improvement in his dress. When he had orated on the sands his costume, except for the fez, was the shabby but respectable costume of any rather unsuccessful English clerk. But now that he had come among aristocrats who petted their souls as they did their senses, there must be no such incongruity. He must be a proper, fresh-picked oriental tulip or lotus. So—he wore long, flowing robes of white, relieved here and there by flame-coloured threads of tracery, and round his head was a turban of a kind of pale golden green. He had to look as if he had come flying across Europe on the magic carpet, or fallen a moment before from his paradise in the moon.

The ladies of Lord Ivywood's world were much as we have already found them. Lady Enid Wimpole still overwhelmed her earnest and timid face with a tremendous costume, that was more like a procession than a dress. It looked rather like the funeral procession of Aubrey Beardsley. Lady Joan Brett still looked like a very beautiful Spaniard with no illusions left about her castle in Spain. The large and resolute lady who had refused to ask any questions at Misysra's earlier lecture, and who was known as Lady Crump, the distinguished Feminist, still had the air of being so full and bursting with questions fatal to Man as to have passed the speaking and reached the speechless stage of hostility. Throughout the proceedings she contributed nothing but bursting silence and a malevolent eye. And old Lady Ivywood, under the oldest and finest lace and the oldest and finest manners, had a look like death on her, which can often be seen in the parents of pure intellectuals. She had that face of a lost mother that is more pathetic than the face of a lost child.

"And what are you going to delight us with today?" Lady Enid was asking of the Prophet.

"My lecture," answered Misysra, gravely, "is on the Pig."

It was part of a simplicity really respectable in him that he never saw any incongruity in the arbitrary and isolated texts or symbols out of which he spun his thousand insane theories. Lady Enid endured the impact of this singular subject for debate without losing that expression of wistful sweetness which she wore on principle when talking to such people.

"The Pig, he is a large subject," continued the Prophet, making curves in the air, as if embracing some particularly prize specimen. "He includes many subjects. It is to me very strange that the Christians should so laugh and be surprised because we hold ourselves to be defiled by pork; we and also another of the Peoples of the Book. But, surely, you Christians yourselves consider the pig as a manner of pollution; since it is your most usual expression of your despising, of your very great dislike. You say 'swine,' my dear lady; you do not say animals far more unpopular, such as the alligator."

"I see," said the lady, "how wonderful!"

"If you are annoyed," went on the encouraged and excited gentleman, "if you are annoyed with anyone, with a—what you say?—a lady's maid, you do not say to her 'Horse.' You do not say to her 'Camel.'"

"Ah, no," said Lady Enid, earnestly.

"'Pig of a lady's maid,' you say in your colloquial English," continued the Prophet, triumphantly. "And yet this great and awful Pig, this monster whose very name, when whispered, you think will wither all your enemies, you allow, my dear lady, to approach yet closer to you. You incorporate this great Pig in the substance of your own person."

Lady Enid Wimpole was looking a little dazed at last, at this description of her habits, and Joan gave Lord Ivywood a hint that the lecturer had better be transferred to his legitimate sphere of lecturing. Ivywood led the way into a larger room that was full of ranked chairs, with a sort of lectern at the other end, and flanked on all four sides with tables laden with all kinds of refreshments. It was typical of the strange, half-fictitious enthusiasm and curiosity of that world, that one long table was set out entirely with vegetarian foods, especially of an eastern sort (like a table spread in the desert for a rather fastidious Indian hermit); but that tables covered with game patties, lobster and champagne were equally provided, and very much more frequented. Even Mr. Hibbs, who would honestly have thought entering a publichouse more disgraceful than entering a brothel, could not connect any conception of disgrace with Lord Ivywood's champagne.

For the purpose of the lecture was not wholly devoted to the great and awful Pig, and the purpose of the meeting even less. Lord Ivywood, the white furnace of whose mind was always full of new fancies hardening into ambitions, wanted to have a debate on the diet of East and West, and felt that Misysra might very appropriately open with an account of the Moslem veto on pork or other coarse forms of flesh food. He reserved it to himself to speak second.

The Prophet began, indeed, with some of his dizziest flights. He informed the Company that they, the English, had always gone in hidden terror and loathing of the Pig, as a sacred symbol of evil. He proved it by the common English custom of drawing a pig with one's eyes shut. Lady Joan smiled, and yet she asked herself (in a doubt that had been darkening round her about many modern things lately) whether it was really much more fanciful than many things the scientists told her: as, the traces of Marriage by Capture which they found in that ornamental and even frivolous being, the Best Man.

He said that the dawn of greater enlightenment is shown in the use of the word "gammon," which still expresses disgust at "the porcine image," but no longer fear of it, but rather a rational disdain and disbelief. "Rowley," said the Prophet, solemnly, and then after a long pause, "Powley, *Gammon* and Spinach."

Lady Joan smiled again, but again asked herself if it was much more farfetched than a history book she had read, which proved the unpopularity of Catholicism in Tudor times from the word "hocus pocus."

He got into a most amazing labyrinth of philology between the red primeval sins of the first pages of Genesis and the Common English word "ham." But, again, Joan wondered whether it was much wilder than the other things she had heard said about Primitive Man by people who had never seen him.

He suggested that the Irish were set to keep pigs because they were a low and defiled caste, and the serfs of the pig-scorning Saxon; and Joan thought it was about as sensible as what the dear old Archdeacon had said about Ireland years ago; which had caused an Irishman of her acquaintance to play "the Shan Van Voght" and then smash the piano.

Joan Brett had been thoughtful for the last few days. It was partly due to the scene in the turret, where she had struck a sensitive and artistic side of Phillip Ivywood she had never seen before, and partly to disturbing news of her mother's health, which, though not menacing, made her feel hypothetically how isolated she was in the world. On all previous occasions she had merely enjoyed the mad lecturer now at the reading-desk. Today she felt a strange desire to analyse him, and imagine how a man could be so connected and so convinced and yet so wildly wide of the mark. As she listened carefully, looking at the hands in her lap, she began to think she understood.

The lecturer did really try to prove that the "porcine image" had never been used in English history or literature, except in contempt. And the lecturer really did know a very great deal about English history and literature: much more than she did; much more than the aristocrats round her did. But she noted that in every case what he knew was a fragmentary fact. In every case what he did not know was the truth behind the fact. What he did not know was the atmosphere. What he did not know was the tradition. She found herself ticking off the cases like counts in an indictment.

Misysra Ammon knew, what next to none of the English present knew, that Richard III was called a "boar" by an eighteenth century poet and a "hog" by a fifteenth century poet. What he did not know was the habit of sport and of heraldry. He did not know (what Joan knew instantly, though she had never thought of it before in her life) that beasts courageous and hard to kill are noble beasts, by the law of chivalry. Therefore, the boar was a noble beast, and a common crest for great captains. Misysra tried to show that Richard had only been called a pig after he was cold pork at Bosworth.

Misysra Ammon knew, what next to none of the English present knew, that there never was such a person as Lord Bacon. The phrase is a falsification of what should be Lord Verulam or Lord St. Albans. What he did not know was exactly what Joan did know (though it had never crossed her mind till that moment) that when all is said and done, a title is a sort of joke, while a surname is a serious thing. Bacon was a gentleman, and his name was Bacon; whatever titles he took. But Misysra seriously tried to prove that "Bacon" was a term of abuse applied to him during his unpopularity or after his fall.

Misysra Ammon knew, what next to none of the English present knew, that the poet Shelley had a friend called Hogg, who treated him on one occasion with grave treachery. He instantly tried to prove that the man was only called "Hogg" because he had treated Shelley with grave treachery. And he actually adduced the fact that another poet, practically contemporary, was called "Hogg" as completing the connection with Shelley. What he did not know was just what Joan had always known without knowing it: the kind of people concerned, the traditions of aristocrats like the Shelleys or of Borderers like the Ettrick Shepherd.

The lecturer concluded with a passage of inpenetrable darkness about pig-iron and pigs of lead, which Joan did not even venture to understand. She could only say that if it did not mean that some day our diet might become so refined that we ate lead and iron, she could form no fancy of what it did mean.

"Can Phillip Ivywood believe this kind of thing?" she asked herself; and even as she did so, Phillip Ivywood rose.

He had, as Pitt and Gladstone had, an impromptu classicism of diction, his words wheeling and deploying into their proper places like a well-disciplined army in its swiftest advance. And it was not long before Joan perceived that the last phase of the picture, obscure and monstrous as it seemed, gave Ivywood exactly the opening he wanted. Indeed, she felt, no doubt, that he had arranged for it beforehand.

"It is within my memory," said Lord Ivywood, "though it need in no case have encumbered yours, that when it was my duty to precede the admired lecturer whom I now feel it a privilege even to follow, I submitted a suggestion which, however simple, would appear to many paradoxical. I affirmed or implied the view that the religion of Mahomet was, in a peculiar sense, a religion of progress. This is so contrary, not only to historical convention but to common platitude, that I shall find no ground either of surprise or censure if it takes a perceptible time before it sinks into the mind of the English public. But I think, ladies and gentlemen, that this period is notably abbreviated by the remarkable exposition which we have heard today. For this question of the attitude of Islam toward food affords as excellent an example of its special mode of progressive purification as the more popular example of its attitude toward drink. For it illustrates that principle which I have ventured to call the principle of the Crescent: the principle of perpetual growth toward an implied and infinite perfection.

"The great religion of Islam does not of itself forbid the eating of flesh foods. But, in accordance with that principle of growth which is its life, it has pointed the way to a perfection not yet perhaps fully attainable by our nature; it has taken a plain and strong example of the dangers of meat-eating; and hung up the repellent carcass as a warning and a sign. In the gradual emergence of mankind from a gross and sanguinary mode of sustenance, the Semite has led the way. He has laid, as it were, a symbolic embargo upon the beast typical, the beast of beasts. With the instinct of the true mystic, he selected for exemption from such cannibal feasts the creature which appeals to both sides of the higher vegetarian ethic. The pig is at once the creature whose helplessness most moves our pity and whose ugliness most repels our taste.

"It would be foolish to affirm that no difficulty arises out of the different stages of moral evolution in which the different races find themselves. Thus it is constantly said, and such things are not said without some excuse in document or incident, that followers of the Prophet have specialised in the arts of war and have come into a contact, not invariably friendly, with those Hindoos of India who have specialised in the arts of Peace. In the same way the Hindoos, it must be confessed, have been almost as much in advance of Islam in the question of meat as Islam is in advance of Christianity in the matter of drink. It must be remembered again and again, ladies and gentlemen, that every allegation we have of any difference between Hindoo and Moslem comes through a Christian channel, and is therefore tainted evidence. But in this matter, even, can we not see the perils of disregarding such plain danger signals as the veto on pork? Did not an Empire nearly slip out of our hands because our hands were greased with cow-fat? And did not the well of Cawnpore brim with blood instead of water because we would not listen to the instinct of the Oriental about the shedding of sacred blood?

"But if it be proposed, with whatever graduation, to approach that repudiation of flesh food which Buddhism mainly and Islam partly recommends, it will always be asked by those who hate the very vision of Progress—'Where do you draw the line? May I eat oysters? May I eat eggs? May I drink milk?' You may. You may eat or drink anything essential to your stage of evolution, so long as you are evolving toward a clearer and cleaner ideal of bodily life. If," he said gravely, "I may employ a phrase of flippancy, I would say that you may eat six dozen oysters today, but I should strongly advise five dozen oysters tomorrow. For how else has all progress in public or private manners been achieved? Would not the primitive cannibals be surprised at the strange distinction we draw between men and beasts? All historians pay high honour to the Huguenots, and the great Huguenot Prince, Henri Quatre. None need deny that his aspiration that every Frenchman should have a chicken in his pot was, for his period, a high aspiration. It is no disrespect to him that we, mounting to higher levels, and looking down longer perspectives, consider the chicken. And this august march of discovery passes figures higher than that of Henry of Navarre. I shall always give a high place, as Islam has always given a high place, to that figure, mythical or no, which we find presiding over the foundations of Christianity. I cannot doubt that the fable, incredible and revolting otherwise, which records the rush of swine into the sea, was an allegory of his early realisation that a spirit, evil indeed, does reside in all animals in so far as they tempt us to devour them. I cannot doubt that the Prodigal leaving his sins among the swine is another illustration of the great thesis of the Prophet of the Moon. But here, also, progress and relativity are relentless in their advance; and not a few of us may have risen today to the point of regretting that the joyful sounds around the return of the Prodigal should be marred by the moaning of a calf.

"For the rest, he who asks us whither we go knows not the meaning of Progress. If we come at last to live on light, as men said of the chameleon, if some cosmic magic closed to us now, as radium was but recently closed, allows us to transmute the very metals into flesh without breaking into the bloody house of life, we shall know these things when we have achieved them. It is enough for us now if we have reached a spiritual station, in which at least the living head we lop has not eyes to reproach us; and the herbs we gather cannot cry against our cruelty like the mandrake."

Lord Ivywood resumed his seat, his colourless lips still moving. By some previous arrangement, probably, Mr. Leveson rose to move a motion about Vegetarianism. Mr. Leveson was of opinion that the Jewish and Moslem veto on pork had been the origin of Vegetarianism. He thought it was a great step, and showed how progressive the creed could be. He thought the persecution of the Hindoos by Moslems had probably been much exaggerated; he thought our experience in the Indian Mutiny showed we considered the feeling of Easterners too little in such matters. He thought Vegetarianism in some ways an advance on orthodox Christianity. He thought we must be ready for yet further advances; and he sat down. And as he had said precisely, clause by clause, everything that Lord Ivywood had said, it is needless to say that that nobleman afterward congratulated him on the boldness and originality of his brilliant speech.

At a similar sort of preconcerted signal, Hibbs However rose rather vaguely to his feet to second the motion. He rather prided himself on being a man of few words, in the vocal sense; he was no orator, as Brutus was. It was only with pen in hand, in an office lined with works of reference, that he could feel that sense of confused responsibility that was the one pleasure of his life. But on this occasion he was brighter than usual; partly because he liked being in a lord's house; partly because he had never tasted champagne before, and he felt as if it agreed with him; partly because he saw in the subject of Progress an infinite opportunity of splitting hairs.

"Whatever," said Hibbs, with a solemn cough, "whatever we may think of the old belief that Moslems have differed from Buddhism in a regrettable way, there can be no doubt the responsibility lay with the Christian Churches. Had the Free Churches put their foot down and met Messrs. Opalstein's demand, we should have heard nothing of these old differences between one belief and another." As it was, it reminded him of Napoleon. He gave his own opinion for what it was worth, but he was not afraid to say at any cost, even there and in that company, that this business of Asiatic vegetation had occupied less of the time of the Wesleyan Conference than it should have done. He would be the last to say, of course, that anyone was in any sense to blame. They all knew

Dr. Coon's qualifications. They all knew as well as he did, that a more strenuous social worker than Charles Chadder had never rallied the forces of progress. But that which was not really an indiscretion might be represented as an indiscretion, and perhaps we had had enough of that just lately. It was all very well to talk about Coffe but it should be remembered, with no disrespect to those in Canada to whom we owe so much, that all that happened before 1891. No one had less desire to offend our Ritualistic friends than he did, but he had no hesitation in saying that the question was a question that could be asked, and though no doubt, from one point of view the goat's—

Lady Joan moved sharply in her chair, as if gripped by sudden pain. And, indeed, she had suddenly felt the chronic and recurrent pain of her life. She was brave about bodily pain, as are most women, even luxurious women: but the torment that from time to time returned and tore her was one to which many philosophical names have been given, but no name so philosophical as Boredom.

She felt she could not stand a minute more of Mr. Hibbs. She felt she would die if she heard about the goats—from one or any point of view. She slipped from her chair and somehow slid round the corner, in pretence of seeking one of the tables of refreshment in the new wing. She was soon among the new oriental apartments, now almost completed; but she took no refreshments, though attenuated tables could still be found here and there. She threw herself on an ottoman and stared toward the empty and elfin turret chamber, in which Ivywood had made her understand that he, also, could thirst for beauty and desire to be at peace. He certainly had a poetry of his own, after all; a poetry that never touched earth; the poetry of Shelley rather than Shakespeare. His phrase about the fairy turret was true: it did look like the end of the world. It did seem to teach her that there is always some serene limit at last.

She started and half rose on her elbow with a small laugh. A dog of ludicrous but familiar appearance came shuffling toward her and she lifted herself in the act of lifting him. She also lifted her head, and saw something that seemed to her, in a sense more Christian and catastrophic, very like the end of the world.

XII

Vegetarianism in the Forest

Humphrey Pump's cooking of a fungus in an old frying-pan (which he had found on the beach) was extremely typical of him. He was, indeed, without any pretence of book-learning, a certain kind of scientific man that science has really been unfortunate in losing. He was the old-fashioned English Naturalist like Gilbert White or even Isaac Walton, who learned things not academically like an American Professor, but actually, like an American Indian. And every truth a man has found out as a man of science is always subtly different from any truth he has found out as a man, because a man's family, friends, habits and social type have always got well under way before he has thoroughly learned the theory of anything. For instance, any eminent botanist at a *Soirée* of the Royal Society could tell you, of course, that other edible fungi exist, as well as mushrooms and truffles. But long before he was a botanist, still less an eminent botanist, he had begun, so to speak, on a basis of mushrooms and truffles. He felt, in a vague way, that these were really edible, that mushrooms were a moderate luxury, proper to the middle classes, while truffles were a much more expensive luxury, more suitable to the Smart Set. But the old English Naturalists, of whom Isaac Walton was perhaps the first, and Humphrey Pump perhaps the last, had in many cases really begun at the other end, and found by experience (often most disastrous experience) that some fungi are wholesome and some are not; but the wholesome ones are, on a whole, the majority. So a man like Pump was no more afraid of a fungus as such than he was of an animal as such. He no more started with the supposition that a grey or purple growth on a stone must be a poisonous growth than he started with the supposition that the dog who came to him out of the wood must be a mad dog. Most of them he knew; those he did not know he treated with rational caution, but to him, as a whole race, these weird-hued and one-legged goblins of the forests were creatures friendly to man.

"You see," he said to his friend the Captain, "eating vegetables isn't half bad, so long as you know what vegetables there are and eat all of them that you can. But there are two ways where it goes wrong among the gentry. First, they've never had to eat a carrot or a potato because it was all there was in the house; so they've never learnt how to be really hungry for carrots, as that donkey might be. They only know the vegetables that are meant to help the meat. They know you take duck and peas; and when they turn vegetarian they can only think of the peas without the duck. They know you take lobster in a salad; and when they turn vegetarian they can only think of the salad without the lobster. But the other reason is worse. There's plenty of good people even round here, and still more in the north, who get meat very seldom. But then, when they do get it, they gobble it up like good 'uns. But the trouble with the gentry is different. The trouble is, the same sort of gentry that don't want to eat meat don't really want to eat anything. The man called a Vegetarian who goes to Ivywood House is generally like a cow trying to live on a blade of grass a day. You and I, Captain, have pretty well been vegetarians for some time, so as not to break into the cheese, and we haven't found it so difficult, because we eat as much as we can."

"It's not so difficult as being teetotallers," answered Dalroy, "so as not to break into the cask. But I'll never deny that I feel the better for that, too, on the whole. But only because I could leave off being one whenever I chose. And, now I come to think of it," he cried, with one of his odd returns of animal energy, "if I'm to be a vegetarian why shouldn't I drink? Why shouldn't I have a purely vegetarian drink? Why shouldn't I take vegetables in their highest form, so to speak? The modest vegetarians ought obviously to stick to wine or beer, plain vegetarian drinks, instead of filling their goblets with the blood of bulls and elephants, as all conventional meat-eaters do, I suppose. What is the matter?"

"Nothing," answered Pump. "I was looking out for somebody who generally turns up about this time. But I think I'm fast."

"I should never have thought so from the look of you," answered the Captain, "but what I'm saying is that the drinking of decent fermented liquor is just simply the triumph of vegetarianism. Why, it's an inspiring idea! I could write a sort of song about it. As, for instance—

> *"You will find me drinking rum*
> *Like a sailor in a slum,*
> *You will find me drinking beer like a Bavarian;*
> *You will find me drinking gin*

In the lowest kind of inn,
Because I am a rigid Vegetarian."

Why, it's a vista of verbal felicity and spiritual edification! It has I don't know how many hundred aspects! Let's see; how could the second verse go? Something like—

> *"So I cleared the inn of wine,*
> *And I tried to climb the Sign;*
> *And I tried to hail the constable as 'Marion';*
> *But he said I couldn't speak,*
> *And he bowled me to the Beak,*
> *Because I was a Happy Vegetarian."*

I really think something instructive to the human race may come out of all this. . . Hullo! Is that what you were looking for?"

The quadruped Quoodle came in out of the woods a whole minute later than the usual time and took his seat beside Humphrey's left foot with a preoccupied air.

"Good old boy," said the Captain. "You seem to have taken quite a fancy to us. I doubt, Hump, if he's properly looked after up at the house. I particularly don't want to talk against Ivywood, Hump. I don't want his soul to be able in all eternity to accuse my soul of a mean detraction. I want to be fair to him, because I hate him like hell, and he has taken from me all for which I lived. But I don't think, with all this in my mind, I don't think I say anything beyond what he would own himself (for his brain is clear) when I say that he could never understand an animal. And so he could never understand the animal side of a man. He doesn't know to this day, Hump, that your sight and hearing are sixty times quicker than his. He doesn't know that I have a better circulation. That explains the extraordinary people he picks up and acts with; he never looks at them as you and I look at that dog. There was a fellow calling himself Gluck who was (mainly by Ivywood's influence, I believe) his colleague on the Turkish Conferences, being supposed to represent Germany. My dear Hump, he was a man that a great gentleman like Ivywood ought not to have touched with a barge-pole. It's not the race he was—if it was one race—it's the Sort he was. A coarse, common, Levantine nark and eavesdropper—but you mustn't lose your temper, Hump. I implore you, Hump, to control this tendency to lose your temper when talking at any length about such people. Have recourse, Hump, to that consoling system of versification which I have already explained to you.

> *"Oh I knew a Doctor Gluck,*
> *And his nose it had a hook,*
> *And his attitudes were anything but Aryan;*
> *So I gave him all the pork*
> *That I had, upon a fork;*
> *Because I am myself a Vegetarian."*

"If you are," said Humphrey Pump, "you'd better come and eat some vegetables. The White Hat can be eaten cold—or raw, for that matter. But Bloodspots wants some cooking."

"You are right, Hump," said Dalroy, seating himself with every appearance of speechless greed. "I will be silent. As the poet says—

> *"I am silent in the Club,*
> *I am silent in the pub,*
> *I am silent on a bally peak in Darien;*
> *For I stuff away for life,*
> *Shoving peas in with a knife,*
> *Because I am at heart a Vegetarian."*

He fell to his food with great gusto, dispatched a good deal of it in a very short time, threw a glance of gloomy envy at the cask, and then sprang to his feet again. He caught up the inn-sign from where it leant against the Pantomime Cottage, and planted it like a pike in the ground beside him. Then he began to sing again, in an even louder voice than before.

> *"O, Lord Ivywood may lop,*
> *And his privilege is sylvan and riparian;*
> *And is also free to top,*
> *But—."*

"Do you know," said Hump, also finishing his lunch, "that I'm rather tired of that particular tune?"

"Tired, is it?" said the indignant Irishman, "then I'll sing you a longer song, to an even worse tune, about more and more vegetarians, and you shall see me dance as well; and I will dance till you burst into tears and offer me the half of your kingdom; and I shall ask for Mr. Leveson's head on the frying-pan. For this, let me tell you, is a song of oriental origin, celebrating the caprices of an ancient Babylonian Sultan and should be performed in palaces of ivory with palm trees and a bulbul accompaniment."

And he began to bellow another and older lyric of his own on vegetarianism.

"Nebuchadnezzar, the King of the Jews,
Suffered from new and original views,
He crawled on his hands and knees it's said,
With grass in his mouth and a crown on his head,
With a wowtyiddly, etc.

"Those in traditional paths that trod,
Thought the thing was a curse from God;
But a Pioneer men always abuse,
Like Nebuchadnezzar the King of the Jews."

Dalroy, as he sang this, actually began to dance about like a ballet girl, an enormous and ridiculous figure in the sunlight, waving the wooden sign around his head. Quoodle opened his eyes and pricked up his ears and seemed much interested in these extraordinary evolutions. Suddenly, with one of those startling changes that will transfigure the most sedentary dogs, Quoodle decided that the dance was a game, and began to bark and bound round the performer, sometimes leaping so far into the air as almost to threaten the man's throat. But, though the sailor naturally knew less about dogs than the countryman, he knew enough about them (as about many other things) not to be afraid, and the voice he sang with might have drowned the baying of a pack.

"Black Lord Foulon the Frenchmen slew,
Thought it a Futurist thing to do;
He offered them grass instead of bread,
So they stuffed him with grass when they cut off his head.
With a wowtyiddly, etc.

"For the pride of his soul he perished then,
But of course it is always of Pride that men

A Man in Advance of his Age accuse
Like Nebuchadnezzar the King of the Jews.

"Simeon Scudder of Styx, in Maine,
Thought of the thing and was at it again;
He gave good grass and water in pails
To a thousand Irishmen hammering rails,
With a wowtyiddly, etc.

"Appetites differ, and tied to a stake,
He was tarred and feathered for Conscience Sake;
But stoning the prophets is ancient news,
Like Nebuchadnezzar the King of the Jews."

In an abandon, unusual even for him, he had danced his way down through the thistles into the jungle of weeds risen round the sunken Chapel. And the dog, now fully convinced that it was not only a game but an expedition, perhaps a hunting expedition, ran barking in front of him, along the path that his own dog's paws had already burst through the tangle. Before Patrick Dalroy well knew what he was doing, or even remembered that he still carried the ridiculous signboard in his hand, he found himself outside the open porch of a sort of narrow tower at the angle of a building which, to the best of his recollection, he had never seen before. Quoodle instantly ran up four or five steps in the dark staircase inside, and then, lifting his ears again, looked back for his companion.

There is, perhaps, such a thing as asking too much of a man. If there is, it was asking too much of Patrick Dalroy to ask him not to accept so eccentric an invitation. Hurriedly plunging his unwieldy wooden ensign upright in the thick of thistles and grass, he bent his gigantic neck and shoulders to enter the porch, and proceeded to climb the stairs. It was quite dark, and it was only after at least two twists of the stone spiral that he saw light ahead of him, and then it was a sort of rent in the wall that seemed to him as ragged as the mouth of a Cornish cave. It was also so low that he had some difficulty in squeezing his bulk through it, but the dog had jumped through with an air of familiarity, and once more looked back to see him follow.

If he had found himself inside any ordinary domestic interior, he would instantly have repented his escapade and gone back. But he found himself in surroundings which he had never seen before, or even, in one sense, believed possible.

His first feeling was that he was walking in the most sealed and secret suite of apartments in the castle of a dream. All the chambers had that air of perpetually opening inwards which is the soul of the Arabian Nights. And the ornament was of the same tradition; gorgeous and flamboyant, yet featureless and stiff. A purple mansion seemed to be built inside a green mansion and a golden mansion inside that. And the quaintly cut doorways or fretted lattices all had wavy lines like a dancing sea, and for some reason (sea-sickness for all he knew) this gave him a feeling as if the place were beautiful but faintly evil: as if it were bored and twisted for the fallen palace of the Worm.

But he had also another sensation which he could not analyze; for it reminded him of being a fly on the ceiling or the wall. Was it the Hanging Gardens of Babylon coming back to his imagination; or the Castle East of the Sun and West of the Moon? Then he remembered that in some boyish illness he had stared at a rather Moorish sort of wall paper, which was like rows and rows of brightly coloured corridors, empty and going on forever. And he remembered that a fly was walking along one of the parallel lines; and it seemed to his childish fancy that the corridors were all dead in front of the fly, but all came to life as he passed.

"By George!" he cried, "I wonder whether that's the real truth about East and West! That the gorgeous East offers everything needed for adventures except the man to enjoy them. It would explain the tradition of the Crusades uncommonly well. Perhaps that's what God meant by Europe and Asia. We dress the characters and they paint the scenery. Well, anyhow, three of the least Asiatic things in the world are lost in this endless Asiatic palace—a good dog, a straight sword, and an Irishman."

But as he went down this telescope of tropical colours he really felt something of that hard fatalistic freedom of the heroes (or should we say villains?) in the Arabian Nights. He was prepared for any impossibility. He would hardly have been surprised if from under the lid of one of the porcelain pots standing in a corner had come a serpentine string of blue or yellow smoke, as if some wizard's oil were within. He would hardly have been surprised if from under the curtains or closed doors had crawled out a snakey track of blood, or if a dumb negro dressed in white had come out with a bow string, having done his work. He would not have been surprised if he had walked suddenly into the still chamber of some Sultan asleep, whom to wake was a death in torments. And yet he was very much more surprised by what he did see, and when he saw it, he was certain at last that he was only wandering in the labyrinth of his own brain. For what he saw was what was really in the core of all his dreams.

What he saw, indeed, was more appropriate to that inmost eastern chamber than anything he had imagined. On a divan of blood-red and orange cushions lay a startlingly beautiful woman, with a skin almost swarthy enough for an Arab's, and who might well have been the Princess proper to such an Arabian tale. But in truth it was not her appropriateness to the scene, but rather her inappropriateness, that made his heart bound. It was not her strangeness but her familiarity that made his big feet suddenly stop.

The dog ran on yet more rapidly, and the princess on the sofa welcomed him warmly, lifting him on his short hind legs. Then she looked up, and seemed turned to stone.

"Bismillah," said the oriental traveller, affably, "may your shadow never grow less—or more, as the ladies would say. The Commander of the Faithful has deputed his least competent slave to bring you back a dog. Owing to temporary delay in collecting the fifteen largest diamonds in the moon, he has been compelled to send the animal without any collar. Those responsible for the delay will instantly be beaten to death with the tails of dragons—"

The frightful shock, which had not yet left the lady's face, brought him back to responsible speech.

"In short," he said, "in the name of the Prophet, dog. I say, Joan, I wish this wasn't a dream."

"It isn't," said the girl, speaking for the first time, "and I don't know yet whether I wish it was."

"Well," argued the dreamer, rationally, "what are you, anytime, if you're not a dream—or a vision? And what are all these rooms, if they aren't a dream—or rather a nightmare?"

"This is the new wing of Ivywood House," said the lady addressed as Joan, speaking with great difficulty. "Lord Ivywood has fitted them up in the eastern style; he is inside conducting a most interesting debate in defence of Eastern Vegetarianism. I only came out because the room was rather hot."

"Vegetarian!" cried Dalroy, with abrupt and rather unreasonable exasperation. "That table seems to fall a bit short of Vegetarianism."

And he pointed to one of the long, narrow tables, laid somewhere in almost all the central rooms, and loaded with elaborate cold meats and expensive wines.

"He must be liberal-minded," cried Joan, who seemed to be on the verge of something, possibly temper. "He can't expect people suddenly to begin being Vegetarians when they've never been before."

"It has been done," said Dalroy, tranquilly, walking across to look at the table. "I say, your ascetical friends seem to have made a pretty good hole in the champagne. You may not believe it, Joan, but I haven't touched what you call alcohol for a month."

With which words he filled with champagne a large tumbler intended for claret cup and swallowed it at a draught.

Lady Joan Brett stood up straight but trembling.

"Now that's really wrong, Pat," she cried. "Oh, don't be silly—you know I don't care about the alcohol or all that. But you're in the man's house, uninvited, and he doesn't know. That wasn't like you."

"He shall know, all right," said the large man, quietly. "I know the exact price of a tumbler of that champagne."

And he scribbled some words in pencil on the back of a bill of fare on the table, and then carefully laid three shillings on top of it.

"And there you do Phillip the worst wrong of all," cried Lady Joan, flaming white. "You know as well as I do, anyhow, that he would not take your money."

Patrick Dalroy stood looking at her for some seconds with an expression on his broad and unusually open face which she found utterly puzzling.

"Curiously enough," he observed, at last, and with absolutely even temper, "curiously enough, it is you who are doing Phillip Ivywood a wrong. I think him quite capable of breaking England or Creation. But I do honestly think he would never break his word. And what is more, I think the more arbitrary and literal his word had been, the more he would keep it. You will never understand a man like that, till you understand that he can have devotion to a definition; even a new definition. He can really feel about an amendment to an Act of Parliament, inserted at the last moment, as you feel about England or your mother."

"Oh, don't philosophise," cried Joan suddenly. "Can't you see this has been a shock?"

"I only want you to see the point," he replied. "Lord Ivywood clearly told me, with his own careful lips, that I might go in and pay for fermented liquor in any place displaying a public sign outside. And he won't go back on that definition or on any definition. If he finds me here, he may quite possibly put me in prison on some other charge, as a thief or a vagabond, or what not. But he will not grudge the champagne. And he will accept the three shillings. And I shall honour him for his glorious consistency."

"I don't understand," said Joan, "one word of what you are talking about. Which way did you come? How can I get you away? You don't seem to grasp that you're in Ivywood House."

"You see there's a new name outside the gate," observed Patrick, conversationally, and led the lady to the end of the corridor by which he had entered and into its ultimate turret chamber.

Following his indications, Lady Joan peered a little over the edge of the window where hung the brilliant purple bird in its brilliant golden cage. Almost immediately below, outside the entrance to the half-closed stairway, stood a wooden tavern sign, as solid and still as if it had been there for centuries.

"All back at the sign of 'The Old Ship,' you see," said the Captain. "Can I offer you anything in a ladylike way?"

There was a vast impudence in the slight, hospitable movement of his hand, that disturbed Lady Joan's features with an emotion other than any that she desired to show.

"Well!" cried Patrick, with a wild geniality, "I've made you laugh again, my dear."

He caught her to him as in a whirlwind, and then vanished from the fairy turret like a blast, leaving her standing with her hand up to her wild black hair.

XIII

THE BATTLE OF THE TUNNEL

What Joan Brett really felt, as she went back from the second tête-à-tête she had experienced in the turret, it is doubtful if anyone will ever know. But she was full of the pungent feminine instinct to "drive at practice," and what she did clearly realise was the pencil writing Dalroy had left on the back of Lord Ivywood's *menu*. Heaven alone knew what it was, and (as it pleased her profane temper to tell herself) she was not satisfied with Heaven alone knowing. She went swiftly back, with swishing skirts, to the table where it had been left. But her skirts fell more softly and her feet trailed slower and more in her usual manner as she came near the table. For standing at it was Lord Ivywood, reading the card with tranquil lowered eyelids, that set off perfectly the long and perfect oval of his face. He put down the card with a quite natural action; and, seeing Joan, smiled at her in his most sympathetic way.

"So you've come out too," he said. "So have I; it's really too hot for anything. Dr. Gluck is making an uncommonly good speech, but I couldn't stop even for that. Don't you think my eastern decorations are rather a success after all? A sort of Vegetarianism in design, isn't it?"

He led her up and down the corridors, pointing out lemon-coloured crescents or crimson pomegranates in the scheme of ornament, with such utter detachment that they twice passed the open mouth of the hall of debate, and Joan could distinctly hear the voice of the diplomatic Gluck saying:

"Indeed, we owe our knowledge of the pollution of the pork primarily to the Jewth and not the Mothlemth. I do not thare that prejudithe against the Jewth, which ith too common in my family and all the arithtocratic and military Prutthian familieth. I think we Prutthian arithocrats owe everything to the Jewth. The Jewth have given to our old Teutonic rugged virtueth, jutht that touch of refinement, jutht that intellectual thuperiority which—."

And then the voice would die away behind, as Lord Ivywood lectured luxuriantly, and very well, on the peacock tail in decoration, or some more extravagant eastern version of the Greek Key. But the third time they turned, they heard the noise of subdued applause and the breaking up the meeting; and people came pouring forth.

With stillness and swiftness, Ivywood pitched on the people he wanted and held them. He button-holed Leveson and was evidently asking him to do something which neither of the two liked doing.

"If your lordship insists," she heard Leveson whispering, "of course I will go myself; but there is a great deal to be done here with your lordship's immediate matters. And if there were anyone else—."

If Phillip, Lord Ivywood, had ever looked at a human being in his life, he would have seen that J. Leveson, Secretary, was suffering from a very ancient human malady, excusable in all men and rather more excusable in one who has had his top-hat smashed over his eyes and has run for his life. As it was, he saw nothing, but merely said, "Oh, well, get someone else. What about your friend Hibbs?"

Leveson ran across to Hibbs, who was drinking another glass of champagne at one of the innumerable buffets.

"Hibbs," said Leveson, rather nervously, "will you do Lord Ivywood a favour? He says you have so much tact. It seems possible that a man may be hanging about the grounds just below that turret there. He is a man it would certainly be Lord Ivywood's public duty to put into the hands of the police, if he is there. But then, again, he is quite capable of not being there at all—I mean of having sent his message from somewhere else and in some other way. Naturally, Lord Ivywood doesn't want to alarm the ladies and perhaps turn the laugh against himself, by getting up a sort of police raid about nothing. He wants some sensible, tactful friend of his to go down and look round the place—it's a sort of disused garden—and report if there's anyone about. I'd go myself, but I'm wanted here."

Hibbs nodded, and filled another glass.

"But there's a further difficulty," went on Leveson. "He's a clever brute, it seems, a 'remarkable and a dangerous man,' were his lordship's words; and it looks as if he'd spotted a very good hiding-place, a disused tunnel leading to the sands, just beyond the disused garden and chapel. It's a smart choice, you see, for he can bolt into the woods if anyone comes from the shore, or on to the shore if anyone comes from the woods. But it would take a good time even to get the police here, and it would take ten times longer to get 'em round to the sea end of the tunnel, especially as the sea comes up to the cliffs once or twice between here and Pebblewick. So we mustn't frighten him away, or he'll get a start. If you meet anyone down there talk to him quite naturally, and come back with the news. We won't send for the police till you come. Talk as if you were just wandering like himself. His lordship wishes your presence to appear quite accidental."

"Wishes my presence to appear quite accidental," repeated Hibbs, gravely.

When the feverish Leveson had flashed off satisfied, Hibbs took a glass or two more of wine; feeling that he was going on a great diplomatic mission to please a lord. Then he went through the opening, picked his way down the stair, and somehow found his way out into the neglected garden and shrubbery.

It was already evening, and an early moon was brightening over the sunken chapel with its dragon-coloured scales of fungus. The night breeze was very fresh and had a marked effect on Mr. Hibbs. He found himself taking a meaningless pleasure in the scene; especially in one fungus that was white with brown spots. He laughed shortly, to think that it should be white with brown spots. Then he said, with carefully accurate articulation, "His lordship wishes my presence to appear quite accidental." Then he tried to remember something else that Leveson had said.

He began to wade through the waves of weed and thorn past the Chapel, but he found the soil much more uneven and obstructive than he had supposed.

He slipped, and sought to save himself by throwing one arm round a broken stone angel at a corner of the heap of Gothic fragments; but it was loose and rocked in its socket.

Mr. Hibbs presented for a moment the appearance of waltzing with the Angel in the moonlight, in a very amorous and irreverent manner. Then the statue rolled over one way and he rolled over the other, and lay on his face in the grass, making inaudible remarks. He might have lain there for some time, or at least found some difficulty in rising, but for another circumstance. The dog Quoodle, with characteristic officiousness, had followed him down the dark stairs and out of the doorway, and, finding him in this unusual posture, began to bark as if the house were on fire.

This brought a heavy human footstep from the more hidden parts of the copse; and in a minute or two the large man with the red hair was looking down at him in undisguised wonder. Hibbs said, in a muffled voice which came obscurely from under his hidden face, "Wish my presence to appear quite accidental."

"It does," said the Captain, "can I help you up? Are you hurt?"

He gently set the prostrate gentleman on his feet, and looked genuinely concerned. The fall had somewhat sobered Lord Ivywood's representative; and he really had a red graze on the left cheek that looked more ugly than it was.

"I am so sorry," said Patrick Dalroy, cordially, "come and sit down in our camp. My friend Pump will be back presently, and he's a capital doctor."

His friend Pump may or may not have been a capital doctor, but the Captain himself was certainly a most inefficient one. So small was his talent for diagnosing the nature of a disease at sight, that having given Mr. Hibbs a seat on a fallen tree by the tunnel, he proceeded to give him (in mere automatic hospitality) a glass of rum.

Mr. Hibbs's eyes awoke again, when he had sipped it, but they awoke to a new world.

"Wharever may be our invidual pinions," he said, and looked into space with an expression of humorous sagacity.

He then put his hand hazily in his pocket, as if to find some letter he had to deliver. He found nothing but his old journalistic note book, which he often carried when there was a chance of interviewing anybody. The feel of it under his fingers changed the whole attitude of his mind. He took it out and said:

"And wha' would you say of Vegetarianism, Colonel Pump?"

"I think it palls," replied the recipient of this complex title, staring.

"Sha' we say," asked Hibbs brightly, turning a leaf in his note book, "sha' we say long been strong vegetarian by conviction?"

"No; I have only once been convicted," answered Dalroy, with restraint, "and I hope to lead a better life when I come out."

"Hopes lead better life," murmured Hibbs, writing eagerly, with the wrong end of his pencil. "And wha' would you shay was best vegable food for really strong veg'tarian by conviction?"

"Thistles," said the Captain, wearily. "But I don't know much about it, you know."

"Lord Ivywoo' strong veg'tarian by conviction," said Mr. Hibbs, shaking his head with unction. "Lord Ivywoo' says tact. Talk to him naturally. And so I do. That's what I do. Talk to him naturally."

Humphrey Pump came through the clearer part of the wood, leading the donkey, who had just partaken of the diet recommended to a vegetarian by conviction; the dog sprang up and ran to them. Pump was, perhaps, the most naturally polite man in the world, and said nothing. But his eyes had accepted, with one snap of surprise, the other fact, also not unconnected with diet, which had escaped Dalroy's notice when he administered rum as a restorative.

"Lord Ivywoo' says," murmured the journalistic diplomatist. "Lord Ivywoo' says, 'talk as if you were just wandering.' That's it. That's tact. That's what I've got to do—talk as if I was just wandering. Long way round to other end tunnel; sea and cliffs. Don' sphose they can swim." He seized his note book again and looked in vain for his pencil. "Good subjec' correspondence. Can policem'n swim?"

"Policemen?" said Dalroy, in a dead silence. The dog looked up, and the innkeeper did not.

"Get to Ivywoo' one thing," reasoned the diplomatist. "Get policemen beach other end other thing. No good do one thing no' do other thing, no goo' do other thing no' do other thing. Wish my presence appear quite accidental. Haw!"

"I'll harness the donkey," said Pump.

"Will he go through that door?" asked Dalroy, with a gesture toward the entrance of the rough boarding with which they had faced the tunnel, "or shall I smash it all at once?"

"He'll go through all right," answered Pump. "I saw to that when I made it. And I think I'll get him to the safe end of the tunnel before I load him up. The best thing you can do is to pull up one of those saplings to bar the door with. That'll delay them a minute or two; though I think we've got warning in pretty easy time."

He led his donkey to the cart, and carefully harnessed the donkey; like all men cunning in the old healthy sense he knew that the last chance of leisure ought to be leisurely, in order that it may be lucid. Then he led the whole equipment through the temporary wooden door of the tunnel, the inquisitive Quoodle, of course, following at his heels.

"Excuse me if I take a tree," said Dalroy, politely, to his guest, like a man reaching across another man for a match. And with that he rent up a young tree by its roots, as he had done in the Island of the Olives, and carried it on his shoulder, like the club of Hercules.

Up in Ivywood House Lord Ivywood had telephoned twice to Pebblewick. It was a delay he seldom suffered; and, though he never expressed impatience in unnecessary words he expressed it in unnecessary walking. He would not yet send for the police without news from his Ambassador, but he thought a preliminary conversation with some police authorities he knew well, might advance matters. Seeing Leveson rather shrunk in a corner, he wheeled round in his walk and said abruptly:

"You must go and see what has happened to Hibbs. If you have any other duties here, I authorize you to neglect them. Otherwise, I can only say—"

At this moment the telephone rang, and the impatient nobleman rushed for his delayed call with a rapidity he seldom showed. There was simply nothing for Leveson to do except to do as he was told, or be sacked. He walked swiftly toward the staircase, and only stopped once at the table where Hibbs had stood and gulped down two goblets of the same wine. But let no man attribute to Mr. Leveson the loose and luxurious social motives of Mr. Hibbs. Mr. Leveson did not drink for pleasure; in fact, he hardly knew what he was drinking. His motive was something far more simple and sincere; a sentiment forcibly described in legal phraseology as going in bodily fear.

He was partly nerved, but by no means reconciled to his adventure, when he crept carefully down the stairs and peered about the thicket for any signs of his diplomatic friend. He could find neither sight nor sound to guide him, except a sort of distant singing, which greatly increased in volume of sound as he pursued it. The first words he heard seemed to run something like—

> "No more the milk of cows
> Shall pollute my private house,
> Than the milk of the wild mares of the Barbarian;
> I will stick to port and sherry,
> For they are so very, very,
> So very, very, very Vegetarian.

Leveson did not know the huge and horrible voice in which these words were shouted, but he had a most strange and even sickening suspicion that he did know the voice, however altered, the quavering and rather refined voice that joined in the chorus and sang,

> "Because they are so vegy,
> So vegy, vegy, vegy Vegetarian."

Terror lit up his wits, and he made a wild guess at what had happened. With a gasp of relief he realised that he had now good excuse for returning to the house with the warning. He ran there like a hare, still hearing the great voice from the woods like the roaring of a lion in his ear.

He found Lord Ivywood in consultation with Dr. Gluck, and also with Mr. Bullrose the Agent, whose froglike eyes hardly seemed to have recovered yet from the fairy-tale of the flying sign-board in the English lane; but who, to do him justice, was more plucky and practical than most of Lord Ivywood's present advisers.

"I'm afraid Mr. Hibbs has inadvertently," stammered Leveson. "I'm afraid he has—I'm afraid the man is making his escape, my lord. You had better send for the police."

Ivywood turned to the agent. "You go and see what's happening," he said simply. "I will come myself when I've rung them up. And get some of the servants up with sticks and things. Fortunately the ladies have gone to bed. Hullo! Is that the Police Station?"

Bullrose went down into the shrubbery and had, for many reasons, less difficulty in crossing it than the hilarious Hibbs. The moon had increased to an almost unnatural brilliancy, so that the whole scene was like a rather silver daylight; and in this clear medium he beheld a very tall man with erect, red hair and a colossal cylinder of cheese carried under one arm, while he employed the other to wag a big forefinger at a dog with whom he was conversing.

It was the Agent's duty and desire to hold the man, whom he recognised from the sign-board mystery, in play and conversation, and prevent his final escape. But there are some people who really cannot be courteous, even when they want to be, and Mr. Bullrose was one of them.

"Lord Ivywood," he said abruptly, "wants to know what you want."

"Do not, however, fall into the common error, Quoodle," Dalroy was saying to the dog, whose unfathomable eyes were fixed on his face, "of supposing that the phrase 'good dog' is used in its absolute sense. A dog is good or bad negatively to a limited scheme of duties created by human civilization—"

"What are you doing here?" asked Mr. Bullrose.

"A dog, my dear Quoodle," continued the Captain, "cannot be either so good or bad as a man. Nay, I should go farther. I would almost say a dog cannot be so stupid as a man. He cannot be utterly wanting as a dog—as some men are as men."

"Answer me, you there!" roared the Agent.

"It is all the more pathetic," continued the Captain, to whose monologue Quoodle seemed to listen with magnetized attention. "It is all the more pathetic because this mental insufficiency is sometimes found in the good; though there are, I should imagine, at least an equal number of opposite examples. The person standing a few feet off us, for example, is both stupid and wicked. But be very careful, Quoodle, to remember that any disadvantage under which we place him should be based on the *moral* and not his *mental* defects. Should I say to you at any time, 'Go for him, Quoodle,' or 'Hold him, Quoodle,' be certain in your own mind, please, that it is solely because he is *wicked* and not because he is *stupid*, that I am entitled to do so. The fact that he is *stupid* would not justify me in saying 'hold him, Quoodle,' with the realistic intonation I now employ—"

"Curse you, call him off!" cried Mr. Bullrose, retreating, for Quoodle was coming toward him with the bulldog part of his pedigree very prominently displayed, like a pennon. "Should Mr. Bullrose find it expedient to climb a tree, or even a sign-post," proceeded Dalroy, for indeed the Agent had already clasped the pole of "The Old Ship," which was stouter than the slender trees standing just around it, "you will keep an eye on him, Quoodle, and, I doubt not, constantly remind him that it is his *wickedness*, and not, as he might hastily be inclined to suppose, *stupidity* that has placed him on so conspicuous an elevation—"

"Some of you'll wish yourself dead for this," said the Agent; who was by this time clinging to the wooden sign like a monkey on a stick, while Quoodle watched him from below with an unsated interest. "Some of you'll see something. Here comes his lordship and the police, I reckon."

"Good morning, my lord," said Dalroy, as Ivywood, paler than ever in the strong moonshine, came through the thicket toward them. It seemed to be his fate that his faultless and hueless face should always be contrasted with richer colours; and even now it was thrown up by the gorgeous diplomatic uniform of Dr. Gluck, who walked just behind him.

"I am glad to see you, my lord," said Dalroy, in a stately manner, "it is always so awkward doing business with an Agent. Especially for the Agent."

"Captain Dalroy," said Lord Ivywood, with a more serious dignity, "I am sorry we meet again like this, and such things are not of my seeking. It is only right to tell you that the police will be here in a moment."

"Quite time, too!" said Dalroy, shaking his head. "I never saw anything so disgraceful in my life. Of course, I am sorry it's a friend of yours; and I hope the police will keep Ivywood House out of the papers. But I won't be a party to one law for the rich and another for the poor, and it would be a great shame if a man in that state got off altogether merely because he had got the stuff at your house."

"I do not understand you," said Ivywood. "What are you talking of?"

"Why of him," replied the Captain, with a genial gesture toward a fallen tree trunk that lay a yard or two from the tunnel wall, "the poor chap the police are coming for."

Lord Ivywood looked at the forest log by the tunnel which he had not glanced at before, and in his pale eyes, perhaps for the first time, stood a simple astonishment.

Above the log appeared two duplicate objects, which, after a prolonged stare, he identified as the soles of a pair of patent leather shoes, offered to his gaze, as if demanding his opinion in the matter of resoling. They were all that was visible of Mr. Hibbs who had fallen backward off his woodland seat and seemed contented with his new situation.

His lordship put up the pince-nez that made him look ten years older, and said with a sharp, steely accent, "What is all this?"

The only effect of his voice upon the faithful Hibbs was to cause him to feebly wave his legs in the air in recognition of a feudal superior. He clearly considered it hopeless to attempt to get up, so Dalroy, striding across to him, lugged him up by his shirt collar and exhibited him, limp and wild-eyed to the company.

"You won't want many policemen to take him to the station," said the Captain. "I'm sorry, Lord Ivywood, I'm afraid it's no use your asking me to overlook it again. We can't afford it," and he shook his head implacably. "We've always kept a respectable house, Mr. Pump and I. 'The Old Ship' has a reputation all over the country—in quite a lot of different parts, in fact. People in the oddest places have found it a quiet, family house. Nothing gadabout in 'The Old Ship.' And if you think you can send all your staggering revellers—"

"Captain Dalroy," said Ivywood, simply, "you seem to be under a misapprehension, which I think it would be hardly honourable to leave undisturbed. Whatever these extraordinary events may mean and whatever be fitting in the case of this gentleman, when I spoke of the police coming, I meant they were coming for you and your confederate."

"For me!" cried the Captain, with a stupendous air of surprise. "Why, I have never done anything naughty in my life."

"You have been selling alcohol contrary to Clause V. of the Act of—"

"But I've got a sign," cried Dalroy, excitedly, "you told me yourself it was all right if I'd got a sign. Oh, do look at our new sign! The 'Sign of the Agile Agent.'"

Mr. Bullrose had remained silent, feeling his position none of the most dignified, and hoping his employer would go away. But Lord Ivywood looked up at him, and thought he had wandered into a planet of monsters.

As he slowly recovered himself Patrick Dalroy said briskly, "All quite correct and conventional, you see. You can't run us in for not having a sign; we've rather an extra life-like one. And you can't run us in as rogues and vagabonds either. Visible means of subsistence," and he slapped the huge cheese under his arm with his great flat hand, so that it reverberated like a drum. "Quite visible. Perceptible," he added, holding it out suddenly almost under Lord Ivywood's nose. "Perceptible to the naked eye through your lordship's eyeglasses."

He turned abruptly, burst open the pantomime door behind him and bowled the big cheese down the tunnel with a noise like thunder, which ended in a cry of acceptation in the distant voice of Mr. Humphrey Pump. It was the last of their belongings left at this end of the tunnel, and Dalroy turned again, a man totally transfigured.

"And now, Ivywood," he said, "what can I be charged with? Well, I have a suggestion to make. I will surrender to the police quite quietly when they come, if you will do me one favour. Let me choose my crime."

"I don't understand you," answered the other coolly, "what crime? What favour?"

Captain Dalroy unsheathed the straight sword that still hung on his now shabby uniform. The slender blade sparkled splendidly in the moonlight as he pointed it straight at Dr. Gluck.

"Take away his sword from the little pawnbroker," he said. "It's about the length of mine; or we'll change if you like. Give me ten minutes on that strip of turf. And then it may be, Ivywood, that I shall be removed from your public path in a way a little worthier of enemies who have once been friends, than if you tripped me up with Bow Street runners, of whose help every ancestor you have would have been ashamed. Or, on the other hand, it may be—that when the police come there will be something to arrest me for."

There was a long silence, and the elf of irresponsibility peeped out again for an instant in Dalroy's mind.

"Mr. Bullrose will see fair play for you, from a throne above the lists," he said. "I have already put my honour in the hands of Mr. Hibbs."

"I must decline Captain Dalroy's invitation," said Ivywood at last, in a curious tone. "Not so much because—"

Before he could proceed, Leveson came racing across the copse, hallooing, "The police are here!"

Dalroy, who loved leaving everything to the last instant, tore up the sign, with Bullrose literally hanging to it, shook him off like a ripe fruit, and then plunged into the tunnel, the clamorous Quoodle at his heels. Before even Ivywood (the promptest of his party) could reach the spot, he had clashed to the wood door and bolted it across with his wooden staple. He had not had time even to sheath his sword.

"Break down this door." said Lord Ivywood, calmly. "I noticed they haven't finished loading their cart."

Under his directions, and vastly against their will, Bullrose and Leveson lifted the tree-trunk vacated by Hibbs, and swinging it thrice as a battering-ram, burst in the door. Lord Ivywood instantly sprang into the entrance.

A voice called out to him quietly from the other end of the tunnel. There was something touching and yet terrible about a voice so human coming out of that inhuman darkness. If Phillip Ivywood had been really a poet, and not rather its opposite, an æsthete, he would have known that all the past and people of England were uttering their oracle out of the cavern. As it was, he only heard a publican wanted by the police.—Yet even he paused, and indeed seemed spellbound.

"My lord, I would like a word. I learned my catechism and never was with the Radicals. I want you to look at what you've done to me. You've stolen a house that was mine as that one's yours. You've made me a dirty tramp, that was a man respected in church and market. Now you send me where I might have cells or the Cat. If I might make so bold, what do you suppose I think of you? Do you think because you go up to London and settle it with lords in Parliament and bring back a lot of papers and long words, that makes any difference to the man you do it to? By what I can see, you're just a bad and cruel master, like those God punished in the old days; like Squire Varney the weasels killed in Holy Wood. Well, parson always said one might shoot at robbers, and I want to tell your lordship," he ended respectfully, "that I have a gun."

Ivywood instantly stepped into the darkness, and spoke in a voice shaken with some emotion, the nature of which was never certainly known.

"The police are here," he said, "but I'll arrest you myself."

A shot shrieked and rattled through the thousand echoes of the tunnel. Lord Ivywood's legs doubled and twisted under him, and he collapsed on the earth with a bullet above his knee.

Almost at the same instant a shout and a bark announced that the cart had started as a complete equipage. It was even more than complete, for the instant before it moved Mr. Quoodle had sprung into it, and, as it was driven off, sat erect in it, looking solemn.

XIV

The Creature that Man Forgets

Despite the natural hubbub round the wound of Lord Ivywood and the difficulties of the police in finding their way to the shore, the fugitives of the Flying Inn must almost certainly have been captured but for a curious accident, which also flowed, as it happened, from the great Ivywood debate on Vegetarianism.

The comparatively late hour at which Lord Ivywood had made his discovery had been largely due to a very long speech which Joan had not heard, and which was delivered immediately before the few concluding observations she had heard from Dr. Gluck. The speech was made by an eccentric, of course. Most of those who attended, and nearly all of those who talked, were eccentric in one way or another. But he was an eccentric of great wealth and good family, an M.P., a J.P., a relation of Lady Enid, a man well known in art and letters; in short, a personality who could not be prevented from being anything he chose, from a revolutionist to a bore. Dorian Wimpole had first become famous outside his own class under the fanciful title of the Poet of the Birds. A volume of verse, expanding the several notes or cries of separate song-birds into fantastic soliloquies of these feathered philosophers, had really contained a great deal of ingenuity and elegance. Unfortunately, he was one of those who always tend to take their own fancies seriously, and in whose otherwise legitimate extravagance there is too little of the juice of jest. Hence, in his later works, when he explained "The Fable of the Angel," by trying to prove that the fowls of the air were creatures higher than man or the anthropoids, his manner was felt to be too austere; and when he moved an amendment to Lord Ivywood's scheme for the model village called Peaceways, urging that its houses should all follow the more hygienic architecture of nests hung in trees, many regretted that he had lost his light touch. But, when he went beyond birds and filled his poems with conjectural psychology about all the Zoological Gardens, his meaning became obscure; and Lady Susan had even described it as his bad period. It was all the more uncomfortable reading because he poured forth the imaginary hymns, love-songs and war-songs of the lower animals, without a word of previous explanation.

Thus, if someone seeking for an ordinary drawing-room song came on lines that were headed "A Desert Love Song," and which began—

> *"Her head is high against the stars,*
> *Her hump is heaved in pride,"*

the compliment to the lady would at first seem startling, until the reader realised that all the characters in the idyll were camels. Or, if he began a poem simply entitled, "The March of Democracy," and found in the first lines—

> *"Comrades, marching evermore,*
> *Fix your teeth in floor and door,"*

he might be doubtful about such a policy for the masses; until he discovered that it was supposed to be addressed by an eloquent and aspiring rat to the social solidarity of his race. Lord Ivywood had nearly quarrelled with his poetic relative over the uproarious realism of the verses called "A Drinking Song," until it was carefully explained to him that the drink was water, and that the festive company consisted of bisons. His vision of the perfect husband, as it exists in the feelings of the young female walrus, is thoughtful and suggestive; but would doubtless receive many emendations from anyone who had experienced those feelings. And in his sonnet called "Motherhood" he has made the young scorpion consistent and convincing, yet somehow not wholly lovable. In justice to him, however, it should be remembered that he attacked the most difficult cases on principle, declaring that there was no earthly creature that a poet should forget.

He was of the blond type of his cousin, with flowing fair hair and mustache, and a bright blue, absent-minded eye; he was very well dressed in the carefully careless manner, with a brown velvet jacket and the image on his ring of one of those beasts men worshipped in Egypt.

His speech was graceful and well worded and enormously long, and it was all about an oyster. He passionately protested against the suggestion of some humanitarians who were vegetarians in other respects, but maintained that organisms so simple might fairly be counted as exceptions. Man, he said, even at his miserable best, was always trying to excommunicate some one citizen of the cosmos, to forget some one creature that he should remember. Now, it seemed that creature was the oyster. He gave a long account of the tragedy of the oyster, a really imaginative and picturesque account; full of fantastic fishes, and coral crags crawling and climbing, and bearded creatures streaking the seashore and the green darkness in the cellars of the sea.

"What a horrid irony it is," he cried, "that this is the only one of the lower creatures whom we call a Native! We speak of him, and of him alone as if he were a native of the country. Whereas, indeed, he is an exile in the universe. What can be conceived more pitiful than the eternal frenzy of the impotent amphibian? What is more terrible than the tear of an oyster? Nature herself has sealed it with the hard seal of eternity. The creature man forgets bears against him a testimony that cannot be forgotten. For the tears of widows and of captives are wiped away at last like the tears of children. They vanish like the mists of morning or the small pools after a flood. But the tear of the oyster is a pearl."

The Poet of the Birds was so excited with his own speech that, after the meeting, he walked out with a wild eye to the motor car, which had been long awaiting him, the chauffeur giving some faint signs of relief.

"Toward home, for the present," said the poet, and stared at the moon with an inspired face.

He was very fond of motoring, finding it fed him with inspirations; and he had been doing it from an early hour that morning, having enjoyed a slightly lessened sleep. He had scarcely spoken to anybody until he spoke to the cultured crowd at Ivywood. He did not wish to speak to anyone for many hours yet. His ideas were racing. He had thrown on a fur coat over his velvet jacket, but he let it fly open, having long forgotten the coldness in the splendour of the moonstruck night. He realised only two things: the swiftness of his car and the swiftness of his thoughts. He felt, as it were, a fury of omniscience; he seemed flying with every bird that sped or spun above the woods, with every squirrel that had leapt and tumbled within them, with every tree that had swung under and sustained the blast.

Yet in a few moments he leaned forward and tapped the glass frontage of the car, and the chauffeur suddenly squaring his shoulders, jarringly stopped the wheels. Dorian Wimpole had just seen something in the clear moonlight by the roadside, which appealed both to this and to the other side of his tradition; something that appealed to Wimpole as well as to Dorian.

Two shabby looking men, one in tattered gaiters and the other in what looked like the remains of fancy dress with the addition of hair, of so wild a red that it looked like a wig, were halted under the hedge, apparently loading a donkey cart. At least two rounded, rudely cylindrical objects, looking more or less like tubs, stood out in the road beside the wheels, along with a sort of loose wooden post that lay along the road beside them. As a matter of fact, the man in the old gaiters had just been feeding and watering the donkey, and was now adjusting its harness more easily. But Dorian Wimpole naturally did not expect that sort of thing from that sort of man. There swelled up in him the sense that his omnipotence went beyond the poetical; that he was a gentleman, a magistrate, an M.P. and J.P., and so on. This callousness or ignorance about animals should not go on while he was a J.P.; especially since Ivywood's last Act. He simply strode across to the stationary cart and said:

"You are overloading that animal, and it is forfeited. And you must come with me to the police station."

Humphrey Pump, who was very considerate to animals, and had always tried to be considerate to gentlemen, in spite of having put a bullet into one of their legs, was simply too astounded and distressed to make any answer at all. He moved a step or two backward and stared with brown, blinking eyes at the poet, the donkey, the cask, the cheese, and the sign-board lying in the road.

But Captain Dalroy, with the quicker recovery of his national temperament, swept the poet and magistrate a vast fantastic bow and said with agreeable impudence, "interested in donkeys, no doubt?"

"I am interested in all things men forget," answered the poet, with a fine touch of pride, "but mostly in those like this, that are most easily forgotten."

Somehow from those two first sentences Pump realised that these two eccentric aristocrats had unconsciously recognised each other. The fact that it was unconscious seemed, somehow, to exclude him all the more. He stirred a little the moonlit dust of the road with his rather dilapidated boots and eventually strolled across to speak to the chauffeur.

"Is the next police station far from here?" he asked.

The chauffeur answered with one syllable of which the nearest literal rendering is "dno." Other spellings have been attempted, but the sentiment expressed is that of agnosticism.

But something of special brutality of abbreviation made the shrewd, and therefore sensitive, Mr. Pump look at the man's face. And he saw it was not only the moonlight that made it white.

With that dumb delicacy that was so English in him, Pump looked at the man again, and saw he was leaning heavily on the car with one arm, and saw that the arm was shaking. He understood his countrymen enough to know that whatever he said he must say in a careless manner.

"I hope it's nearer to your place. You must be a bit done up."

"Oh hell!" said the driver and spat on the road.

Pump was sympathetically silent, and Mr. Wimpole's chauffeur broke out incoherently, as if in another place.

"Blarsted beauties o' dibrike and no breakfast. Blarsted lunch Hivywood and no lunch. Blarsted black everlastin' hours artside while 'e 'as 'is cike an' champine. And then it's a dornkey."

"You don't mean to say," said Pump in a very serious voice, "that you've had no food today?"

"Ow no!" replied the cockney, with the irony of the deathbed. "Ow, of course not."

Pump strolled back into the road again, picked up the cheese in his left hand, and landed it on the seat beside the driver. Then his right hand went to one of his large loose equivocal pockets, and the blade of a big jack-knife caught and recaught the steady splendours of the moon.

The driver stared for several instants at the cheese, with the knife shaking in his hand. Then he began to hack it, and in that white witchlike light the happiness of his face was almost horrible.

Pump was wise in all such things, and knew that just as a little food will sometimes prevent sheer intoxication, so a little stimulant will sometimes prevent sudden and dangerous indigestion. It was practically impossible to make the man stop eating cheese. It was far better to give him a very little of the rum, especially as it was very good rum, and better than anything he could find in any of the public-houses that were still permitted. He walked across the road again and picked up the small cask, which he put on the other side of the cheese and from which he filled, in his own manner, the little cup he carried in his pocket.

But at the sight of this the cockney's eyes lit at once with terror and desire.

"But yer cawnt do it," he whispered hoarsely, "its the pleece. It's gile for that, with no doctor's letter nor sign-board nor nothink."

Mr. Humphrey Pump made yet another march back into the road. When he got there he hesitated for the first time, but it was quite clear from the attitude of the two insane aristocrats who were arguing and posturing in the road that they would notice nothing except each other. He picked the loose post off the road and brought it to the car, humorously propping it erect in the aperture between keg and cheese.

The little glass of rum was wavering in the poor chauffeur's hand exactly as the big knife had done, but when he looked up and actually saw the wooden sign above him, he seemed not so much to pluck up his courage, but rather to drag up some forgotten courage from the foundations of some unfathomable sea. It was indeed the forgotten courage of the people.

He looked once at the bleak, black pinewoods around him and took the mouthful of golden liquid at a gulp, as if it were a fairy potion. He sat silent; and then, very slowly, a sort of stony glitter began to come into his eyes. The brown and vigilant eyes of Humphrey Pump were studying him with some anxiety or even fear. He did look rather like a man enchanted or turned to stone. But he spoke very suddenly.

"The blighter!" he said. "I'll give 'im 'ell. I'll give 'im bleeding 'ell. I'll give 'im somethink wot 'e don't expect."

"What do you mean?" asked the inn-keeper.

"Why," answered the chauffeur, with abrupt composure, "I'll give 'im a little dornkey."

Mr. Pump looked troubled. "Do you think," he observed, affecting to speak lightly, "that he's fit to be trusted even with a little donkey?"

"Ow, yes," said the man. "He's very amiable with donkeys, and donkeys we is to be amiable with 'im."

Pump still looked at him doubtfully, appearing or affecting not to follow his meaning. Then he looked equally anxiously across at the other two men; but they were still talking. Different as they were in every other way, they were of the sort who forget everything, class, quarrel, time, place and physical facts in front of them, in the lust of lucid explanation and equal argument.

Thus, when the Captain began by lightly alluding to the fact that after all it was his donkey, since he had bought it from a tinker for a just price, the police station practically vanished from Wimpole's mind— and I fear the donkey-cart also. Nothing remained but the necessity of dissipating the superstition of personal property.

"I own nothing," said the poet, waving his hands outward, "I own nothing save in the sense that I own everything. All depends whether wealth or power be used for or against the higher purposes of the cosmos."

"Indeed," replied Dalroy, "and how does your motor car serve the higher purposes of the cosmos?"

"It helps me," said Mr. Wimpole, with honourable simplicity, "to produce my poems."

"And if it could be used for some higher purpose (if such a thing could be), if some new purpose had come into the cosmos's head by accident," inquired the other, "I suppose it would cease to be your property."

"Certainly," replied the dignified Dorian. "I should not complain. Nor have you any title to complain when the donkey ceases to be yours when you depress it in the cosmic scale."

"What makes you think," asked Dalroy, "that I wanted to depress it?"

"It is my firm belief," replied Dorian Wimpole, sternly, "that you wanted to ride on it" (for indeed the Captain had once repeated his playful gesture of putting his large leg across). "Is not that so?"

"No," answered the Captain, innocently, "I never ride on a donkey. I'm afraid of it."

"Afraid of a donkey!" cried Wimpole, incredulously.

"Afraid of an historical comparison," said Dalroy.

There was a short pause, and Wimpole said coolly enough, "Oh, well, we've outlived those comparisons."

"Easily," answered the Irish Captain. "It is wonderful how easily one outlives someone else's crucifixion."

"In this case," said the other grimly, "I think it is the donkey's crucifixion."

"Why, you must have drawn that old Roman caricature of the crucified donkey," said Patrick Dalroy, with an air of some wonder. "How well you have worn; why, you look quite young! Well, of course, if this donkey is crucified, he must be uncrucified. But are you quite sure," he added, very gravely, "that you know how to uncrucify a donkey? I assure you it's one of the rarest of human arts. All a matter of knack. It's like the doctors with the rare diseases, you know; the necessity so seldom arises. Granted that, by the higher purposes of the cosmos, I am unfit to look after this donkey, I must still feel a faint shiver of responsibility in passing him on to you. Will you understand this donkey? He is a delicate-minded donkey. He is a complex donkey. How can I be certain that, on so short an acquaintance, you will understand every shade of his little likes and dislikes?"

The dog Quoodle, who had been sitting as still as the sphinx under the shadow of the pine trees, waddled out for an instant into the middle of the road and then returned. He ran out when a slight noise as of rotatory grinding was heard; and ran back when it had ceased. But Dorian Wimpole was much too keen on his philosophical discovery to notice either dog or wheel.

"I shall not sit on its back, anyhow," he said proudly, "but if that were all it would be a small matter. It is enough for you that you have left it in the hands of the only person who could really understand it; one who searches the skies and seas so as not to neglect the smallest creature."

"This is a very curious creature," said the Captain, anxiously, "he has all sorts of odd antipathies. He can't stand a motor-car, for instance, especially one that throbs like that while it's standing still. He doesn't mind a fur coat so much, but if you wear a brown velvet jacket under it, he bites you. And you must keep him out of the way of a certain kind of people. I don't suppose you've met them; but they always think that anybody with less than two hundred a year is drunk and very cruel, and that anybody with more than two thousand a year is conducting the Day of Judgment. If you will keep our dear donkey from the society of such persons—Hullo! Hullo! Hullo!"

He turned in genuine disturbance, and dashed after the dog, who had dashed after the motor-car and jumped inside. The Captain jumped in after the dog, to pull him out again. But before he could do so, he found the car was flying along too fast for any such leap. He looked up and saw the sign of "The Old Ship" erect in the front like a rigid banner; and Pump, with his cask and cheese, sitting solidly beside the driver.

The thing was more of an earthquake and transformation to him even than to any of the others; but he rose waveringly to his feet and shouted out to Wimpole.

"You've left it in the right hands. I've never been cruel to a motor."

In the moonlight of the magic pine-wood far behind, Dorian and the donkey were left looking at each other.

To the mystical mind, when it is a mind at all (which is by no means always the case), there are no two things more impressive and symbolical than a poet and a donkey. And the donkey was a very genuine donkey, and the poet was a very genuine poet; however lawfully he might be mistaken for the other animal at times. The interest of the donkey in the poet will never be known. The interest of the poet in the donkey was perfectly genuine; and survived even that appalling private interview in the owlish secrecy of the woods.

But I think even the poet would have been enlightened if he had seen the white, set, frantic face of the man on the driver's seat of his vanishing motor. If he had seen it he might have remembered the name, or, perhaps, even begun to understand the nature of a certain animal which is neither the donkey nor the oyster; but the creature whom man has always found it easiest to forget, since the hour he forgot God in a Garden.

XV

The Songs of the Car Club

More than once as the car flew through black and silver fairylands of fir wood and pine wood, Dalroy put his head out of the side window and remonstrated with the chauffeur without effect. He was reduced at last to asking him where he was going.

"I'm goin' 'ome," said the driver in an undecipherable voice. "I'm a goin' 'ome to my mar."

"And where does she live?" asked Dalroy, with something more like diffidence than he had ever shown before in his life.

"Wiles," said the man, "but I ain't seen 'er since I was born. But she'll do."

"You must realise," said Dalroy, with difficulty, "that you may be arrested—it's the man's own car; and he's left behind with nothing to eat, so to speak."

"'E's got 'is dornkey," grunted the man. "Let the stinker eat 'is dornkey, with thistle sauce. 'E would if 'e was as 'ollow as I was."

Humphrey Pump opened the glass window that separated him from the rear part of the car, and turned to speak to his friend over his square elbow and shoulder.

"I'm afraid," he said, "he won't stop for anything just yet. He's as mad as Moody's aunt, as they say."

"Do they say it?" asked the Captain, with a sort of anxiety. "They never said it in Ithaca."

"Honestly, I think you'd better leave him alone," answered Pump, with his sagacious face. "He'd just run us into a Scotch Express like Dandy Mutton did, when they said he was driving carelessly. We can send the car back to Ivywood somehow later on, and really, I don't think it'll do the gentleman any harm to spend a night with a donkey. The donkey might teach him something, I tell you."

"It's true he denied the Principle of Private Property," said Dalroy, reflectively, "but I fancy he was thinking of a plain house fixed on the ground. A house on wheels, such as this, he might perhaps think a more permanent possession. But I never understand it;" and again he passed a weary palm across his open forehead. "Have you ever noticed, Hump, what is really odd about those people?"

The car shot on amid the comfortable silence of Pump, and then the Irishman said again:

"That poet in the pussy-cat clothes wasn't half bad. Lord Ivywood isn't cruel; but he's inhuman. But that man wasn't inhuman. He was ignorant, like most cultured fellows. But what's odd about them is that they try to be simple and never clear away a single thing that's complicated. If they have to choose between beef and pickles, they always abolish the beef. If they have to choose between a meadow and a motor, they forbid the meadow. Shall I tell you the secret? These men only surrender the things that bind them to other men. Go and dine with a temperance millionaire and you won't find he's abolished the *hors d'œuvres* or the five courses or even the coffee. What he's abolished is the port and sherry, because poor men like that as well as rich. Go a step farther, and you won't find he's abolished the fine silver forks and spoons, but he's abolished the meat, because poor men like meat—when they can get it. Go a step farther, and you won't find he goes without gardens or gorgeous rooms, which poor men can't enjoy at all. But you will find he boasts of early rising, because sleep is a thing poor men can still enjoy. About the only thing they can still enjoy. Nobody ever heard of a modern philanthropist giving up petrol or typewriting or troops of servants. No, no! What he gives up must be some simple and universal thing. He will give up beef or beer or sleep—because these pleasures remind him that he is only a man."

Humphrey Pump nodded, but still answered nothing; and the voice of the sprawling Dalroy took one of its upward turns of a sort of soaring flippancy; which commonly embodied itself in remembering some song he had composed.

"Such," he said, "was the case of the late Mr. Mandragon, so long popular in English aristocratic society as a bluff and simple democrat from the West, until he was unfortunately sand-bagged by six men whose wives he had had shot by private detectives, on his incautiously landing on American soil.

"Mr. Mandragon the Millionaire, he wouldn't have wine or wife,
He couldn't endure complexity; he lived the simple life;
He ordered his lunch by megaphone in manly, simple tones,
And used all his motors for canvassing voters, and twenty telephones;
Besides a dandy little machine,
Cunning and neat as ever was seen,

> With a hundred pulleys and cranks between,
> Made of iron and kept quite clean,
> To hoist him out of his healthful bed on every day of his life,
> And wash him and brush him and shave him and dress him to live
> the Simple Life.

> "Mr. Mandragon was most refined and quietly, neatly dressed,
> Say all the American newspapers that know refinement best;
> Quiet and neat the hair and hat, and the coat quiet and neat,
> A trouser worn upon either leg, while boots adorned the feet;
> And not, as anyone might expect,
> A Tiger Skin, all striped and specked,
> And a Peacock Hat with the tail erect,
> A scarlet tunic with sunflowers decked—
> That might have had a more marked effect,
> And pleased the pride of a weaker man that yearned for wine or wife;
> But fame and the flagon for Mr. Mandragon obscured the Simple Life.

> "Mr. Mandragon the Millionaire, I am happy to say, is dead.
> He enjoyed a quiet funeral in a crematorium shed,
> And he lies there fluffy and soft and grey and certainly quite refined,
> When he might have rotted to flowers and fruit with Adam
> and all mankind.
> Or been eaten by bears that fancy blood,
> Or burnt on a big tall tower of wood,
> In a towering flame as a heathen should,
> Or even sat with us here at food,
> Merrily taking twopenny rum and cheese with a pocket knife,
> But these were luxuries lost for him that lived for the Simple Life."

Mr. Pump had made many attempts to arrest this song, but they were as vain as all attempts to arrest the car. The angry chauffeur seemed, indeed, rather inspired to further energy by the violent vocal noises behind; and Pump again found it best to fall back on conversation.

"Well, Captain," he said, amicably. "I can't quite agree with you about those things. Of course, you can trust foreigners too much as poor Thompson did; but then you can go too far the other way. Aunt Sarah lost a thousand pounds that way. I told her again and again he wasn't a nigger, but she wouldn't believe me. And, of course, that was just the kind of thing to offend an ambassador if he was an Austrian. It seems to me, Captain, you aren't quite fair to these foreign chaps. Take these Americans, now! There were many Americans went by Pebblewick, you may suppose. But in all the lot there was never a bad lot; never a nasty American, nor a stupid American—nor, well, never an American that I didn't rather like."

"I know," said Dalroy, "you mean there was never an American who did not appreciate 'The Old Ship.'"

"I suppose I do mean that," answered the inn-keeper, "and somehow, I feel 'The Old Ship' might appreciate the American too."

"You English are an extraordinary lot," said the Irishman, with a sudden and sombre quietude. "I sometimes feel you may pull through after all."

After another silence he said, "You're always right, Hump, and one oughtn't to think of Yankees like that. The rich are the scum of the earth in every country. And a vast proportion of the real Americans are among the most courteous, intelligent, self-respecting people in the world. Some attribute this to the fact that a vast proportion of the real Americans are Irishmen."

Pump was still silent, and the Captain resumed in a moment.

"All the same," he said, "it's very hard for a man, especially a man of a small country like me, to understand how it must feel to be an American; especially in the matter of nationality. I shouldn't like to have to write the American National Anthem, but fortunately there is no great probability of the commission being given. The shameful secret of my inability to write an American patriotic song is one that will die with me."

"Well, what about an English one," said Pump, sturdily. "You might do worse, Captain."

"English, you bloody tyrant," said Patrick, indignantly. "I could no more fancy a song by an Englishman than you could one by that dog."

Mr. Humphrey Pump gravely took the paper from his pocket, on which he had previously inscribed the sin and desolation of grocers, and felt in another of his innumerable pockets for a pencil.

"Hullo," cried Dalroy. "Are you going to have a shy at the Ballad of Quoodle?"

Quoodle lifted his ears at his name. Mr. Pump smiled a slight and embarrassed smile. He was secretly proud of Dalroy's admiration for his previous literary attempts and he had some natural knack for verse as a game, as he had for all games; and his reading, though desultory, had not been merely rustic or low.

"On condition," he said, deprecatingly, "that you write a song for the English."

"Oh, very well," said Patrick, with a huge sigh that really indicated the very opposite of reluctance. "We must do something till the thing stops, I suppose, and this seems a blameless parlour game. 'Songs of the Car Club.' Sounds quite aristocratic."

And he began to make marks with a pencil on the fly-leaf of a little book he had in his pocket—Wilson's *Noctes Ambrosianæ*. Every now and then, however, he looked up and delayed his own composition by watching Pump and the dog, whose proceedings amused him very much. For the owner of "The Old Ship" sat sucking his pencil and looking at Mr. Quoodle with eyes of fathomless attention. Every now and then he slightly scratched his brown hair with the pencil, and wrote down a word. And the dog Quoodle, with that curious canine power of either understanding or most brazenly pretending to understand what is going on, sat erect with his head at an angle, as if he were sitting for his portrait.

Hence it happened that though Pump's poem was a little long, as are often the poems of inexperienced poets, and though Dalroy's poem was very short (being much hurried toward the end) the long poem was finished some time before the short one.

Therefore it was that there was first produced for the world the song more familiarly known as "No Noses," or more correctly called "The Song of Quoodle." Part of it ran eventually thus:—

> *"They haven't got no noses*
> *The fallen sons of Eve,*
> *Even the smell of roses*
> *Is not what they supposes,*
> *But more than mind discloses,*
> *And more than men believe.*
>
> *"They haven't got no noses,*
> *They cannot even tell*
> *When door and darkness closes*
> *The park a Jew encloses,*
> *Where even the Law of Moses*
> *Will let you steal a smell;*

"The brilliant smell of water,
The brave smell of a stone,
The smell of dew and thunder
And old bones buried under,
Are things in which they blunder
And err, if left alone.

"The wind from winter forests,
The scent of scentless flowers,
The breath of bride's adorning,
The smell of snare and warning,
The smell of Sunday morning,
God gave to us for ours.

*　　*　　*　　*　　*

"And Quoodle here discloses
All things that Quoodle can;
They haven't got no noses,
They haven't got no noses,
And goodness only knowses
The Noselessness of Man."

This poem also shows traces of haste in its termination, and the present editor (who has no aim save truth) is bound to confess that parts of it were supplied in the criticisms of the Captain, and even enriched (in later and livelier circumstances) by the Poet of the Birds himself. At the actual moment the chief features of this realistic song about dogs was a crashing chorus of "Bow-wow, wow," begun by Mr. Patrick Dalroy; but immediately imitated (much more successfully) by Mr. Quoodle. In the face of all this Dalroy suffered some real difficulty in fulfilling the bargain by reading out his much shorter poem about what he imagined an Englishman might feel. Indeed there was something very rough and vague in his very voice as he read it out; as of one who had not found the key to his problem. The present compiler (who has no aim save truth) must confess that the verses ran as follows:—

"St. George he was for England,
And before he killed the dragon

He drank a pint of English ale
Out of an English flagon.
For though he fast right readily
In hair-shirt or in mail,
It isn't safe to give him cakes
Unless you give him ale.

St. George he was for England,
And right gallantly set free
The lady left for dragon's meat
And tied up to a tree;
But since he stood for England
And knew what England means,
Unless you give him bacon,
You mustn't give him beans.

"St. George he was for England,
And shall wear the shield he wore
When we go out in armour,
With the battle-cross before;
But though he is jolly company
And very pleased to dine,
It isn't safe to give him nuts
Unless you give him wine."

"Very philosophical song that," said Dalroy, shaking his head solemnly, "full of deep thought. I really think that is about the truth of the matter, in the case of the Englishman. Your enemies say you're stupid, and you boast of being illogical—which is about the only thing you do that really *is* stupid. As if anybody ever made an Empire or anything else by saying that two and two make five. Or as if anyone was ever the stronger for *not* understanding anything—if it were only tip-cat or chemistry. But this *is* true about you Hump. You English are supremely an artistic people, and therefore you go by associations, as I said in my song. You won't have one thing without the other thing that goes with it. And as you can't imagine a village without a squire and parson, or a college without port and old oak, you get the reputation of a Conservative people. But it's because you're sensitive, Hump, not because you're stupid, that you won't part with things. It's lies, lies and flattery they tell you, Hump, when they tell you you're fond of compromise. I tell ye, Hump, every real revolution is a compromise. D'ye think Wolfe Tone or Charles Stuart Parnell never compromised? But it's just because you're afraid of a compromise that you won't have a revolution. If you really overhauled 'The Old Ship'—or Oxford—you'd have to make up your mind what to take and what to leave, and it would break your heart, Humphrey Pump."

He stared in front of him with a red and ruminant face, and at length added, somewhat more gloomily.

"This æsthetic way we have, Hump, has only two little disadvantages which I will now explain to you. The first is exactly what has sent us flying in this contraption. When the beautiful, smooth, harmonious thing you've made is worked by a new type, in a new spirit, then I tell you it would be better for you a thousand times to be living under the thousand paper constitutions of Condorcet and Sieyès. When the English oligarchy is run by an Englishman who hasn't got an English mind—then you have Lord Ivywood and all this nightmare, of which God could only guess the end."

The car had beaten some roods of dust behind it, and he ended still more darkly:

"And the other disadvantage, my amiable æsthete, is this. If ever, in blundering about the planet, you come on an island in the Atlantic—Atlantis, let us say—which won't accept *all* your pretty picture—to which you can't give everything—*why* you will probably decide to give nothing. You will say in your hearts: 'Perhaps they will starve soon'; and you will become, for that island, the deafest and the most evil of all the princes of the earth."

It was already daybreak, and Pump, who knew the English boundaries almost by intuition, could tell even through the twilight that the tail of the little town they were leaving behind was of a new sort, the sort to be seen in the western border. The chauffeur's phrase about his mother might merely have been a music-hall joke; but certainly he had driven darkly in that direction.

White morning lay about the grey stoney streets like spilt milk. A few proletarian early risers, wearier at morning than most men at night, seemed merely of opinion that it was no use crying over it. The two or three last houses, which looked almost too tired to stand upright, seemed to have moved the Captain into another sleepy explosion.

"There are two kinds of idealists, as everybody knows—or must have thought of. There are those who idealize the real and those who (precious seldom) realize the ideal. Artistic and poetical people like the English generally idealize the real. This I have expressed in a song, which—"

"No, really," protested the innkeeper, "really now, Captain—"

"This I have expressed in a song," repeated Dalroy, in an adamantine manner, "which I will now sing with every circumstance of leisure, loudness, or any other—"

He stopped because the flying universe seemed to stop. Charging hedgerows came to a halt, as if challenged by the bugle. The racing forests stood rigid. The last few tottering houses stood suddenly at attention. For a noise like a pistol-shot from the car itself had stopped all that race, as a pistol-shot might start any other.

The driver clambered out very slowly, and stood about in various tragic attitudes round the car. He opened an unsuspected number of doors and windows in the car, and touched things and twisted things and felt things.

"I must back as best I can to that there garrige, sir," he said, in a heavy and husky tone they had not heard from him before.

Then he looked round on the long woods and the last houses, and seemed to gnaw his lip, like a great general who has made a great mistake. His brow seemed as black as ever, yet his voice, when he spoke again, had fallen many further degrees toward its dull and daily tone.

"Yer see, this is a bit bad," he said. "It'll be a beastly job even at the best plices, if I'm gettin' back at all."

"Getting back," repeated Dalroy, opening the blue eyes of a bull. "Back where?"

"Well, yer see," said the chauffeur, reasonably, "I was bloody keen to show 'im it was me drove the car and not 'im. By a bit o' bad luck, I done damage to 'is car. Well—if *you* can stick in 'is car—"

Captain Patrick Dalroy sprang out of the car so rapidly that he almost reeled and slipped upon the road. The dog sprang after him, barking furiously.

"Hump," said Patrick, quietly. "I've found out everything about you. I know what always bothered me about the Englishman."

Then, after an instant's silence, he said, "That Frenchman was right who said (I forget how he put it) that you march to Trafalgar Square to rid yourself of your temper; not to rid yourself of your tyrant. Our friend was quite ready to rebel, rushing away. To rebel sitting still was too much for him. Do you read *Punch*? I am sure you do. Pump and

Punch must be almost the only survivors of the Victorian Age. Do you remember an old joke in an excellent picture, representing two ragged Irishmen with guns, waiting behind a stone wall to shoot a landlord? One of the Irishmen says the landlord is late, and adds, 'I hope no accident's happened to the poor gintleman.' Well, it's all perfectly true; I knew that Irishman intimately, but I want to tell you a secret about him. He was an Englishman."

The chauffeur had backed with breathless care to the entrance of the garage, which was next door to a milkman's or merely separated from it by a black and lean lane, looking no larger than the crack of a door. It must, however, have been larger than it looked, because Captain Dalroy disappeared down it.

He seemed to have beckoned the driver after him; at any rate that functionary instantly followed. The functionary came out again in an almost guilty haste, touching his cap and stuffing loose papers into his pocket. Then the functionary returned yet again from what he called the "garrige," carrying larger and looser things over his arm.

All this did Mr. Humphrey Pump observe, not without interest. The place, remote as it was, was evidently a *rendez-vous* for motorists. Otherwise a very tall motorist, throttled and masked in the most impenetrable degree, would hardly have strolled up to speak to him. Still less would the tall motorist have handed him a similar horrid disguise of wraps and goggles, in a bundle over his arm. Least of all would any motorist, however tall, have said to him from behind the cap and goggles, "Put on these things, Hump, and then we'll go into the milk shop. I'm waiting for the car. Which car, my seeker after truth? Why the car I'm going to buy for you to drive."

The remorseful chauffeur, after many adventures, did actually find his way back to the little moonlit wood where he had left his master and the donkey. But his master and the donkey had vanished.

XVI

The Seven Moods of Dorian

That timeless clock of all lunatics, which was so bright in the sky that night, may really have had some elfin luck about it, like a silver penny. Not only had it initiated Mr. Hibbs into the mysteries of Dionysius, and Mr. Bullrose into the arboreal habits of his ancestors, but one night of it made a very considerable and rather valuable change in Mr. Dorian Wimpole, the Poet of the Birds. He was a man neither foolish nor evil, any more than Shelley; only a man made sterile by living in a world of indirectness and insincerity, with words rather than with things. He had not had the smallest intention of starving his chauffeur; he did not realize that there was worse spiritual murder in merely forgetting him. But as hour after hour passed over him, alone with the donkey and the moon, he went through a raging and shifting series of frames of mind, such as his cultured friends would have described as moods.

The First Mood, I regret to say, was one of black and grinding hatred. He had no notion of the chauffeur's grievance, and could only suppose he had been bribed or intimidated by the demonic donkey-torturers. But Mr. Wimpole was much more capable at that moment of torturing a chauffeur than Mr. Pump had ever been of torturing a donkey; for no sane man can hate an animal. He kicked the stones in the road, sending them flying into the forest, and wished that each one of them was a chauffeur. The bracken by the roadside he tore up by the roots, as representing the hair of the chauffeur, to which it bore no resemblance. He hit with his fist such trees, as, I suppose, seemed in form and expression most reminiscent of the chauffeur; but desisted from this, finding that in this apparently one-sided contest the tree had rather the best of it. But the whole wood and the whole world had become a kind of omnipresent and pantheistic chauffeur, and he hit at him everywhere.

The thoughtful reader will realise that Mr. Wimpole had already taken a considerable upward stride in what he would have called the cosmic scale. The next best thing to really loving a fellow creature is really hating him: especially when he is a poorer man separated from you otherwise by mere social stiffness. The desire to murder him is at least an acknowledgment that he is alive. Many a man has owed the first white gleams of the dawn of Democracy in his soul to a desire to find a stick and beat the butler. And we have it on the unimpeachable local authority of Mr. Humphrey Pump that Squire Merriman chased his librarian through three villages with a horse-pistol; and was a Radical ever after.

His rage also did him good merely as a relief, and he soon passed into a second and more positive mood of meditation.

"The damnable monkeys go on like this," he muttered, "and then they call a donkey one of the Lower Animals. Ride on a donkey would he? I'd like to see the donkey riding on him for a bit. Good old man."

The patient ass turned mild eyes on him when he patted it, and Dorian Wimpole discovered, with a sort of subconscious surprise, that he really was fond of the donkey. Deeper still in his subliminal self he knew that he had never been fond of an animal before. His poems about fantastic creatures had been quite sincere, and quite cold. When he said he loved a shark, he meant he saw no reason for hating a shark, which was right enough. There is no reason for hating a shark, however much reason there may be for avoiding one. There is no harm in a craken if you keep it in a tank—or in a sonnet.

But he also realised that his love of creatures had been turned round and was working from the other end. The donkey was a companion, and not a monstrosity. It was dear because it was near, not because it was distant. The oyster had attracted him because it was utterly unlike a man; unless it be counted a touch of masculine vanity to grow a beard. The fancy is no idler than that he had himself used, in suggesting a sort of feminine vanity in the permanence of a pearl. But in that maddening vigil among the mystic pines, he found himself more and more drawn toward the donkey, because it was more like a man than anything else around him; because it had eyes to see, and ears to hear—and the latter even unduly developed.

"He that hath ears to hear, let him hear," he said, scratching those grey hairy flappers with affection. "Haven't you lifted your ears toward Heaven? And will you be the first to hear the Last Trumpet?"

The ass rubbed his nose against him with what seemed almost like a human caress. And Dorian caught himself wondering how a caress from an oyster could be managed. Everything else around him was beautiful, but inhuman. Only in the first glory of anger could he really trace in a

G.K. CHESTERTON

tall pine-tree the features of an ex-taxi-cabman from Kennington. Trees and ferns had no living ears that they could wag nor mild eyes that they could move. He patted the donkey again.

But the donkey had reconciled him to the landscape, and in his third mood he began to realize how beautiful it was. On a second study, he was not sure it was so inhuman. Rather he felt that its beauty at least was half human; that the aureole of the sinking moon behind the woods was chiefly lovely because it was like the tender-coloured aureole of an early saint; and that the young trees were, after all, noble because they held up their heads like virgins. Cloudily there crowded into his mind ideas with which it was imperfectly familiar, especially an idea which he had heard called "The Image of God." It seemed to him more and more that all these things, from the donkey to the very docks and ferns by the roadside, were dignified and sanctified by their partial resemblance to something else. It was as if they were baby drawings: the wild, crude sketches of Nature in her first sketch-books of stone.

He had flung himself on a pile of pine-needles to enjoy the gathering darkness of the pinewoods as the moon sank behind them. There is nothing more deep and wonderful than really impenetrable pinewoods where the nearer trees show against the more shadowy; a tracery of silver upon grey and of grey upon black.

It was, by this time, in pure pleasure and idleness that he picked up a pine-needle to philosophise about it.

"Think of sitting on needles!" he said. "Yet, I suppose this is the sort of needle that Eve, in the old legend, used in Eden. Aye, and the old legend was right, too! Think of sitting on all the needles in London! Think of sitting on all the needles in Sheffield! Think of sitting on any needles, except on all the needles of Paradise! Oh, yes, the old legend was right enough. The very needles of God are softer than the carpets of men."

He took a pleasure in watching the weird little forest animals creeping out from under the green curtains of the wood. He reminded himself that in the old legend they had been as tame as the ass, as well as being as comic. He thought of Adam naming the animals, and said to a beetle, "I should call *you* Budger."

The slugs gave him great entertainment, and so did the worms. He felt a new and realistic interest in them which he had not known before; it was, indeed, the interest that a man feels in a mouse in a dungeon;

the interest of any man tied by the leg and forced to see the fascination of small things. Creatures of the wormy kind, especially, crept out at very long intervals; yet he found himself waiting patiently for hours for the pleasure of their acquaintance. One of them rather specially arrested his eye, because it was a little longer than most worms and seemed to be turning its head in the direction of the donkey's left foreleg. Also, it had a head to turn, which most worms have not.

Dorian Wimpole did not know much about exact Natural History, except what he had once got up very thoroughly from an encyclopedia for the purposes of a sympathetic *vilanelle*. But as this information was entirely concerned with the conjectural causes of laughter in the Hyena, it was not directly helpful in this case. But though he did not know much Natural History, he knew some. He knew enough to know that a worm ought not to have a head, and especially not a squared and flattened head, shaped like a spade or a chisel. He knew enough to know that a creeping thing with a head of that pattern survives in the English country sides, though it is not common. In short, he knew enough to step across the road and set a sharp and savage boot-heel on the neck and spine of the creature, breaking it into three black bits that writhed once more before they stiffened.

Then he gave out a great explosive sigh. The donkey, whose leg had been in such danger, looked at the dead adder with eyes that had never lost their moony mildness. Even Dorian, himself, looked at it for a long time, and with feelings he could neither arrest nor understand, before he remembered that he had been comparing the little wood to Eden.

"And even in Eden," he said at last; and then the words of Fitzgerald failed upon his lips.

And while he was warring with such words and thoughts, something happened about him and behind him; something he had written about a hundred times and read about a thousand; something he had never seen in his life. It flung faintly across the broad foliage a wan and pearly light far more mysterious than the lost moonshine. It seemed to enter through all the doors and windows of the woodland, pale and silent but confident, like men that keep a tryst; soon its white robes had threads of gold and scarlet: and the name of it was morning.

For some time past, loud and in vain, all the birds had been singing to the Poet of the Birds. But when that minstrel actually saw broad daylight breaking over wood and road, the effect on him was somewhat curious. He stood staring at it in gaping astonishment, until it had fulfilled the fulness of its shining fate; and the pine-cones and the curling ferns and the live donkey and the dead viper were almost as distinct as they could be at noon, or in a Preraphaelite picture. And then the Fourth Mood fell upon him like a bolt from the blue, and he strode across and took the donkey's bridle, as if to lead it along.

"Damn it all," he cried, in a voice as cheerful as the cockcrow that rang recently from the remote village, "it's not everybody who's killed a snake." Then he added, reflectively, "I bet Dr. Gluck never did. Come along, donkey, let's have some adventures."

The finding and fighting of positive evil is the beginning of all fun—and even of all farce. All the wild woodland looked jolly now the snake was killed. It was one of the fallacies of his literary clique to refer all natural emotions to literary names, but it might not untruly be said that he had passed out of the mood of Maeterlinck into the mood of Whitman, and out of the mood of Whitman into the mood of Stevenson. He had not been a hypocrite when he asked for gilded birds of Asia or purple polypi out of the Southern Seas; he was not a hypocrite now, when he asked for mere comic adventures along a common English road. It was his misfortune and not his fault if his first adventure was his last; and was much too comic to laugh at.

Already the wan morning had warmed into a pale blue and was spotted with those little plump pink clouds which must surely have been the origin of the story that pigs might fly. The insects of the grass chattered so cheerfully that every green tongue seemed to be talking. The skyline on every side was broken only by objects that encouraged such swashbucklering comedy. There was a windmill that Chaucer's Miller might have inhabited or Cervantes' champion charged. There was an old leaden church spire that might have been climbed by Robert Clive. Away toward Pebblewick and the sea, there were the two broken stumps of wood which Humphrey Pump declares to this day to have been the stands for an unsuccessful children's swing; but which tourists always accept as the remains of the antique gallows. In the gaiety of such surroundings, it is small wonder if Dorian and the donkey stepped briskly along the road. The very donkey reminded him of Sancho Panza.

He did not wake out of this boisterous reverie of the white road and the wind till a motor horn had first hooted and then howled, till the ground had shaken with the shock of a stoppage, and till a human hand fell heavily and tightly on his shoulder. He looked up and saw the complete costume of a Police Inspector. He did not worry about the face. And there fell on him the Fifth, or Unexpected Mood, which is called by the vulgar Astonishment.

In despair he looked at the motor car itself that had anchored so abruptly under the opposite hedge. The man at the steering wheel was so erect and unresponsive that Dorian felt sure he was feasting his eyes on yet another policeman. But on the seat behind was a very different figure, a figure that baffled him all the more because he felt certain he had seen it somewhere. The figure was long and slim, with sloping shoulders, and the costume, which was untidy, yet contrived to give the impression that it was tidy on other occasions. The individual had bright yellow hair, one lock of which stuck straight up and was exalted, like the little horn in his favorite scriptures. Another tuft of it, in a bright but blinding manner, fell across and obscured the left optic, as in literal fulfilment of the parable of a beam in the eye. The eyes, with or without beams in them, looked a little bewildered, and the individual was always nervously resettling his necktie. For the individual went by the name of Hibbs, and had only recently recovered from experiences wholly new to him.

"What on earth do you want?" asked Wimpole of the policeman.

His innocent and startled face, and perhaps other things about his appearance, evidently caused the Inspector to waver.

"Well, it's about this 'ere donkey, sir," he said.

"Do you think I stole it?" cried the indignant aristocrat. "Well, of all the mad worlds! A pack of thieves steal my Limousine, I save their damned donkey's life at the risk of my own—and *I'm* run in for stealing."

The clothes of the indignant aristocrat probably spoke louder than his tongue; the officer dropped his hand, and after consulting some papers in his hand, walked across to consult with the unkempt gentleman in the car.

"That seems to be a similar cart and donkey," Dorian heard him saying, "but the clothes don't seem to fit your description of the men you saw."

Now, Mr. Hibbs had extremely vague and wild recollections of the men he saw; he could not even tell what he had done and what he had merely dreamed. If he had spoken sincerely, he would have described a sort of green nightmare of forests, in which he found himself in the power of an ogre about twelve feet high, with scarlet flames for hair and dressed rather like Robin Hood. But a long course of what is known as "keeping the party together" had made it as unnatural to him to tell anyone (even himself) what he really thought about anything, as it would have been to spit—or to sing. He had at present only three motives and strong resolves: (1) not to admit that he had been drunk; (2) not to let anyone escape whom Lord Ivywood might possibly want to question; and (3) not to lose his reputation for sagacity and tact.

"This party has a brown velvet suit, you see, and a fur overcoat," the Inspector continued, "and in the notes I have from you, you say the man wore a uniform."

"When we say uniform," said Mr. Hibbs, frowning intellectually, "when we say *uniform*, of course—we must distinguish some of our friends who don't quite see eye to eye with us, you know," and he smiled with tender leniency, "some of our friends wouldn't like it called a *uniform* perhaps. But—of course—well, it wasn't a police uniform, for instance. Ha! Ha!"

"I should hope not," said the official, shortly.

"So—in a way—however," said Hibbs, clutching his verbal talisman at last, "it might be brown velvet in the dark."

The Inspector replied to this helpful suggestion with some wonder. "But it was a moon, like limelight," he protested.

"Yars, yars," cried Hibbs, in a high tone that can only be described as a hasty drawl. "Yars—discolours everything of course. The flowers and things—"

"But look here," said the Inspector, "you said the principal man's hair was red."

"A blond type! A blond type!" said Hibbs, waving his hand with a solemn lightness. "Reddish, yellowish, brownish sort of hair, you know." Then he shook his head and said with the heaviest solemnity the word was capable of carrying, "Teutonic, purely Teutonic."

The Inspector began to feel some wonder that, even in the confusion following on Lord Ivywood's fall, he had been put under the guidance of this particular guide. The truth was that Leveson, once more masking his own fears under his usual parade of hurry, had found Hibbs at a table by an open window, with wild hair and sleepy eyes, picking himself up with some sort of medicine. Finding him already fairly clear-headed in a dreary way, he had not scrupled to use the remains of his bewilderment to despatch him with the police in the first pursuit. Even the mind of a semi-recovered drunkard, he thought, could be trusted to recognise anyone so unmistakable as the Captain.

But, though the diplomatist's debauch was barely over, his strange, soft fear and cunning were awake. He felt fairly certain the man in the fur coat had something to do with the mystery, as men with fur coats do not commonly wander about with donkeys. He was afraid of offending Lord Ivywood, and at the same time, afraid of exposing himself to a policeman.

"You have large discretion," he said, gravely. "Very right you should have large discretion in the interests of the public. I think you would be quite authorised, for the present, in preventing the man's escape."

"And the other man?" inquired the officer, with knitted brow. "Do you suppose he has escaped?"

"The *other* man," repeated Hibbs. However, regarding the distant windmill through half-closed lids, as if this were a new fine shade introduced into an already delicate question.

"Well, hang it all," said the police officer, "you must know whether there were two men or one."

Gradually it dawned, in a grey dawn of horror, over the brain of Hibbs that this was what he specially couldn't know. He had always heard, and read in comic papers, that a drunken man "sees double" and beholds two lamp-posts, one of which is (as the Higher Critic would have said) purely subjective. For all he knew (being a mere novice) inebriation might produce the impression of the two men of his dream-like adventure, when in truth there had only been one.

"Two men, you know—one man," he said with a sort of moody carelessness. "Well we can go into their numbers later; they can't have a very large following." Here he shook his head very firmly. "Quite impossible. And as the late Lord Goschen used to say, 'You can prove anything by statistics.'"

And here came an interruption from the other side of the road.

"And how long am I to wait here for you and your Goschens, you silly goat," were the intemperate wood-notes issuing from the Poet of the Birds. "I'm shot if I'll stand this! Come along, donkey, and let's pray for a better adventure next time. These are very inferior specimens of your own race."

And seizing the bridle of the ass again, he strode past them swiftly, and almost as if urging the animal to a gallop.

Unfortunately this disdainful dash for liberty was precisely what was wanting to weigh down the rocking intelligence of the Inspector on the wrong side. If Wimpole had stood still a minute or two longer, the official, who was no fool, might have ended in disbelieving Hibbs's story altogether. As it was, there was a scuffle, not without blows on both sides, and eventually the Honourable Dorian Wimpole, donkey and all, was marched off to the village, in which there was a Police Station; in which was a temporary cell; in which a Sixth Mood was experienced.

His complaints, however, were at once so clamorous and so convincing, and his coat was so unquestionably covered with fur, that after some questioning and cross purposes they agreed to take him in the afternoon to Ivywood House, where there was a magistrate incapacitated by a shot only recently extracted from his leg.

They found Lord Ivywood lying on a purple ottoman, in the midst of his Chinese puzzle of oriental apartments. He continued to look away as they entered, as if expecting, with Roman calm, the entrance of a recognised enemy. But Lady Enid Wimpole, who was attending to the wants of the invalid, gave a sharp cry of astonishment; and the next moment the three cousins were looking at each other. One could almost have guessed they were cousins, all being (as Mr. Hibbs subtly put it) a blond type. But two of the blond types expressed amazement, and one blond type merely rage.

"I am sorry, Dorian," said Ivywood, when he had heard the whole story. "These fanatics are capable of anything, I fear, and you very rightly resent their stealing your car—"

"You are wrong, Phillip," answered the poet, emphatically. "I do not even faintly resent their stealing my car. What I do resent is the continued existence on God's earth of this Fool" (pointing to the serious Hibbs) "and of that Fool" (pointing to the Inspector) "and—yes, by thunder, of *that* Fool, too" (and he pointed straight at Lord Ivywood). "And I tell you frankly, Phillip, if there really are, as you say, two men who are bent on smashing your schemes and making your life a hell—I am very happy to put my car at their disposal. And now I'm off."

"You'll stop to dinner?" inquired Ivywood, with frigid forgiveness.

"No, thanks," said the disappearing bard, "I'm going up to town."

The Seventh Mood of Dorian Wimpole had a grand finale at the Café Royal, and consisted largely of oysters.

XVII

The Poet in Parliament

During the singular entrance and exit of Dorian Wimpole, M.P., J.P., etc., Lady Joan was looking out of the magic casements of that turret room which was now literally, and not only poetically, the last limit of Ivywood House. The old broken hole and black staircase up which the lost dog Quoodle used to come and go, had long ago been sealed up and cemented with a wall of exquisite Eastern workmanship. All through the patterns Lord Ivywood had preserved and repeated the principle that no animal shape must appear. But, like all lucid dogmatists, he perceived all the liberties his dogma allowed him. And he had irradiated this remote end of Ivywood with sun and moon and solar and starry systems, with the Milky Way for a dado and a few comets for comic relief. The thing was well done of its kind (as were all the things that Phillip Ivywood got done for him); and if all the windows of the turret were closed with their peacock curtains, a poet with anything like a Hibbsian appreciation of the family champagne might almost fancy he was looking out across the sea on a night crowded with stars. And (what was yet more important) even Misysra (that exact thinker) could not call the moon a live animal without falling into idolatry.

But Joan, looking out of real windows on a real sky and sea, thought no more about the astronomical wall-paper than about any other wall-paper. She was asking herself in sullen emotionalism, and for the thousandth time, a question she had never been able to decide. It was the final choice between an ambition and a memory. And there was this heavy weight in the scale: that the ambition would probably materialise, and the memory probably wouldn't. It has been the same weight in the same scale a million times, since Satan became the prince of this world. But the evening stars were strengthening over the old sea-shore, and they also wanted weighing like diamonds.

As once before at the same stage of brooding, she heard behind her the swish of Lady Enid's skirts, that never came so fast save for serious cause.

"Joan! Please do come! Nobody but you, I do believe, could move him." Joan looked at Lady Enid and realised that the lady was close on crying. She turned a trifle pale and asked quietly for the question. "Phillip says he's going to London now, with that leg and all," cried Enid, "and he won't let us say a word."

"But how did it all happen?" asked Joan.

Lady Enid Wimpole was quite incapable of explaining how it all happened, so the task must for the moment devolve on the author. The simple fact was that Ivywood in the course of turning over magazines on his sofa, happened to look at a paper from the Midlands.

"The Turkish news," said Mr. Leveson, rather nervously, "is on the other side of the page."

But Lord Ivywood continued to look at the side of the paper that did not contain the Turkish news, with the same dignity of lowered eyelids and unconscious brow with which he had looked at the Captain's message when Joan found him by the turret.

On the page covered merely with casual, provincial happenings was a paragraph, "Echo of Pebblewick Mystery. Reported Reappearance of the Vanishing Inn." Underneath was printed, in smaller letters:

"An almost incredible report from Wyddington announces that the mysterious 'Sign of the Old Ship' has once more been seen in this country; though it has long been relegated by scientific investigators to the limbo of old rustic superstitions. According to the local version, Mr. Simmons, a dairyman of Wyddington, was serving in his shop when two motorists entered, one of them asking for a glass of milk. They were in the most impenetrable motoring panoply, with darkened goggles and waterproof collars turned up, so that nothing can be recalled of them personally, except that one was a person of unusual stature. In a few moments, this latter individual went out of the shop again and returned with a miserable specimen out of the street, one of the tattered loafers that linger about our most prosperous towns, tramping the streets all night and even begging in defiance of the police. The filth and disease of the creature were so squalid that Mr. Simmons at first refused to serve him with the glass of milk which the taller motorist wished to provide for him. At length, however, Mr. Simmons consented, and was immediately astonished by an incident against which he certainly had a more assured right to protest.

"The taller motorist, saying to the loafer, 'but, man, you're blue in the face,' made a species of signs to the smaller motorist, who thereupon appears to have pierced a sort of cylindrical trunk or chest that seemed to be his only luggage, and drawn from it a few drops of a yellow liquid which he deliberately dropped into the ragged creature's milk. It was afterward discovered to be rum, and the protests of Mr. Simmons may be imagined. The tall motorist, however, warmly defended his action, having apparently some wild idea that he was doing an act of kindness. 'Why, I found the man nearly fainting,' he said. 'If you'd picked him off a raft, he couldn't be more collapsed with cold and sickness; and if you'd picked him off a raft you'd have given him rum—yes, by St. Patrick, if you were a bloody pirate and made him walk the plank afterward.' Mr. Simmons replied with dignity, that he did not know how it was with rafts, and could not permit such language in his shop. He added that he would lay himself open to a police prosecution if he permitted the consumption of alcohol in his shop; since he did not display a sign. The motorist then made the amazing reply, 'But you *do* display a sign, you jolly old man. Did you think I couldn't find my way to the sign of The Old Ship, you sly boots?' Mr. Simmons was now fully convinced of the intoxication of his visitors, and refusing a glass of rum rather boisterously offered him, went outside his shop to look round for a policeman. To his surprise he found the officer engaged in dispersing a considerable crowd, which was staring up at some object behind him. On looking round (he states in his deposition) he 'saw what was undoubtedly one of the low tavern signs at one time common in England.' He was wholly unable to explain its presence outside his premises, and as it undoubtedly legalised the motorist's action, the police declined to move in the matter.

"Later. The two motorists have apparently left the town, unmolested, in a small second-hand two-seater. There is no clue to their destination, except it be indicated by a single incident. It appears that when they were waiting for the second glass of milk, one of them drew attention to a milk-can of a shape seemingly unfamiliar to him, which was, of course, the Mountain Milk now so much recommended by doctors. The taller motorist (who seemed in every way strangely ignorant of modern science and social life) asked his companion where it came from, receiving, of course, the reply that it is manufactured in the model village of Peaceways, under the personal superintendence of its distinguished and philanthropic inventor, Dr. Meadows. Upon this the taller person, who appeared highly irresponsible, actually bought the whole can; observing, as he tucked it under his arm, that it would help him to remember the address.

"Later. Our readers will be glad to hear that the legend of 'The Old Ship' sign has once more yielded to the wholesome scepticism of science. Our representative reached Wyddington after the practical jokers, or whatever they were, had left; but he searched the whole frontage of Mr. Simmons's shop, and we are in a position to assure the public that there is no trace of the alleged sign."

Lord Ivywood laid down the newspaper and looked at the rich and serpentine embroideries on the wall with the expression that a great general might have if he saw a chance of really ruining his enemy, if he would also ruin all his previous plan of campaign. His pallid and classic profile was as immovable as a cameo; but anyone who had known him at all would have known that his brain was going like a motor car that has broken the speed limit long ago.

Then he turned his head and said, "Please tell Hicks to bring round the long blue car in half an hour; it can be fitted up for a sofa. And ask the gardener to cut a pole of about four feet nine inches, and put a cross-piece for a crutch. I'm going up to London tonight."

Mr. Leveson's lower jaw literally fell with astonishment.

"The Doctor said three weeks," he said. "If I may ask it, where are you going?"

"St. Stephens, Westminster," answered Ivywood.

"Surely," said Mr. Leveson, "I could take a message."

"You could take a message," assented Ivywood, "I'm afraid they would not allow you to make a speech."

It was a moment or two afterward that Enid Wimpole had come into the room, and striven in vain to shake his decision. Then it was that Joan had been brought out of the turret and saw Phillip standing, sustained upon a crutch of garden timber; and admired him as she had never admired him before. While he was being helped downstairs, while he was being propped in the car with such limited comfort as was possible, she did really feel in him something worthy of his ancient roots, worthy of such hills and of such a sea. For she felt God's wind from nowhere which is called the Will; and is man's only excuse upon this earth. In the small toot of the starting motor she could hear a hundred trumpets, such as might have called her ancestors and his to the glories of the Third Crusade.

Such imaginary military honours were not, at least in the strategic sense, undeserved. Lord Ivywood really had seen the whole map of the situation in front of him, and swiftly formed a plan to meet it, in a manner not unworthy of Napoleon. The realities of the situation unrolled themselves before him, and his mind was marking them one by one as with a pencil.

First, he knew that Dalroy would probably go to the Model Village. It was just the sort of place he would go to. He knew Dalroy was almost constitutionally incapable of not kicking up some kind of row in a place of that kind.

Second, he knew that if he missed Dalroy at this address, it was very likely to be his last address; he and Mr. Pump were quite clever enough to leave no more hints behind.

Third, he guessed, by careful consideration of map and clock, that they could not get to so remote a region in so cheap a car under something like two days, nor do anything very conclusive in less than three. Thus, he had just time to turn round in.

Fourth, he realised that ever since that day when Dalroy swung round the sign-board and smote the policeman into the ditch, Dalroy had swung round the Ivywood Act on Lord Ivywood. He (Lord Ivywood) had thought, and might well have thought rightly, that by restricting the old sign-posts to a few places so select that they can afford to be eccentric, and forbidding such artistic symbols to all other places, he could sweep fermented liquor for all practical purposes out of the land. The arrangement was exactly that at which all such legislation is consciously or unconsciously aiming. A sign-board could be a favour granted by the governing class to itself. If a gentleman wished to claim the liberties of a Bohemian, the path would be open. If a Bohemian wished to claim the liberties of a gentleman, the path would be shut. So, gradually, Lord Ivywood had thought, the old signs which can alone sell alcohol, will dwindle down to mere curiosities, like Audit Ale or the Mead that may still be found in the New Forest. The calculation was by no means unstatesmanlike. But, like many other statesmanlike calculations, it did not take into account the idea of dead wood walking about. So long as his flying foes might set up their sign anywhere, it mattered little whether the result was enjoyment or disappointment for the populace. In either case it must mean constant scandal or riot. If there was one thing worse than the appearance of "The Old Ship" it was its disappearance.

He realised that his own law was letting them loose every time; for the local authorities hesitated to act on the spot, in defiance of a symbol now so exclusive and therefore impressive. He realised that the law must be altered. Must be altered at once. Must be altered, if possible, before the fugitives broke away from the Model Village of Peaceways.

He realised that it was Thursday. This was the day on which any private member of Parliament could introduce any private bill of the kind called "non-contentious," and pass it without a division, so long as no particular member made any particular fuss. He realised that it was improbable that any particular member would make any particular fuss about Lord Ivywood's own improvement on Lord Ivywood's own Act.

Finally, he realised that the whole case could be met by so slight an improvement as this. Change the words of the Act (which he knew by heart, as happier men might know a song): "If such sign be present liquids containing alcohol can be sold on the premises," to these other words: "Liquids containing alcohol can be sold, if previously preserved for three days on the premises"; it was mate in a few moves. Parliament could never reject or even examine so slight an emendation. And the revolution of "The Old Ship" and the late King of Ithaca would be crushed for ever.

It does undoubtedly show, as we have said, something Napoleonic in the man's mind that the whole of this excellent and even successful plan was complete long before he saw the great glowing clock on the towers of Westminster; and knew he was in time.

It was unfortunate, perhaps, that about the same time, or not long after, another gentleman of the same rank, and indirectly of the same family, having left the restaurant in Regent Street and the tangle of Piccadilly, had drifted serenely down Whitehall, and had seen the same great golden goblin's eye on the tall tower of St. Stephen.

The Poet of the Birds, like most æsthetes, had known as little of the real town as he had of the real country. But he had remembered a good place for supper; and as he passed certain great cold clubs, built of stone and looking like Assyrian Sarcophagi, he remembered that he belonged to many of them. And so when he saw afar off, sitting above the river, what has been very erroneously described as the best club in London, he suddenly remembered that he belonged to that too. He could not at the moment recall what constituency in South England it was that he sat for; but he knew he could walk into the place if he wanted to. He might not so have expressed the matter, but he knew that in an oligarchy things go by respect for persons and not for claims; by visiting cards and not by voting cards. He had not been near the place for years, being permanently paired against a famous Patriot who had accepted an important government appointment in a private madhouse. Even in his silliest days, he had never pretended to feel any respect for modern politics, and made all haste to put his "leaders" and the mad patriot's "leaders" on the well selected list of the creatures whom man forgets. He had made one really eloquent speech in the House (on the subject of gorillas), and then found he was speaking against his party. It was an indescribable sort of place, anyhow. Even Lord Ivywood did not go to it except to do some business that could be done nowhere else; as was the case that night.

Ivywood was what is called a peer by courtesy; his place was in the Commons, and for the time being on the Opposition side. But, though he visited the House but seldom, he knew far too much about it to go into the Chamber itself. He limped into the Smoking Room (though he did not smoke), procured a needless cigarette and a much-needed sheet of note-paper, and composed a curt but careful note to the one member of the government whom he knew must be in the House. Having sent it up to him, he waited.

Outside, Mr. Dorian Wimpole also waited, leaning on the parapet of Westminster Bridge and looking down the river. He was becoming one with the oysters in a more solemn and solid sense than he had hitherto conceived possible, and also with a strictly Vegetarian beverage which bears the noble and starry name of Nuits. He felt at peace with all things, even in a manner with politics. It was one of those magic hours of evening when the red and golden lights of men are already lit along the river, and look like the lights of goblins, but daylight still lingers in a cold and delicate green. He felt about the river something of that smiling and glorious sadness which two Englishmen have expressed under the figure of the white wood of an old ship fading like a phantom; Turner, in painting, and Henry Newbolt, in poetry. He had come back to earth like a man fallen from the moon; he was at bottom not only a poet but a patriot, and a patriot is always a little sad. Yet his melancholy was mixed up with that immutable yet meaningless faith which few Englishmen, even in modern times, fail to feel at the unexpected sight either of Westminster or of that height on which stands the temple of St. Paul.

> *"While flows the sacred river,*
> *While stands the sacred hill,"*

he murmured in some schoolboy echo of the ballad of Lake Regillus,

> *"While flows the sacred river,*
> *While stands the sacred hill,*
> *The proud old pantaloons and nincompoops,*
> *Who yawn at the very length of their own lies*
> *in that accursed sanhedrim where*
> *people put each other's hats on in a poisonous*
> *room with no more windows than hell*
> *Shall have such honour still."*

Relieved by this rendering of Macaulay in the style known among his cultured friends as *vers libre*, or poesy set free from the shackles of formal metre, he strolled toward the members' entrance and went in.

Lacking Lord Ivywood's experience, he strolled into the Common's Chamber itself and sat down on a green bench, under the impression that the House was not sitting. He was, however, gradually able to distinguish some six or eight drowsy human forms from the seats on which they sat; and to hear a senile voice with an Essex accent, saying, all on one note, and without beginning or end, in a manner which it is quite impossible to punctuate,

". . . no wish at all that this proposal should be regarded except in the right way and have tried to put it in the right way and cannot think the honourable member was altogether adding to his reputation in putting it in what those who think with me must of course consider the wrong way and I for one am free to say that if in his desire to settle this great question he takes this hasty course and this revolutionary course about slate pencils he may not be able to prevent the extremists behind him from applying it to lead pencils and while I should be the last to increase the heat and the excitement and the personalities of this debate if I could possibly help it I must confess that in my opinion the honourable gentleman has himself encouraged that heat and personality in a manner that he now doubtless regrets I have no desire to use abusive terms indeed you Mr. Speaker would not allow me of course to use abusive terms but I must tell the honourable member face to face that the perambulators with which he has twitted me cannot be germane to this discussion I should be the last person. . ."

Dorian Wimpole had softly risen to go, when he was arrested by the sight of someone sliding into the House and handing a note to the solitary young man with heavy eyelids who was at that moment governing all England from the Treasury Bench. Seeing him go out, Dorian had a sickening sweetness of hope (as he might have said in his earlier poems), that something intelligible might happen after all, and followed him out almost with alacrity.

The solitary and sleepy governor of Great Britain went down into the lower crypts of its temple of freedom and turned into an apartment where Wimpole was astonished to see his cousin Ivywood sitting at a little table with a large crutch leaning beside him, as serene as Long John Silver. The young man with the heavy eyelids sat down opposite him and they had a conversation which Wimpole, of course, did not hear. He withdrew into an adjoining room where he managed to procure coffee and a liqueur; an excellent liqueur which he had forgotten and of which he had more than one glass.

But he had so posted himself that Ivywood could not come out without passing him, and he waited for what might happen with exquisite patience. The only thing that seemed to him queer was that every now and then a bell rang in several rooms at once. And whenever the bell rang, Lord Ivywood nodded, as if he were part of the electrical machinery. And whenever Lord Ivywood nodded the young man turned and sped upstairs like a mountaineer, returning in a short time to resume the conversation. On the third occasion the poet began to observe that many others from the other rooms could be heard running upstairs at the sound of this bell, and returning with the slightly less rapid step which expresses relief after a duty done. Yet did he not know that this duty was Representative Government; and that it is thus that the cry of Cumberland or Cornwall can come to the ears of an English King.

Suddenly the sleepy young man sprang erect, uninspired by any bell, and strode out once more. The poet could not help hearing him say as he left the table, jotting down something with a pencil: "Alcohol can be sold if previously preserved for three days on the premises. I think we can do it, but you can't come on for half an hour."

Saying this, he darted upstairs again, and when Dorian saw Ivywood come out laboriously, afterward, on his large country crutch, he had exactly the same revulsion in his favour that Joan had had. Jumping up from his table, which was in one of the private dining-rooms, he touched the other on the elbow and said:

"I want to apologise to you, Phillip, for my rudeness this afternoon. Honestly, I am sorry. Pinewoods and prison-cells try a man's temper, but I had no rag of excuse for not seeing that for neither of them were you to blame. I'd no notion you were coming up to town tonight; with your leg and all. You mustn't knock yourself up like this. Do sit down a minute."

It seemed to him that the bleak face of Phillip softened a little; how far he really softened will never be known until such men as he are understood by their fellows. It is certain that he carefully unhooked himself from his crutch and sat down opposite his cousin. Whereupon his cousin struck the table so that it rang like a dinner-bell and called out, "Waiter!" as if he were in a crowded restaurant. Then, before Lord Ivywood could protest, he said:

"It's awfully jolly that we've met. I suppose you've come up to make a speech. I *should* like to hear it. We haven't always agreed; but, by God, if there's anything good left in literature it's your speeches reported in a newspaper. That thing of yours that ended, 'death and the last shutting of the iron doors of defeat'—Why you must go back to Strafford's last speech for such English. Do let me hear your speech! I've got a seat upstairs, you know."

"If you wish it," said Ivywood hurriedly, "but I shan't make much of a speech tonight." And he looked at the wall behind Wimpole's head with thunderous wrinkles thickening on his brow. It was essential to his brilliant and rapid scheme, of course, that the Commons should make no comment at all on his little alteration in the law.

An attendant hovered near in response to the demand for a waiter, and was much impressed by the presence and condition of Lord Ivywood. But as that exalted cripple resolutely refused anything in the way of liquor, his cousin was so kind as to have a little more himself, and resumed his remarks.

"It's about this public-house affair of yours, I suppose. I'd like to hear you speak on that. P'raps I'll speak myself. I've been thinking about it a good deal all day, and a good deal of last night, too. Now, here's what I should say to the House, if I were you. To begin with, can you abolish the public-house? Are you *important* enough now to abolish the public-house? Whether it's right or wrong, can you in the long run prevent haymakers having ale any more than you can prevent me having this glass of Chartreuse?"

The attendant, hearing the word, once more drew near; but heard no further order; or, rather, the orders he heard were such as he was less able to cope with.

"Remember the curate!" said Dorian, abstractedly shaking his head at the functionary, "remember the sensible little High-Church curate, who when asked for a Temperance Sermon preached on the text 'Suffer us not to be overwhelmed in the water-floods.' Indeed, indeed, Phillip, you are in deeper waters than you know. *You* will abolish ale! *You* will make Kent forget hop-poles, and Devonshire forget cider! The fate of the Inn is to be settled in that hot little room upstairs! Take care its fate and yours are not settled in the Inn. Take care Englishmen don't sit in judgment on you as they do on many another corpse at an inquest—at a common public-house! Take care that the one tavern that is really neglected and shut up and passed like a house of pestilence is not the tavern in which I drink tonight, and that merely because it is the worst tavern on the King's highway. Take care this place where we sit does not get a name like any pub where sailors are hocussed or girls debauched. That is what I shall say to them," said he, rising cheerfully, "that's what I shall say. See you to it," he cried with sudden passion and apparently to the waiter, "see you to it if the sign that is destroyed is not the sign of 'The Old Ship' but the sign of the Mace and Bauble, and, in the words of a highly historical brewer, if we see a dog bark at your going."

Lord Ivywood was observing him with a deathly quietude; another idea had come into his fertile mind. He knew his cousin, though excited, was not in the least intoxicated; he knew he was quite capable of making a speech and even a good one. He knew that any speech, good or bad, would wreck his whole plan and send the wild inn flying again. But the orator had resumed his seat and drained his glass, passing a hand across his brow. And he remembered that a man who keeps a vigil in a wood all night and drinks wine on the following evening is liable to an accident that is not drunkenness, but something much healthier.

"I suppose your speech will come on pretty soon," said Dorian, looking at the table. "You'll let me know when it does, of course. Really and truly, I don't want to miss it. And I've forgotten all the ways here, and feel pretty tired. You'll let me know?"

"Yes," said Lord Ivywood.

Stillness fell along all the rooms until Lord Ivywood broke it by saying:

"Debate is a most necessary thing; but there are times when it rather impedes than assists parliamentary government."

He received no reply. Dorian still sat as if looking at the table, but his eyelids had lightly fallen; he was asleep. Almost at the same moment the Member of Government, who was nearly asleep, appeared at the entrance of the long room and made some sort of weary signal.

Phillip Ivywood raised himself on his crutch and stood for a moment looking at the sleeping man. Then he and his crutch trailed out of the long room, leaving the sleeping man behind. Nor was that the only thing that he left behind. He also left behind an unlighted cigarette and his honour and all the England of his father's; everything that could really distinguish that high house beside the river from any tavern for the hocussing of sailors. He went upstairs and did his business in twenty minutes in the only speech he had ever delivered without any trace of eloquence. And from that hour forth he was the naked fanatic; and could feed on nothing but the future.

XVIII

THE REPUBLIC OF PEACEWAYS

In a hamlet round about Windermere, let us say, or somewhere in Wordsworth's country, there could be found a cottage, in which could be found a cottager. So far all is as it should be; and the visitor would first be conscious of a hearty and even noisy elderly man, with an apple face and a short white beard. This person would then loudly proffer to the visitor the opportunity of seeing his father, a somewhat more elderly man, with a somewhat longer white beard, but still "up and about." And these two together would then initiate the neophyte into the joys of the society of a grandfather, who was more than a hundred years old, and still very proud of the fact.

This miracle, it seemed, had been worked entirely on milk. The subject of this diet the oldest of the three men continued to discuss in enormous detail. For the rest, it might be said that his pleasures were purely arithmetical. Some men count their years with dismay, and he counted his with a juvenile vanity. Some men collect stamps or coins, and he collected days. Newspaper men interviewed him about the historic times through which he had lived, without eliciting anything whatever; except that he had apparently taken to an exclusive milk diet at about the age when most of us leave it off. Asked if he was alive in 1815, he said that was the very year he found it wasn't any milk, but must be Mountain Milk, like Dr. Meadows says. Nor would his calculating creed of life have allowed him to understand you if you had said that in a meadowland oversea that lies before the city of Brussels, boys of his old school in that year gained the love of the gods and died young.

It was the philanthropic Dr. Meadows, of course, who discovered this deathless tribe, and erected on it the whole of his great dietetic philosophy, to say nothing of the houses and dairies of Peaceways. He attracted many pupils and backers among the wealthy and influential; young men who were, so to speak, training for extreme old age, infant old men, embryo nonagenarians. It would be an exaggeration to say that they watched joyfully for the first white hair as Fascination Fledgeby watched for his first whisker; but it is quite true to say that they seemed to have scorned the beauty of woman and the feasting of friends and, above all, the old idea of death with glory; in comparison with this vision of the sports of second childhood.

Peaceways was in its essential plan much like what we call a Garden City; a ring of buildings where the work people did their work, with a pretty ornamental town in the centre, where they lived in the open country outside. This was no doubt much healthier than the factory system in the great towns and may have partly accounted for the serene expression of Dr. Meadows and his friends, if any part of the credit can be spared from the splendours of Mountain Milk. The place lay far from the common highways of England, and its inhabitants were enabled to enjoy their quiet skies and level woods almost undisturbed, and fully absorb whatever may be valuable in the Meadows method and view; until one day a small and very dirty motor drove into the middle of their town. It stopped beside one of those triangular islets of grass that are common at forked roads, and two men in goggles, one tall and the other short, got out and stood on the central space of grass, as if they were buffoons about to do tricks. As, indeed, they were.

Before entering the town they had stopped by a splendid mountain stream quickening and thickening rapidly into a river; unhelmed and otherwise eased themselves, eaten a little bread bought at Wyddington and drank the water of the widening current which opened on the valley of Peaceways.

"I'm beginning quite to like water," said the taller of the two knights. "I used to think it a most dangerous drink. In theory, of course, it ought only to be given to people who are fainting. It's really good for them, much better than brandy. Besides, think of wasting good brandy on people who are fainting! But I don't go so far as I did; I shouldn't insist on a doctor's prescription before I allow people water. That was the too severe morality of youth; that was my innocence and goodness. I thought that if I fell once, water-drinking might become a habit. But I do see the good side of water now. How good it is when you're really thirsty, how it glitters and gurgles! How alive it is! After all, it's the best of drinks, after the other. As it says in the song:

> *"Feast on wine or fast on water,*
> *And your honour shall stand sure;*
> *God Almighty's son and daughter,*
> *He the valiant, she the pure.*

If an angel out of heaven
Brings you other things to drink,
Thank him for his kind intentions,
Go and pour them down the sink.

"Tea is like the East he grows in,
A great yellow Mandarin,
With urbanity of manner,
And unconsciousness of sin;
All the women, like a harem,
At his pig-tail troop along,
And, like all the East he grows in,
He is Poison when he's strong.

"Tea, although an Oriental,
Is a gentleman at least;
Cocoa is a cad and coward,
Cocoa is a vulgar beast;
Cocoa is a dull, disloyal,
Lying, crawling cad and clown,
And may very well be grateful
To the fool that takes him down.

"As for all the windy waters,
They were rained like trumpets down,
When good drink had been dishonoured
By the tipplers of the town.
When red wine had brought red ruin,
And the death-dance of our times,
Heaven sent us Soda Water
As a torment for our crimes."

"Upon my soul, this water tastes quite nice. I wonder what vintage now?" and he smacked his lips with solemnity. "It tastes just like the year 1881 tasted."

"You can fancy anything in the tasting way," returned his shorter companion. "Mr. Jack, who was always up to his tricks, did serve plain water in those little glasses they drink liqueurs out of, and everyone swore it was a delicious liqueur, and wanted to know where they could get it—all except old Admiral Guffin, who said it tasted too strong of olives. But water's much the best for our game, certainly."

Patrick nodded, and then said:

"I doubt if I could do it, if it weren't for the comfort of looking at that," and he kicked the rum-keg, "and feeling we shall have a good swig at it some day. It feels like a fairy-tale, carrying that about—as if rum were a pirate's treasure, as if it were molten gold. Besides, we can have such fun with it with other people—what was that joke I thought of this morning? Oh, I remember! Where's that milk-can of mine?"

For the next twenty minutes he was industriously occupied with his milk-can and the cask; Pump watching him with an interest amounting to anxiety. Lifting his head, however, at the end of that time, he knotted his red brows and said, "What's that?"

"What's what?" asked the other traveller.

"That!" said Captain Patrick Dalroy, and pointed to a figure approaching on the road parallel to the river, "I mean, what's it for?"

The figure had a longish beard and very long hair falling far below its shoulders. It had a serious and steadfast expression. It was dressed in what the inexperienced Mr. Pump at first took to be its night-gown; but afterward learned to be its complete goats' hair tunic, unmixed even with a thread of the destructive and deadly wool of the sheep. It had no boots on its feet. It walked very swiftly to a particular turn of the stream and then turned very sharply (since it had accomplished its constitutional), and walked back toward the perfect town of Peaceways.

"I suppose it's somebody from that milk place," said Humphrey Pump, indulgently. "They seem to be pretty mad."

"I don't mind that so much," said Dalroy, "I'm mad myself sometimes. But a madman has only one merit and last link with God. A madman is always logical. Now what is the logical connection between living on milk and wearing your hair long? Most of us lived on milk when we had no hair at all. How do they connect it up? Are there any heads even for a synopsis? Is it, say, 'milk—water—shaving-water—shaving—hair?' Is it 'milk—kindness—unkindness—convicts—hair?' What is the logical connection between having too much hair and having far too few boots? What *can* it be? Is it 'hair—hair-trunk—leather-trunk—leather-boots?' Is it 'hair—beard—oysters—seaside—paddling—no boots?' Man is liable to err—especially when every mistake he makes is called a movement—but why should all the lunacies live together?"

"Because all the lunatics should live together," said Humphrey, "and if you'd seen what happened up at Crampton, with the farming-out idea, you'd know. It's all very well, Captain; but if people can prevent a guest of great importance being buried up to the neck in farm manure, they will. They will, really." He coughed almost apologetically. He was about to attempt a resumption of the conversation, when he saw his companion slap the milk-can and keg back into the car, and get into it himself. "You drive," he said, "drive me where those things live; you know, Hump."

They did not, however, arrive in the civic centre of such things without yet another delay. They left the river and followed the man with the long hair and the goatskin frock; and he stopped as it happened at a house on the outskirts of the village. The adventurers stopped also, out of curiosity, and were at first relieved to see the man almost instantly reappear, having transacted his business with a quickness that seemed incredible. A second glance showed them it was not the man, but another man dressed exactly like him. A few minutes more of inquisitive delay, showed them many of the kilty and goatish sect going in and out of this particular place, each clad in his innocent uniform.

"This must be the temple and chapel," muttered Patrick, "it must be here they sacrifice a glass of milk to a cow, or whatever it is they do. Well, the joke is pretty obvious, but we must wait for a lull in the crowding of the congregation."

When the last long-haired phantom had faded up the road, Dalroy sprang from the car and drove the sign-board deep into the earth with savage violence, and then very quietly knocked at the door.

The apparent owner of the place, of whom the two last of the long-haired and bare-footed idealists were taking a rather hurried farewell, was a man curiously ill-fitted for the part he seemed cast for in the only possible plot.

Both Pump and Dalroy thought they had never seen a man look so sullen. His face was of the rubicund sort that does not suggest jollity, but merely a stagnant indigestion in the head. His mustache hung heavy and dark, his brows yet heavier and darker. Dalroy had seen something of the sort on the faces of defeated people disgracefully forced into submission, but he could not make head or tail of it in connection with the priggish perfections of Peaceways. It was all the odder because he was manifestly prosperous; his clothes were smartly cut in something of the sporting manner, and the inside of his house was at least four times grander than the outside.

But what mystified them most was this, that he did not so much exhibit the natural curiosity of a gentleman whose private house is entered by strangers, but rather an embarrassed and restless expectation. During Dalroy's eager apologies and courteous inquiries about the direction and accommodations of Peaceways, his eye (which was of the boiled gooseberry order) perpetually wandered from them to the cupboard and then again to the window, and at last he got up and went to look out into the road.

"Oh, yes, sir; very healthy place, Peaceways," he said, peering through the lattice. "Very. . . dash it, what do they mean? . . . Very healthy place. Of course they have their little ways."

"Only drink pure milk, don't they?" asked Dalroy.

The householder looked at him with a rather wild eye and grunted.

"Yes; so they say," and he went again to the window.

"I've bought some of it," said Patrick, patting his pet milk-can, which he carried under his arm, as if unable to be separated from Dr. Meadows's discovery. "Have a glass of milk, sir."

The man's boiled eye began to bulge in anger—or some other emotion.

"What do you want?" he muttered, "are you 'tecs or what?"

"Agents and Distributors of the Meadows' Mountain Milk," said the Captain, with simple pride, "taste it?"

The dazed householder took a glass of the blameless liquid and sipped it; and the change on his face was extraordinary.

"Well, I'm jiggered," he said, with a broad and rather coarse grin. "That's a queer dodge. You're in the joke, I see." Then he went again restlessly to the window; and added, "but if we're all friends, why the blazes don't the others come in? I've never known trade so slow before."

"Who are the others?" asked Mr. Pump.

"Oh, the usual Peaceways people," said the other. "They generally come here before work. Dr. Meadows don't work them for very long hours, that wouldn't be healthy or whatever he calls it; but he's particular about their being punctual. I've seen 'em running, with all their pure-minded togs on, when the hooter gave the last call."

Then he abruptly opened the front door and called out impatiently, but not loudly:

"Come along in if you're coming. You'll give the show away if you play the fool out there."

Patrick looked out also and the view of the road outside was certainly rather singular. He was used to crowds, large and small, collecting outside houses which he had honoured with the sign of "The Old Ship," but they generally stared up at it in unaffected wonder and amusement. But outside this open door, some twenty or thirty persons in what Pump had called their night-gowns were moving to and fro like somnambulists, apparently blind to the presence of the sign; looking at the other side of the road, looking at the horizon, looking at the clouds of morning; and only occasionally stopping to whisper to each other. But when the owner of the house called to one of these ostentatiously abstracted beings and asked him hoarsely what the devil was the matter, it was natural for the milk-fed one to turn his feeble eye toward the sign. The gooseberry eyes followed his, and the face to which they belonged was a study in apoplectic astonishment.

"What the hell have you done to my house?" he demanded. "Of course they can't come in if this thing's here."

"I'll take it down, if you like," said Dalroy, stepping out and picking it up like a flower from the front garden (to the amazement of the men in the road, who thought they had strayed into a nursery fairy-tale), "but I wish, in return, you'd give me some idea of what the blazes all this means."

"Wait till I've served these men," replied his host.

The goat-garbed persons went very sheepishly (or goatishly) into the now signless building, and were rapidly served with raw spirits, which Mr. Pump suspected to be of no very superior quality. When the last goat was gone, Captain Dalroy said:

"I mean that all this seems to me topsy-turvy. I understood that as the law stands now, if there's a sign they are allowed to drink and if there isn't they aren't."

"The Law!" said the man, in a voice thick with scorn. "Do you think these poor brutes are afraid of the Law as they are of the Doctor?"

"Why should they be afraid of the Doctor?" asked Dalroy, innocently. "I always heard that Peaceways was a self-governing republic."

"Self-governing be damned," was the illiberal reply. "Don't he own all the houses and could turn 'em out in a snow storm? Don't 'e pay all the wages and could starve 'em stiff in a month? The Law!" And he snorted. A moment after he squared his elbows on the table and began to explain more fully.

"I was a brewer about here and had the biggest brewery in these parts. There were only two houses which didn't belong to me, and the magistrates took away their licenses after a time. Ten years ago you could see Hugby's Ales written beside every sign in the county. Then came these cursed Radicals, and our leader, Lord Ivywood, must go over to their side about it, and let this Doctor buy all the land under some new law that there shan't be any pubs at all. And so my business is ruined so that he can sell his milk. Luckily I'd done pretty well before and had some compensation, of course; and I still do a fair trade on the Q.T., as you see. But of course that don't amount to half the old one, for they're afraid of old Meadows finding out. Snuffling old blighter!"

And the gentleman with the good clothes spat on the carpet.

"I am a Radical myself," said the Irishman, rather coldly, "for all information on the Conservative party I must refer you to my friend, Mr. Pump, who is, of course, in the inmost secrets of his leaders. But it seems to me a very rum sort of Radicalism to eat and drink at the orders of a master who is a madman, merely because he's also a millionaire. O Liberty, what very complicated and even unsatisfactory social developments are committed in thy name! Why don't they kick the old ass round the town a bit? No boots? Is that why they're allowed no boots? Oh, roll him down hill in a milk can: he can't object to that."

"I don't know," said Pump, in his ruminant way, "Master Christian's aunt did, but ladies are more particular, of course."

"Look here!" cried Dalroy, in some excitement, "if I stick up that sign outside, and stay here to help, will you defy them? You'd be strictly within the law, and any private coercion I can promise you they shall repent. Plant the sign and sell the stuff openly like a man, and you may stand in English history like a deliverer."

Mr. Hugby, of Hugby's Ales, only looked gloomily at the table. His was not the sort of drinking nor the sort of drink-selling on which the revolutionary sentiment flourishes.

"Well," said the Captain, "will you come with me and say 'Hear, hear!' and 'How true!'—'What matchless eloquence!' if I make a speech in the marketplace? Come along! There's room in our car."

"Well, I'll come with you, if you like," replied Mr. Hugby, heavily. "It's true if yours is allowed we might get our trade back, too." And putting on a silk hat he followed the Captain and the innkeeper out to their little car. The model village was not an appropriate background for

Mr. Hugby's silk hat. Indeed, the hat somehow seemed to bring out by contrast all that was fantastic in the place.

It was a superb morning, some hours after sunrise. The edges of the sky touching the ring of dim woods and distant hills were still jewelled with the tiny transparent clouds of daybreak, delicate red and green or yellow. But above the vault of Heaven rose through turquoise into a torrid and solid blue in which the other clouds, the colossal cumuli, tumbled about like a celestial pillow-fight. The bulk of the houses were as white as the clouds, so that it looked (to use another simile) as if some of the whitewashed cottages were flying and falling about the sky. But most of the white houses were picked out here and there with bright colours, here an ornament in orange or there a stripe of lemon yellow, as if by the brush of a baby giant. The houses had no thatching (thatching is not hygienic) but were mostly covered with a sort of peacock green tiles bought cheap at a Preraphaelite Bazaar; or, less frequently, by some still more esoteric sort of terra cotta bricks. The houses were not English, nor homelike, nor suited to the landscape; for the houses had not been built by free men for themselves, but at the fancy of a whimsical lord. But considered as a sort of elfin city in a pantomime it was a really picturesque background for pantomimic proceedings.

I fear Mr. Dalroy's proceedings from the first rather deserved that name. To begin with, he left the sign, the cask, and the keg all wrapped and concealed in the car, but removed all the wraps of his own disguise, and stood on the central patch of grass in that green uniform that looked all the more insolent for being as ragged as the grass. Even that was less ragged than his red hair, which no red jungle of the East could imitate. Then he took out, almost tenderly, the large milk-can, and deposited it, almost reverently, on the island of turf. Then he stood beside it, like Napoleon beside a gun, with an expression of tremendous seriousness and even severity. Then he drew his sword, and with that flashing weapon, as with a flail, lashed and thrashed the echoing metal can till the din was deafening, and Mr. Hugby hastily got out of the car and withdrew to a slight distance, stopping his ears. Mr. Pump sat solidly at the steering wheel, well knowing it might be necessary to start in some haste.

"Gather, gather, gather, Peaceways," shouted Patrick, still banging on the can and lamenting the difficulties of adapting "Macgregor's Gathering" to the name and occasion, "We're landless, *landless*, landless, Peaceways!"

Two or three of the goat-clad, recognising Mr. Hugby with a guilty look, drew near with great caution, and the Captain shouted at them as if they were an army covering Salisbury Plain.

"Citizens," he roared, saying anything that came into his head, "try the only original unadulterated Mountain Milk, for which alone Mahomet came to the mountain. The original milk of the land flowing with milk and honey; the high quality of which could alone have popularised so unappetising a combination. Try our milk! None others are genuine! Who can do without milk. Even whales can't do without milk. If any lady or gentleman keeps a favourite whale at home, now's their chance! The early whale catches the milk. Just look at our milk! If you say you can't look at the milk, because it's in the can—well, look at the can! You must look at the can! You simply must! When Duty whispers low 'Thou Must!'" he bellowed at the top of his voice in a highly impromptu peroration, "When Duty whispers low 'Thou Must,' the Youth replies, 'I can!'" And with the word "Can" he hit the can with a shocking and shattering noise, like a peal of demoniac bells of steel.

This introductory speech is open to criticism from those who regard it as intended for the study rather than the stage. The present chronicler (who has no aim save truth) is bound to record that for its own unscrupulous purpose it was extremely successful: a great mass of the citizens of Peaceways having been attracted by the noise of one man shouting like a crowd. There are crowds who do not care to revolt; but there are no crowds who do not like someone else to do it for them; a fact which the safest oligarchs may be wise to learn.

But Dalroy's ultimate triumph (I regret to say) consisted in actually handing to a few of the foremost of his audience some samples of his blameless beverage. The fact was certainly striking. Some were paralysed with surprise. Some were abruptly broken double with laughter. Many chuckled. Some cheered. All looked radiantly toward the eccentric orator.

And yet the radiance died quietly and suddenly from their faces. And only because one little old man had joined the group; a little old man in white linen with a white pointed beard and a white powder-puff of hair like thistledown: a man whom almost every man present could have killed with the left arm.

XIX

The Hospitality of the Captain

D r. Moses Meadows, whether that was his name or an Anglicised version of it, had certainly come in the first instance from a little town in Germany and his first two books were written in German. His first two books were his best, for he began with a genuine enthusiasm for physical science, and this was adulterated with nothing worse than a hatred of what he thought was superstition, and what many of us think is the soul of the state. The first enthusiasm was most notable in the first book, which was concerned to show that "in the female not upsprouting of the whiskers was from the therewith increasing arrested mentality derived." In his second book he came more to grips with delusions, and for some time he was held to have proved (to everyone who agreed with him already) that the Time Ghost had been walking particularly "rapidly, lately; and that the Christus Mythus was by the alcoholic mind's trouble explained." Then, unfortunately, he came across the institution called Death, and began to argue with it. Not seeing any rational explanation of this custom of dying, so prevalent among his fellow-citizens, he concluded that it was merely traditional (which he thought meant "effete"), and began to think of nothing but ways of evading or delaying it. This had a rather narrowing effect on him, and he lost much of that acrid ardour which had humanised the atheism of his youth, when he would almost have committed suicide for the pleasure of taunting God with not being there. His later idealism grew more and more into materialism and consisted of his changing hypotheses and discoveries about the healthiest foods. There is no need to detain the reader over what has been called his Oil Period; his Sea-weed Period has been authoritatively expounded in Professor Nym's valuable little work; and on the events of his Glue Period it is, perhaps, not very generous to dwell. It was during his prolonged stay in England that he chanced on the instance of the longevity of milk consumers, and built on it a theory which was, at the beginning at least, sincere. Unfortunately it was also successful: wealth flowed in to the inventor and proprietor of Mountain Milk, and he began to feel a fourth and last enthusiasm, which, also, can come late in life and have a narrowing effect on the mind.

In the altercation which naturally followed on his discovery of the antics of Mr. Patrick Dalroy, he was very dignified, but naturally not very tolerant; for he was quite unused to anything happening in spite of him, or anything important even happening without him, in the land that lay around. At first he hinted severely that the Captain had stolen the milk-can from the milk-producing premises, and sent several workmen to count the cans in each shed; but Dalroy soon put him right about that.

"I bought it in a shop at Wyddington," he said, "and since then I have used no other. You'll hardly believe me," he said, with some truth, "but when I went into that shop I was quite a little man. I had one glass of your Mountain Milk; and look at me now."

"You have no right to sell the milk here," said Dr. Meadows, with the faintest trace of a German accent. "You are not in my employment; I am not responsible for your methods. You are not a representative of the business."

"I'm an Advertisement," said the Captain. "We advertise you all over England. You see that lean, skimpy, little man over there," pointing to the indignant Mr. Pump, "He's Before Taking Meadows's Mountain Milk. I'm After," added Mr. Dalroy, with satisfaction.

"You shall laugh at the magistrate," said the other, with a thickening accent.

"I shall," agreed Patrick. "Well, I'll make a clean breast of it, sir. The truth is it isn't your milk at all. It has quite a different taste. These gentlemen will tell you so."

A smothered giggle sent all the blood to the eminent capitalist's face.

"Then, either you have stolen my can and are a thief," he said, stamping, "or you have introduced inferior substances into my discovery and are an adulterer—er—"

"Try adulteratist," said Dalroy, kindly. "Prince Albert always said 'adulteratarian.' Dear old Albert! It seems like yesterday! But it is, of course, today. And it's as true as daylight that this stuff tastes different. I can't tell you what the taste is" (subdued guffaws from the outskirts of the crowd). "It's something between the taste of your first sugar-stick and the fag-end of your father's cigar. It's as innocent as Heaven and as hot as hell. It tastes like a paradox. It tastes like a prehistoric inconsistency—I trust I make myself clear. The men who taste it most are the simplest men that God has made, and it always reminds them of the salt, because it is made out of sugar. Have some!"

And with a gesture of staggering hospitality, he shot out his long arm with the little glass at the end of it. The despotic curiosity in the Prussian overcame even his despotic dignity. He took a sip of the liquid, and his eyes stood out from his face.

"You've been mixing something with the milk," were the first words that came to him.

"Yes," answered Dalroy, "and so have you, unless you're a swindler. Why is your milk advertised as different from everyone else's milk, if you haven't made the difference? Why does a glass of your milk cost threepence, and a glass of ordinary milk, a penny, if you haven't put twopennorth of something into it? Now, look here, Dr. Meadows. The Public Analyst who would judge this, happens to be an honest man. I have a list of the twenty-one and a half honest men still employed in such posts. I make you a fair offer. He shall decide what it is I add to the milk, if you let him decide what it is you add to the milk. You must add something to the milk, or what can all these wheels and pumps and pulleys be for? Will you tell me, here and now, what you add to the milk which makes it so exceedingly Mountain?"

There was a long silence, full of the same sense of submerged mirth in the mob. But the philanthropist had fallen into a naked frenzy in the sunlight, and shaking his fists aloft in a way unknown to all the English around him, he cried out:

"Ach! but I know what you add! I know what you add! It is the Alcohol! And you have no sign and you shall laugh at a magistrate."

Dalroy, with a bow, retired to the car, removed a number of wrappings and produced the prodigious wooden sign-post of "The Old Ship," with its blue three-decker and red St. George's cross conspicuously displayed. This he planted on his narrow territory of turf and looked round serenely.

"In this old oak-panelled inn of mine," he said, "I will laugh at a million magistrates. Not that there's anything unhygienic about this inn. No low ceilings or stuffiness here. Windows open everywhere, except in the floor. And as I hear some are saying there ought always to be food sold with fermented liquor, why, my dear Dr. Meadows, I've got a cheese here that will make another man of you. At least, we'll hope so. We can but try."

But Dr. Meadows was long past being merely angry. The exhibition of the sign had put him into a serious difficulty. Like most sceptics, like even the most genuine sceptics such as Bradlaugh, he was as legal as he was sceptical. He had a profound fear, which also had in it something better than fear, of being ultimately found in the wrong in a police court or a public inquiry. And he also suffered the tragedy of all such men living in modern England; that he must always be certain to respect the law, while never being certain of what it was. He could only remember generally that Lord Ivywood, when introducing or defending the great Ivywood Act on this matter, had dwelt very strongly on the unique and significant nature of the sign. And he could not be certain that if he disregarded it altogether, he might not eventually be cast in heavy damages—or even go to prison, in spite of his success in business. Of course he knew quite well that he had a thousand answers to such nonsense: that a patch of grass in the road couldn't be an inn; that the sign wasn't even produced when the Captain began to hand round the rum. But he also knew quite well that in the black peril we call British law, that is not the point. He had heard points quite as obvious urged to a judge and urged in vain. At the bottom of his mind he found this fact: rich as he was, Lord Ivywood had made him—and on which side would Lord Ivywood be?

"Captain," said Humphrey Pump, speaking for the first time, "we'd better be getting away. I feel it in my bones."

"Inhospitable innkeeper!" cried the Captain, indignantly. "And after I have gone out of the way to license your premises! Why, this is the dawn of peace in the great city of Peaceways. I don't despair of Dr. Meadows tossing off another bumper before we've done. For the moment, Brother Hugby will engage."

As he spoke, he served out milk and rum at random; and still the Doctor had too much terror of our legal technicalities to make a final interference. But when Mr. Hugby, of Hugby's Ales, heard his name called, he first of all jumped so as almost to dislodge the silk hat, then he stood quite still. Then he accepted a glass of the new Mountain Milk; and then his very face became full of speech, before he had spoken a word.

"There's a motor coming along the road from the far hills," said Humphrey, quietly. "It'll be across the last bridge down stream in ten minutes and come up on this side."

"Well," said the Captain, impatiently, "I suppose you've seen a motor before."

"Not in this valley all this morning," answered Pump.

"Mr. Chairman," said Mr. Hugby, feeling a dim disposition to say "Mr. Vice," in memory of old commercial banquets, "I'm sure we're all law-abiding people here, and wish to remain friends, especially with our good friend the Doctor; may he never want a friend or a bottle—that is in short, anything he wants, as we go up the hill of prosperity, and so on. But, as our friend here with the sign-board seems to be within his rights, well, I think the time's come when we can look at these things more broadly, so to speak. Now I know it's quite true those dirty little pubs do a lot of harm to a property, and you get a lot of ignorant people there who are just like pigs; and I don't say our friend the Doctor hasn't done good by clearing 'em away. But a big, well-managed business with plenty of capital behind it is quite another thing. Well, friends, you all know that I was originally in the Trade; though I have, of course, left off selling under the new regulations." Here the goats looked rather guiltily at their cloven hoofs. "But I've got my little bit and I wouldn't mind putting it into this 'Old Ship' here, if our friend would allow it to be run on business lines. And especially if he'd enlarge the premises a bit. Ha! ha! And if our good friend, the Doctor—"

"You rascal fellow!" spluttered Meadows, "your goot friend the doctor will make you dance before a magistrate."

"Now, don't be unbusinesslike," reasoned the brewer. "It won't hurt your sales. It's quite a different public, don't you see? Do talk like a business man."

"I am not a business man," said the scientist, with fiery eyes, "I am a servant of humanity."

"Then," said Dalroy, "why do you never do what your master tells you?"

"The motor has crossed the river," said Humphrey Pump.

"You would undo all my works," cried the Doctor, with sincere passion. "When I have built this town myself, when I have made it sober and healthful myself, when I am awake and about before anyone in the town myself, watching over its interests—you would ruin all to sell your barbaric and fundamentally beastly beer. And then you call me a goot friend. I am not a goot friend!"

"That I can't say," growled Hugby, "but if it comes to that—aren't you trying to sell—"

A motor car drove up with a white explosion of dust, and about six very dusty people got out of it. Even through the densest disguise of the swift motorist, Pump perceived in many of them the peculiar style and bodily carriage of the police. The most evident exception was a long and more slender figure, which, on removing its cap and goggles, disclosed the dark and drooping features of J. Leveson, Secretary. He walked across to the little, old millionaire, who instantly recognized him and shook hands. They confabulated for some little time, turning over some official documents. Dr. Meadows cleared his throat and said to the whole crowd.

"I am very glad to be able to announce to you all that this extraordinary outrage has been too late attempted. Lord Ivywood, with the promptitude he so invariably shows, has immediately communicated to places of importance such as this a most just and right alteration of the law, which exactly meets the present case."

"We shall sleep in jail tonight," said Humphrey Pump. "I know it in my bones."

"It is enough to say," proceeded the millionaire, "that by the law as it now stands, any innkeeper, even if he display a sign, is subject to imprisonment if he sells alcohol on premises where it has not been previously kept for three days."

"I thought it would be something like that," muttered Pump. "Shall we give up, Captain, or shall we try a bolt for it?"

Even the impudence of Dalroy appeared for the instant dazed and stilled. He was staring forlornly up into the abyss of sky above him, as if, like Shelley, he could get inspiration from the last and purest clouds and the perfect hues of the ends of Heaven.

At last he said, in a soft and meditative voice, the single syllable,
"Sells!"

Pump looked at him sharply with a remarkable expression growing on his grim face. But the Doctor was far too rabidly rejoicing in his triumph to understand the Captain's meaning.

"Sells alcohol, are the exact words," he insisted, brandishing the blue oblong of the new Act of Parliament.

"So far as I am concerned they are inexact words," said Captain Dalroy, with polite indifference. "I have not been selling alcohol, I have been giving it away. Has anybody here paid me money? Has anybody here seen anybody else pay me money? I'm a philanthropist just like Dr. Meadows. I'm his living image!"

Mr. Leveson and Dr. Meadows looked across at each other, and on the face of the first was consternation, and on the second a full return of all his terrors of the complicated law.

"I shall remain here for several weeks," continued the Captain, leaning elegantly on the can, "and shall give away, gratis, such supplies of this excellent drink as may be demanded by the citizens. It appears that there is no such supply at present in this district, and I feel sure that no person present can object to so strictly legal and highly charitable an arrangement."

In this he was apparently in error; for several persons present seemed to object to it. But curiously enough it was not the withered and fanatical face of the philanthropist Meadows, nor the dark and equine face of the official Leveson, which stood out most vividly as a picture of protest. The face most strangely unsympathetic with this form of charity was that of the ex-proprietor of Hugby's Ales. His gooseberry eyes were almost dropping from his head and his words sprang from his lips before he could stop them.

"And you blooming well think you can come here like a big buffoon, you beast, and take away all my trade—"

Old Meadows turned on him with the swiftness of an adder.

"And what is your trade, Mr. Hugby?" he asked.

The brewer bubbled with a sort of bursting anger. The goats all looked at the ground as is, according to a Roman poet, the habit of the lower animals. Man (in the character of Mr. Patrick Dalroy) taking advantage of a free but fine translation of the Latin passage, "looked aloft, and with uplifted eyes beheld his own hereditary skies."

"Well, all I can say is," roared Mr. Hugby, "if the police come all this way and can't lock up a dirty loafer whose coat's all in rags, there's an end of me paying these fat infernal taxes and—"

"Yes," said Dalroy, in a voice that fell like an axe, "there is an end of you, please God. It's brewers like you that have made the inns stink with poison, till even good men asked for no inns at all. And you are worse than the teetotalers, for you prevented what they never knew. And as for you, eminent man of science, great philanthropist, idealist and destroyer of inns, let me give one cold fact for your information. You are not respected. You are obeyed. Why should I or anyone respect you particularly? You say you built this town and get up at daybreak to watch this town. You built it for money and you watch it for more money. Why should I respect you because you are fastidious about food, that your poor old digestion may outlive the hearts of better men? Why should you be the god of this valley, whose god is your belly, merely because you do not even love your god, but only fear him? Go home to your prayers, old man; for all men shall die. Read the Bible, if you like, as they do in your German home; and I suppose you once read it to pick texts as you now read it to pick holes. I don't read it myself, I'm afraid, but I remember some words in old Mulligan's translation; and I leave them with you. 'Unless God,'" and he made a movement with his arm, so natural and yet so vast that for an instant the town really looked like a toy of bright coloured cardboard at the feet of the giant; "'unless God build the city, their labour is but lost that build it; unless God keep the city, the watchman watcheth in vain. It is lost labour that you rise up early in the morning and eat the bread of carefulness; while He giveth His beloved sleep.' Try and understand what that means, and never mind whether it's Elohistic. And now, Hump, we'll away and away. I'm tired of the green tiles over there. Come, fill up my cup," and he banged down the cask in the car, "come saddle my horses and call out my men. And tremble, gay goats, in the midst of your glee; for you've no' seen the last of my milk-can and me."

This song was joyously borne away with Mr. Dalroy in the disappearing car; and the motorists were miles beyond pursuit from Peaceways before they thought of halting again. But they were still beside the bank of that noble and enlarging river; and in a place of deep fern and fairy-ribboned birches with the glowing and gleaming water behind them, Patrick asked his friend to stop the car.

"By the way," said Humphrey, suddenly, "there was one thing I didn't understand. Why was he so afraid of the Public Analyst? What poison and chemicals does he put in the milk?"

"H_2O," answered the Captain, "I take it without milk myself."

And he bent over as if to drink of the stream, as he had done at daybreak.

XX

The Turk and the Futurists

MR. Adrian Crooke was a successful chemist whose shop was in the neighbourhood of Victoria, but his face expressed more than is generally required in a successful chemist. It was a curious face, prematurely old and like parchment, but acute and decisive, with real headwork in every line of it. Nor was his conversation, when he did converse, out of keeping with this: he had lived in many countries, and had a rich store of anecdote about the more quaint and sometimes the more sinister side of his work, visions of the vapour of eastern drugs or guesses at the ingredients of Renascence poisons. He himself, it need hardly be said, was a most respectable and reliable apothecary, or he would not have had the custom of families, especially among the upper classes; but he enjoyed as a hobby, the study of the dark days and lands where his science had lain sometimes on the borders of magic and sometimes upon the borders of murder. Hence it often happened that persons, who in their serious senses were well aware of his harmless and useful habits, would leave his shop on some murky and foggy night, with their heads so full of wild tales of the eating of hemp or the poisoning of roses, they could hardly help fancying that the shop, with its glowing moon of crimson or saffron, like bowls of blood and sulphur, was really a house of the Black Art.

It was doubtless for such conversational pleasures, in part, that Hibbs However entered the shop; as well as for a small glass of the same restorative medicine which he had been taking when Leveson found him by the open window. But this did not prevent Hibbs from expressing considerable surprise and some embarrassment when Leveson entered the same chemist's and asked for the same chemical. Indeed, Leveson looked harassed and weary enough to want it.

"You've been out of town, haven't you?" said Leveson. "No luck. They got away again on some quibble. The police wouldn't make the arrest; and even old Meadows thought it might be illegal. I'm sick of it. Where are you going?"

"I thought," said Mr. Hibbs, "of dropping in at this Post-Futurist exhibition. I believe Lord Ivywood will be there; he is showing it to the

Prophet. I don't pretend to know much about art, but I hear it's very fine."

There was a long silence and Mr. Leveson said, "People always prejudiced against new ideas."

Then there was another long silence and Mr. Hibbs said, "After all, they said the same of Whistler."

Refreshed by this ritual, Mr. Leveson became conscious of the existence of Crooke, and said to him, cheerfully, "That's so in your department, too, isn't it? I suppose the greatest pioneers in chemistry were unpopular in their own time."

"Look at the Borgias," said Mr. Crooke. "They got themselves quite disliked."

"You're very flippant, you know," said Leveson, in a fatigued way. "Well, so long. Are you coming, Hibbs?"

And the two gentlemen, who were both attired in high hats and afternoon callers' coats, betook themselves down the street. It was a fine, sunny day, the twin of the day before that had shone so brightly on the white town of Peaceways; and their walk was a pleasant one, along a handsome street with high houses and small trees that overlooked the river all the way. For the pictures were exhibited in a small but famous gallery, a rather rococo building of which the entrance steps almost descended upon the Thames. The building was girt on both sides and behind with gaudy flower-beds, and on the top of the steps, in front of the Byzantine doorway, stood their old friend, Misysra Ammon, smiling broadly, and in an unusually sumptuous costume. But even the sight of that fragrant eastern flower did not seem to revive altogether the spirits of the drooping Secretary.

"You have coome," said the beaming Prophet, "to see the decoration? It is approo-ooved. I haf approo-ooved it."

"We came to see the Post-Futurist pictures," began Hibbs; but Leveson was silent.

"There are no pictures," said the Turk, simply, "if there had been I could not haf approo-ooved. For those of our Religion pictures are not goo-ood; they are Idols, my friendss. Loo-ook in there," and he turned and darted a solemn forefinger just under his nose toward the gates of the gallery; "Loo-ook in there and you will find no Idols. No Idols at all. I have most carefully loo-ooked into every one of the frames. Every one I have approo-ooved. No trace of ze Man form. No trace of ze Animal form. All decoration as goo-ood as the goo-oodest of carpets; it harms not. Lord Ivywood smile of happiness; for I tell him Islam indeed progresses. Ze old Moslems allow to draw the picture of the vegetable. Here I hunt even for the vegetable. And there is no vegetable."

Hibbs, whose trade was tact, naturally did not think it wise that the eminent Misysra should go on lecturing from a tall flight of steps to the whole street and river, so he had slipped past with a general proposal to go in and see. The Prophet and the Secretary followed; and all entered the outer hall where Lord Ivywood stood with the white face of a statue. He was the only statue the New Moslems were allowed to worship.

On a sofa like a purple island in the middle of the sea of floor sat Enid Wimpole, talking eagerly to her cousin, Dorian; doing, in fact, her best to prevent the family quarrel, which threatened to follow hard on the incident at Westminster. In the deeper perspective of the rooms Lady Joan Brett was floating about. And if her attitude before the Post-Futurist pictures could not be called humble, or even inquiring, it is but just to that school to say that she seemed to be quite as bored with the floor that she walked on, and the parasol she held. Bit by bit other figures or groups of that world drifted through the Exhibition of the Post-Futurists. It is a very small world, but it is just big enough and just small enough to govern a country—that is, a country with no religion. And it has all the vanity of a mob; and all the reticence of a secret society.

Leveson instantly went up to Lord Ivywood, pulled papers from his pocket and was plainly telling him of the escape from Peaceways. Ivywood's face hardly changed; he was, or felt, above some things; and one of them was blaming a servant before the servant's social superiors. But no one could say he looked less like cold marble than before.

"I made all possible inquiries about their subsequent route," the Secretary was heard saying, "and the most serious feature is that they seem to have taken the road for London."

"Quite so," replied the statue, "they will be easier to capture here."

Lady Enid, by a series of assurances (most of which were, I regret to say, lies) had succeeded in preventing the scandal of her cousin, Dorian, actually cutting her cousin, Phillip. But she knew very little of the masculine temper if she really thought she had prevented the profound intellectual revolt of the poet against the politician. Ever since he heard Mr. Hibbs say, "Yars! Yars!", and order his arrest by a common policeman, the feelings of Dorian Wimpole had flowed for some four days and nights in a direction highly contrary to the ideals of Mr. Hibbs, and the sudden appearance of that blameless diplomatist quickened the mental current to a cataract. But as he could not insult Hibbs, whom socially he did not even know; and could not insult Ivywood, with whom he had just had a formal reconciliation, it was absolutely necessary that he should insult something else instead. All watchers for the Dawn will be deeply distressed to know that the Post-Futurist School of Painting received the full effects of this perverted wrath. In vain did Mr. Leveson affirm from time to time, "People always prejudiced against new ideas." Vainly did Mr. Hibbs say at the proper intervals, "After all, they said the same of Whistler." Not by such decent formalities was the frenzy of Dorian to be appeased.

"That little Turk has more sense than you have," he said, "he passes it as a good wall-paper. I should say it was a bad wall-paper; the sort of wall-paper that gives a sick man fever when he hasn't got it. But to call it pictures—you might as well call it seats for the Lord Mayor's Show. A seat isn't a seat if you can't see the Lord Mayor's Show. A picture isn't a picture if you can't see any picture. You can sit down at home more comfortably than you can at a procession. And you can walk about at home more comfortably than you can at a picture gallery. There's only one thing to be said for a street show or a picture show— and that is whether there is anything to be shown. Now, then! Show me something!"

"Well," said Lord Ivywood, good humouredly, motioning toward the wall in front of him, "let me show you the 'Portrait of an Old Lady.'"

"Well," said Dorian, stolidly, "which is it?"

Mr. Hibbs made a hasty gesture of identification, but was so unfortunate as to point to the picture of "Rain in the Apennines," instead of the "Portrait of an Old Lady," and his intervention increased the irritation of Dorian Wimpole. Most probably, as Mr. Hibbs afterward explained, it was because a vivacious movement of the elbow of Mr. Wimpole interfered with the exact pointing of the forefinger of Mr. Hibbs. In any case, Mr. Hibbs was sharply and horridly fixed by embarrassment; so that he had to go away to the refreshment bar and eat three lobster-patties, and even drink a glass of that champagne that had once been his ruin. But on this occasion he stopped at one glass, and returned with a full diplomatic responsibility.

He returned to find that Dorian Wimpole had forgotten all the facts of time, place, and personal pride, in an argument with Lord Ivywood, exactly as he had forgotten such facts in an argument with Patrick Dalroy, in a dark wood with a donkey-cart. And Phillip Ivywood was interested also; his cold eyes even shone; for though his pleasure was almost purely intellectual, it was utterly sincere.

"And I do trust the untried; I do follow the inexperienced," he was saying quietly, with his fine inflections of voice. "You say this is changing the very nature of Art. I want to change the very nature of Art. Everything lives by turning into something else. Exaggeration is growth."

"But exaggeration of what?" demanded Dorian. "I cannot see a trace of exaggeration in these pictures; because I cannot find a hint of what it is they want to exaggerate. You can't exaggerate the feathers of a cow or the legs of a whale. You can draw a cow with feathers or a whale with legs for a joke—though I hardly think such jokes are in your line. But don't you see, my good Phillip, that even then the joke depends on its looking like a cow and not only like a thing with feathers. Even then the joke depends on the whale as well as the legs. You can combine up to a certain point; you can distort up to a certain point; after that you lose the identity; and with that you lose everything. A Centaur is so much of a man with so much of a horse. The Centaur must not be hastily identified with the Horsey Man. And the Mermaid must be maidenly; even if there is something fishy about her social conduct."

"No," said Lord Ivywood, in the same quiet way, "I understand what you mean, and I don't agree. I should like the Centaur to turn into something else, that is neither man nor horse."

"But not something that has nothing of either?" asked the poet.

"Yes," answered Ivywood, with the same queer, quiet gleam in his colourless eyes, "something that has nothing of either."

"But what's the good?" argued Dorian. "A thing that has changed entirely has not changed at all. It has no bridge of crisis. It can remember no change. If you wake up tomorrow and you simply *are* Mrs. Dope, an old woman who lets lodgings at Broadstairs—well, I don't doubt Mrs. Dope is a saner and happier person than you are. But in what way have *you* progressed? What part of *you* is better? Don't you see this prime fact of identity is the limit set on all living things?"

"No," said Phillip, with suppressed but sudden violence, "I deny that any limit is set upon living things."

"Why, then I understand," said Dorian, "why, though you make such good speeches, you have never written any poetry."

Lady Joan, who was looking with tedium at a rich pattern of purple and green in which Misysra attempted to interest her (imploring her to disregard the mere title, which idolatrously stated it as "First Communion in the Snow"), abruptly turned her full face to Dorian. It was a face to which few men could feel indifferent, especially when thus suddenly shown them.

"Why can't he write poetry?" she asked. "Do you mean he would resent the limits of metre and rhyme and so on?"

The poet reflected for a moment and then said, "Well, partly; but I mean more than that too. As one can be candid in the family, I may say that what everyone says about him is that he has no humour. But that's not my complaint at all. I think my complaint is that he has no pathos. That is, he does not feel human limitations. That is, he will not write poetry."

Lord Ivywood was looking with his cold, unconscious profile into a little black and yellow picture called "Enthusiasm"; but Joan Brett leaned across to him with swarthy eagerness and cried quite provocatively,

"Dorian says you've no pathos. Have you any pathos? He says it's a sense of human limitations."

Ivywood did not remove his gaze from the picture of "Enthusiasm," but simply said "No; I have no sense of human limitations." Then he put up his elderly eyeglass to examine the picture better. Then he dropped it again and confronted Joan with a face paler than usual.

"Joan," he said, "I would walk where no man has walked; and find something beyond tears and laughter. My road shall be my road indeed; for I will make it, like the Romans. And my adventures shall not be in the hedges and the gutters, but in the borders of the ever advancing brain. I will think what was unthinkable until I thought it; I will love what never lived until I loved it—I will be as lonely as the First Man."

"They say," she said, after a silence, "that the first man fell."

"You mean the priests?" he answered. "Yes, but even they admit that he discovered good and evil. So are these artists trying to discover some distinction that is still dark to us."

"Oh," said Joan, looking at him with a real and unusual interest, "then you don't *see* anything in the pictures, yourself?"

"I see the breaking of the barriers," he answered, "beyond that I see nothing."

She looked at the floor for a little time and traced patterns with her parasol, like one who has really received food for thought. Then she said, suddenly,

"But perhaps the breaking of barriers might be the breaking of everything."

The clear and colourless eyes looked at her quite steadily.

"Perhaps," said Lord Ivywood.

Dorian Wimpole made a sudden movement a few yards off, where he was looking at a picture, and said, "Hullo! What's this?" Mr. Hibbs was literally gaping in the direction of the entrance.

Framed in that fine Byzantine archway stood a great big, boney man in threadbare but careful clothes, with a harsh, high-featured, intelligent face, to which a dark beard under the chin gave something of the Puritanic cast. Somehow his whole personality seemed to be pulled together and explained when he spoke with a North Country accent.

"Weel, lards," he said, genially, "t'hoose be main great on t'pictures. But I coom for suthin' in a moog. Haw! Haw!"

Leveson and Hibbs looked at each other. Then Leveson rushed from the room. Lord Ivywood did not move a finger; but Mr. Wimpole, with a sort of poetic curiosity, drew nearer to the stranger, and studied him.

"It's perfectly awful," cried Enid Wimpole, in a loud whisper, "the man must be drunk."

"Na, lass," said the man with gallantry, "a've not been droonk, nobbut at Hurley Fair, these years and all; a'm a decent lad and workin' ma way back t'Wharfdale. No harm in a moog of ale, lass."

"Are you quite sure," asked Dorian Wimpole, with a singular sort of delicate curiosity, "are you quite *sure* you're not drunk."

"A'm not droonk," said the man, jovially.

"Even if these were licensed premises," began Dorian, in the same diplomatic manner.

"There's t'sign on t'hoose," said the stranger.

The black, bewildered look on the face of Joan Brett suddenly altered. She took four steps toward the doorway, and then went back and sat on the purple ottoman. But Dorian seemed fascinated with his inquiry into the alleged decency of the lad who was working his way to Wharfdale.

"Even if these were licensed premises," he repeated, "drink could be refused you if you were drunk. Now, are you *really* sure you're not drunk. Would you know if it was raining, say?"

"Aye," said the man, with conviction.

"Would you know any common object of your countryside," inquired Dorian, scientifically, "a woman—let us say an old woman."

"Aye," said the man, with good humour.

"What on earth are you doing with the creature?" whispered Enid, feverishly.

"I am trying," answered the poet, "to prevent a very sensible man from smashing a very silly shop. I beg your pardon, sir. As I was saying, would you know these things in a picture, now? Do you know what a landscape is and what a portrait is? Forgive my asking; you see we are responsible while we keep the place going."

There soared up into the sky like a cloud of rooks the eager vanity of the North.

"We collier lads are none so badly educated, lad," he said. "In the town a' was born in there was a gallery of pictures as fine as Lunnon. Aye, and a' knew 'em, too."

"Thank you," said Wimpole, pointing suddenly at the wall. "Would you be so kind, for instance, as to look at those two pictures. One represents an old woman and the other rain in the hills. It's a mere formality. You shall have your drink when you've said which is which."

The northerner bowed his huge body before the two frames and peered into them patiently. The long stillness that followed seemed to be something of a strain on Joan, who rose in a restless manner, first went to look out of a window and then went out of the front door.

At length the art-critic lifted a large, puzzled but still philosophical face.

"Soomehow or other," he said, "a' mun be droonk after all."

"You have testified," cried Dorian with animation. "You have all but saved civilization. And by God, you shall have your drink."

And he brought from the refreshment table a huge bumper of the Hibbsian champagne, and declined payment by the rapid method of running out of the gallery on to the steps outside.

Joan was already standing there. Out the little side window she had seen the incredible thing she expected to see; which explained the ludicrous scene inside. She saw the red and blue wooden flag of Mr. Pump standing up in the flower-beds in the sun, as serenely as if it were a tall and tropical flower; and yet, in the brief interval between the window and the door it had vanished, as if to remind her it was a flying dream. But two men were in a little motor outside, which was in the very act of starting. They were in motoring disguise, but she knew who they were. All that was deep in her, all that was sceptical, all that was stoical, all that was noble, made her stand as still as one of the pillars of the porch; but a dog, bearing the name of Quoodle, sprang up in the moving car, and barked with joy at the mere sight of her, and though she had borne all else, something in that bestial innocence of an animal suddenly blinded her with tears.

It could not, however, blind her to the extraordinary fact that followed. Mr. Dorian Wimpole, attired in anything but motoring costume, dressed in that compromise between fashion and art which seems proper to the visiting of picture-galleries, did not by any means stand as still as one of the pillars of the porch. He rushed down the steps, ran after the car and actually sprang into it, without disarranging his Whistlerian silk hat.

"Good afternoon," he said to Dalroy, pleasantly. "You owe me a motor-ride, you know."

XXI

The Road to Roundabout

Patrick Dalroy looked at the invader with a heavy and yet humourous expression, and merely said, "I didn't steal your car; really, I didn't."

"Oh, no," answered Dorian, "I've heard all about it since, and as you're rather the persecuted party, so to speak, it wouldn't be fair not to tell you that I don't agree much with Ivywood about all this. I disagree with him; or rather, to speak medically, he disagrees with me. He has, ever since I woke up after an oyster supper and found myself in the House of Commons with policemen calling out, 'Who goes home?'"

"Indeed," inquired Dalroy, drawing his red bushy eyebrows together. "Do the officials in Parliament say, 'Who goes home?'"

"Yes," answered Wimpole, indifferently, "it's a part of some old custom in the days when Members of Parliament might be attacked in the street."

"Well," inquired Patrick, in a rational tone, "why aren't they attacked in the street?"

There was a silence. "It is a holy mystery," said the Captain at last. "But, 'Who goes home?'—that is uncommonly good."

The Captain had received the poet into the car with all possible expressions of affability and satisfaction, but the poet, who was keen-sighted enough about people of his own sort, could not help thinking that the Captain was a little absent-minded. As they flew thundering through the mazes of South London (for Pump had crossed Westminster Bridge and was making for the Surrey hills), the big blue eyes of the big red-haired man rolled perpetually up and down the streets; and, after longer and longer silences, he found expression for his thoughts.

"Doesn't it strike you that there are a very large number of chemists in London nowadays?"

"Are there?" asked Wimpole, carelessly. "Well, there certainly are two very close to each other just over there."

"Yes, and both the same name," replied Dalroy, "Crooke. And I saw the same Mr. Crooke chemicalizing round the corner. He seems to be a highly omnipresent deity."

"A large business, I suppose," observed Dorian Wimpole.

"Too large for its profits, I should say," said Dalroy. "What can people want with two chemists of the same sort within a few yards of each other? Do they put one leg into one shop and one into the other and have their corns done in both at once? Or, do they take an acid in one shop and an alkali in the next, and wait for the fizz? Or, do they take the poison in the first shop and the emetic in the second shop? It seems like carrying delicacy too far. It almost amounts to living a double life."

"But, perhaps," said Dorian, "he is an uproariously popular chemist, this Mr. Crooke. Perhaps there's a rush on some specialty of his."

"It seems to me," said the Captain, "that there are certain limitations to such popularity in the case of a chemist. If a man sells very good tobacco, people may smoke more and more of it from sheer self-indulgence. But I never heard of anybody exceeding in cod-liver oil. Even castor-oil, I should say, is regarded with respect rather than true affection."

After a few minutes of silence, he said, "Is it safe to stop here for an instant, Pump?"

"I think so," replied Humphrey, "if you'll promise me not to have any adventures in the shop."

The motor car stopped before yet a fourth arsenal of Mr. Crooke and his pharmacy, and Dalroy went in. Before Pump and his companion could exchange a word, the Captain came out again, with a curious expression on his countenance, especially round the mouth.

"Mr. Wimpole," said Dalroy, "will you give us the pleasure of dining with us this evening? Many would consider it an unceremonious invitation to an unconventional meal; and it may be necessary to eat it under a hedge or even up a tree; but you are a man of taste, and one does not apologise for Hump's rum or Hump's cheese to persons of taste. We will eat and drink of our best tonight. It is a banquet. I am not very certain whether you and I are friends or enemies, but at least there shall be peace tonight."

"Friends, I hope," said the poet, smiling, "but why peace especially tonight?"

"Because there will be war tomorrow," answered Patrick Dalroy, "whichever side of it you may be on. I have just made a singular discovery."

And he relapsed into his silence as they flew out of the fringe of London into the woods and hills beyond Croydon. Dalroy remained in the same mood of brooding, Dorian was brushed by the butterfly wing of that fleeting slumber that will come on a man hurried, through the air, after long lounging in hot drawing rooms; even the dog Quoodle was asleep at the bottom of the car. As for Humphrey Pump, he very seldom talked when he had anything else to do. Thus it happened that long landscapes and perspectives were shot past them like suddenly shifted slides, and long stretches of time elapsed before any of them spoke again. The sky was changing from the pale golds and greens of evening to the burning blue of a strong summer night, a night of strong stars. The walls of woodland that flew past them like long assegais, were mostly, at first, of the fenced and park-like sort; endless oblong blocks of black pinewood shut in by boxes of thin grey wood. But soon fences began to sink, and pinewoods to straggle, and roads to split and even to sprawl. Half an hour later Dalroy had begun to realise something romantic and even faintly reminiscent in the roll of the country, and Humphrey Pump had long known he was on the marches of his native land.

So far as the difference could be defined by a detail, it seemed to consist not so much in the road rising as in the road perpetually winding. It was more like a path; and even where it was abrupt or aimless, it seemed the more alive. They appeared to be ascending a big, dim hill that was built of a crowd of little hills with rounded tops; it was like a cluster of domes. Among these domes the road climbed and curled in multitudinous curves and angles. It was almost impossible to believe that it could turn itself and round on itself so often without tying itself in a knot and choking.

"I say," said Dalroy, breaking the silence suddenly, "this car will get giddy and fall down."

"Perhaps," said Dorian, beaming at him, "my car, as you may have noticed, was much steadier."

Patrick laughed, but not without a shade of confusion. "I hope you got back your car all right," he said. "This is really nothing for speed; but it's an uncommonly good little climber, and it seems to have some climbing to do just now. And even more wandering."

"The roads certainly seem to be very irregular," said Dorian, reflectively.

"Well," cried Patrick, with a queer kind of impatience, "you're English and I'm not. You ought to know why the road winds about like this. Why, the Saints deliver us!" he cried, "it's one of the wrongs of Ireland that she can't understand England. England won't understand herself, England won't tell us why these roads go wriggling about. Englishmen won't tell us! You won't tell us!"

"Don't be too sure," said Dorian, with a quiet irony.

Dalroy, with an irony far from quiet, emitted a loud yell of victory.

"Right," he shouted. "More songs of the car club! We're all poets here, I hope. Each shall write something about why the road jerks about so much. So much as this, for example," he added, as the whole vehicle nearly rolled over in a ditch.

For, indeed, Pump appeared to be attacking such inclines as are more suitable for a goat than a small motor-car. This may have been exaggerated in the emotions of his companions, who had both, for different reasons, seen much of mere flat country lately. The sensation was like a combination of trying to get into the middle of the maze at Hampton Court, and climbing the spiral staircase to the Belfry at Bruges.

"This is the right way to Roundabout," said Dalroy, cheerfully, "charming place; salubrious spot. You can't miss it. First to the left and right and straight on round the corner and back again. That'll do for my poem. Get on, you slackers; why aren't you writing your poems?"

"I'll try one if you like," said Dorian, treating his flattered egotism lightly. "But it's too dark to write; and getting darker."

Indeed they had come under a shadow between them and the stars, like the brim of a giant's hat; only through the holes and rents in which the summer stars could now look down on them. The hill, like a cluster of domes, though smooth and even bare in its lower contours was topped with a tangle of spanning trees that sat above them like a bird brooding over its nest. The wood was larger and vaguer than the clump that is the crown of the hill at Chanctonbury, but was rather like it and held much the same high and romantic position. The next moment they were in the wood itself, and winding in and out among the trees by a ribbon of paths. The emerald twilight between the stems, combined with the dragon-like contortions of the great grey roots of the beeches, had a suggestion of monsters and the deep sea; especially as a long litter of crimson and copper-coloured fungi, which might well have been the more gorgeous types of anemone or jelly-fish, reddened the ground like a sunset dropped from the sky. And yet, contradictorily enough, they had also a strong sense of being high up; and even near to heaven; and the brilliant summer stars that stared through the chinks of the leafy roof might almost have been white starry blossoms on the trees of the wood.

But though they had entered the wood as if it were a house, their strongest sensation still was the rotatory; it seemed as if that high green

G.K. CHESTERTON

house went round and round like a revolving lighthouse or the whiz-gig temple in the old pantomimes. The stars seemed to circle over their heads; and Dorian felt almost certain he had seen the same beech-tree twice.

At length they came to a central place where the hill rose in a sort of cone in the thick of its trees, lifting its trees with it. Here Pump stopped the car, and clambering up the slope, came to the crawling colossal roots of a very large but very low beech-tree. It spread out to the four quarters of heaven more in the manner of an octopus than a tree, and within its low crown of branches there was a kind of hollow, like a cup, into which Mr. Humphrey Pump, of "The Old Ship," Pebblewick, suddenly and entirely disappeared.

When he appeared it was with a kind of rope ladder, which he politely hung over the side for his companions to ascend by, but the Captain preferred to swing himself onto one of the octopine branches with a whirl of large wild legs worthy of a chimpanzee. When they were established there, each propped in the hollow against a branch, almost as comfortably as in an arm chair, Humphrey himself descended once more and began to take out their simple stores. The dog was still asleep in the car.

"An old haunt of yours, Hump, I suppose," said the Captain. "You seem quite at home."

"I am at home," answered Pump, with gravity, "at the sign of 'The Old Ship.'" And he stuck the old blue and red sign-board erect among the toadstools, as if inviting the passer-by to climb the trees for a drink.

The tree just topped the mound or clump of trees, and from it they could see the whole champaign of the country they had passed, with the silver roads roaming about in it like rivers. They were so exalted they could almost fancy the stars would burn them.

"Those roads remind me of the songs you've all promised," said Dalroy at last. "Let's have some supper, Hump, and then recite."

Humphrey had hung one of the motor lanterns onto a branch above him, and proceeded by the light of it to tap the keg of rum and hand round the cheese.

"What an extraordinary thing," exclaimed Dorian Wimpole, suddenly. "Why, I'm quite comfortable! Such a thing has never happened before, I should imagine. And how holy this cheese tastes."

"It has gone on a pilgrimage," answered Dalroy, "or rather a Crusade. It's a heroic, a fighting cheese. 'Cheese of all Cheeses, Cheeses of all the world,' as my compatriot, Mr. Yeats, says to the Something-or-other of Battle. It's almost impossible that this cheese can have come out of such a coward as a cow. I suppose," he added, wistfully, "I suppose it wouldn't do to explain that in this case Hump had milked the bull. That would be classed by scientists among Irish legends—those that have the Celtic glamour and all that. No, I think this cheese must have come from that Dun Cow of Dunsmore Heath, who had horns bigger than elephant's tusks, and who was so ferocious that one of the greatest of the old heroes of chivalry was required to do battle with it. The rum's good, too. I've earned this glass of rum—earned it by Christian humility. For nearly a month I've lowered myself to the beasts of the field, and gone about on all fours like a teetotaler. Hump, circulate the bottle—I mean the cask—and let us have some of this poetry you're so keen about. Each poem must have the same title, you know; it's a rattling good title. It's called "An Inquiry into the Causes geological, historical, agricultural, psychological, psychical, moral, spiritual and theological of the alleged cases of double, treble, quadruple and other curvature in the English Road, conducted by a specially appointed secret commission in a hole in a tree, by admittedly judicious and academic authorities specially appointed by themselves to report to the Dog Quoodle, having power to add to their number and also to take away the number they first thought of; God save the King." Having delivered this formula with blinding rapidity, he added rather breathlessly, "that's the note to strike, the lyric note."

For all his rather formless hilarity, Dalroy still impressed the poet as being more *distrait* than the others, as if his mind were labouring with some bigger thing in the background. He was in a sort of creative trance; and Humphrey Pump, who knew him like his own soul, knew well that it was not mere literary creation. Rather it was a kind of creation which many modern moralists would call destruction. For Patrick Dalroy was, not a little to his misfortune, what is called a man of action; as Captain Dawson realised when he found his entire person a bright pea-green. Fond as he was of jokes and rhymes, nothing he could write or even sing ever satisfied him like something he could do.

Thus it happened that his contribution to the metrical inquiry into the crooked roads was avowedly hasty and flippant. While Dorian who was of the opposite temper, the temper that receives impressions instead of pushing out to make them, found his artist's love of beauty fulfilled as it had never been before in that noble nest; and was far more serious and human than usual. Patrick's verses ran:

"Some say that Guy of Warwick,
The man that killed the Cow,
And brake the mighty Boar alive,
Beyond the Bridge at Slough,
Went up against a Loathly Worm
That wasted all the Downs,
And so the roads they twist and squirm
(If I may be allowed the term)
From the writhing of the stricken Worm
That died in seven towns.
I see no scientific proof
That this idea is sound,
And I should say they wound about
To find the town of Roundabout,
The merry town of Roundabout
That makes the world go round.

"Some say that Robin Goodfellow,
Whose lantern lights the meads,
(To steal a phrase Sir Walter Scott
In heaven no longer needs)
Such dance around the trysting-place
The moonstruck lover leads;
Which superstition I should scout;
There is more faith in honest doubt,
(As Tennyson has pointed out)
Than in those nasty creeds.
But peace and righteousness (St. John)
In Roundabout can kiss,
And since that's all that's found about
The pleasant town of Roundabout,
The roads they simply bound about
To find out where it is.

"Some say that when Sir Lancelot
Went forth to find the Grail,
Grey Merlin wrinkled up the roads
For hope that he should fail;
All roads led back to Lyonesse

> *And Camelot in the Vale;*
> *I cannot yield assent to this*
> *Extravagant hypothesis,*
> *The plain, shrewd Briton will dismiss*
> *Such rumours (Daily Mail).*
> *But in the streets of Roundabout*
> *Are no such factions found,*
> *Or theories to expound about*
> *Or roll upon the ground about,*
> *In the happy town of Roundabout*
> *That makes the world go round."*

Patrick Dalroy relieved his feelings by finishing with a shout, draining a stiff glass of his sailor's wine, turning restlessly on his elbow and looking across the landscape toward London.

Dorian Wimpole had been drinking golden rum and strong starlight and the fragrance of forests; and, though his verses, too, were burlesque, he read them more emotionally than was his wont.

> *"Before the Roman came to Rye or out to Severn strode,*
> *The rolling English drunkard made the rolling English road.*
> *A reeling road, a rolling road, that rambles round the shire,*
> *And after him the parson ran, the sexton and the squire.*
> *A merry road, a mazy road, and such as we did tread*
> *That night we went to Birmingham by way of Beachy Head.*
>
> *"I knew no harm of Bonaparte and plenty of the Squire,*
> *And for to fight the Frenchmen I did not much desire;*
> *But I did bash their baggonets because they came arrayed*
> *To straighten out the crooked road an English drunkard made,*
> *Where you and I went down the lane with ale-mugs in our hands*
> *The night we went to Glastonbury by way of Goodwin Sands.*
>
> *"His sins they were forgiven him; or why do flowers run*
> *Behind him; and the hedges all strengthening in the sun?*
> *The wild thing went from left to right and knew not which was which,*
> *But the wild rose was above him when they found him in the ditch.*
> *God pardon us, nor harden us; we did not see so clear*
> *The night we went to Bannockburn by way of Brighton Pier.*

> "My friends, we will not go again or ape an ancient rage,
> Or stretch the folly of our youth to be the shame of age,
> But walk with clearer eyes and ears this path that wandereth,
> And see undrugged in evening light the decent inn of death;
> For there is good news yet to hear and fine things to be seen
> Before we go to Paradise by way of Kensal Green."

"Have you written one, Hump?" asked Dalroy. Humphrey, who had been scribbling hard under the lamp, looked up with a dismal face.

"Yes," he said. "But I write under a great disadvantage. You see, I know why the road curves about." And he read very rapidly, all on one note:

> "The road turned first toward the left
> Where Pinker's quarry made the cleft;
> The path turned next toward the right
> Because the mastiff used to bite;
> Then left, because of Slippery Height,
> And then again toward the right.
> We could not take the left because
> It would have been against the laws;
> Squire closed it in King William's day
> Because it was a Right of Way.
> Still right; to dodge the ridge of chalk
> Where Parson's Ghost it used to walk,
> Till someone Parson used to know
> Met him blind drunk in Callao.
> Then left, a long way round, to skirt
> The good land where old Doggy Burt
> Was owner of the Crown and Cup,
> And would not give his freehold up;
> Right, missing the old river-bed,
> They tried to make him take instead
> Right, since they say Sir Gregory
> Went mad and let the Gypsies be,
> And so they have their camp secure.
> And, though not honest, they are poor,
> And that is something; then along
> And first to right—no, I am wrong!

Second to right, of course; the first
Is what the holy sisters cursed,
And none defy their awful oaths
Since the policeman lost his clothes
Because of fairies; right again,
What used to be High Toby Lane,
Left by the double larch and right
Until the milestone is in sight,
Because the road is firm and good
From past the milestone to the wood;
And I was told by Dr. Lowe
Whom Mr. Wimpole's aunt would know,
Who lives at Oxford writing books,
And ain't so silly as he looks;
The Romans did that little bit
And we've done all the rest of it;
By which we hardly seem to score;
Left, and then forward as before
To where they nearly hanged Miss Browne,
Who told them not to cut her down,
But loose the rope or let her swing,
Because it was a waste of string;
Left once again by Hunker's Cleft,
And right beyond the elm, and left,
By Pill's right by Nineteen Nicks
And left—"

"No! No! No! Hump! Hump! Hump!" cried Dalroy in a sort of terror. "Don't be exhaustive! Don't be a scientist, Hump, and lay waste fairyland! How long does it go on? Is there a lot more of it?"

"Yes," said Pump, in a stony manner. "There is a lot more of it."

"And it's all true?" inquired Dorian Wimpole, with interest.

"Yes," replied Pump with a smile, "it's all true."

"My complaint, exactly," said the Captain. "What you want is legends. What you want is lies, especially at this time of night, and on rum like this, and on our first and our last holiday. What do you think about rum?" he asked Wimpole.

"About this particular rum, in this particular tree, at this particular moment," answered Wimpole, "I think it is the nectar of the younger gods. If you ask me in a general, synthetic sense what I think of rum—well, I think it's rather rum."

"You find it a trifle sweet, I suppose," said Dalroy, with some bitterness. "Sybarite! By the way," he said abruptly, "what a silly word that word 'Hedonist' is! The really self-indulgent people generally like sour things and not sweet; bitter things like caviare and curries or what not. It's the Saints who like the sweets. At least I've known at least five women who were practically saints, and they all preferred sweet champagne. Look here, Wimpole! Shall I tell you the ancient oral legend about the origin of rum? I told you what you wanted was legends. Be careful to preserve this one, and hand it on to your children; for, unfortunately, my parents carelessly neglected the duty of handing it on to me. After the words 'A Farmer had three sons. . .' all that I owe to tradition ceases. But when the three boys last met in the village market-place, they were all sucking sugar-sticks. Nevertheless, they were all discontented, and on that day parted for ever. One remained on his father's farm, hungering for his inheritance. One went up to London to seek his fortune, as fortunes are found today in that town forgotten of God. The third ran away to sea. And the first two flung away their sugar-sticks in shame; and he on the farm was always drinking smaller and sourer beer for the love of money; and he that was in town was always drinking richer and richer wines, that men might see that he was rich. But he who ran away to sea actually ran on board with the sugar-stick in his mouth; and St. Peter or St. Andrew, or whoever is the patron of men in boats, touched it and turned it into a fountain for the comfort of men upon the sea. That is the sailor's theory of the origin of rum. Inquiry addressed to any busy Captain with a new crew in the act of shipping an unprecedented cargo, will elicit a sympathetic agreement."

"Your rum at least," said Dorian, good-humouredly, "may well produce a fairy-tale. But, indeed, I think all this would have been a fairy-tale without it."

Patrick raised himself from his arboreal throne, and leaned against his branch with a curious and sincere sense of being rebuked.

"Yours was a good poem," he said, with seeming irrelevance, "and mine was a bad one. Mine was bad, partly because I'm not a poet as you are; but almost as much because I was trying to make up another song at the same time. And it went to another tune, you see."

He looked out over the rolling roads and said almost to himself:

"In the city set upon slime and loam
They cry in their parliament 'Who goes home?'
And there is no answer in arch or dome,
For none in the city of graves goes home.
Yet these shall perish and understand,
For God has pity on this great land.
Men that are men again; who goes home?
Tocsin and trumpeter! Who goes home?
For there's blood on the field and blood on the foam,
And blood on the body when man goes home.
And a voice valedictory—Who is for Victory?
Who is for Liberty? Who goes home?"

Softly and idly as he had said this second rhyme, there were circumstances about his attitude that must have troubled or interested anyone who did not know him well.

"May I ask," asked Dorian, laughing, "why it is necessary to draw your sword at this stage of the affair?"

"Because we have left the place called Roundabout," answered Patrick, "and we have come to a place called Rightabout."

And he lifted his sword toward London, and the grey glint upon it came from a low, grey light in the east.

XXII

THE CHEMISTRY OF MR. CROOKE

When the celebrated Hibbs next visited the shop of Crooke, that mystic and criminologist chemist, he found the premises were impressively and even amazingly enlarged with decorations in the eastern style. Indeed, it would not have been too much to say that Mr. Crooke's shop occupied the whole of one side of a showy street in the West End; the other side being a blank façade of public buildings. It would be no exaggeration to say that Mr. Crooke was the only shopkeeper for some distance round. Mr. Crooke still served in his shop, however; and politely hastened to serve his customer with the medicine that was customary. Unfortunately, for some reason or other, history was, in connection with this shop, only too prone to repeat itself. And after a vague but soothing conversation with the chemist (on the subject of vitriol and its effects on human happiness), Mr. Hibbs experienced the acute annoyance of once more beholding his most intimate friend, Mr. Joseph Leveson, enter the same fashionable emporium. But, indeed, Leveson's own annoyance was much too acute for him to notice any on the part of Hibbs.

"Well," he said, stopping dead in the middle of the shop, "here is a fine confounded kettle of fish!"

It is one of the tragedies of the diplomatic that they are not allowed to admit either knowledge or ignorance; so Hibbs looked gloomily wise; and said, pursing his lips, "you mean the *general* situation."

"I mean the situation about this everlasting business of the inn-signs," said Leveson, impatiently. "Lord Ivywood went up specially, when his leg was really bad, to get it settled in the House in a small non-contentious bill, providing that the sign shouldn't be enough if the liquor hadn't been on the spot three days."

"Oh, but," said Hibbs, sinking his voice to a soft solemnity, as being one of the initiate, "a thing like *that* can be managed, don't you know."

"Of course it can," said the other, still with the same slightly irritable air. "It was. But it doesn't seem to occur to you, any more than it did to his lordship, that there is rather a weak point after all in this business of passing acts quietly because they're un-popular. Has it ever occurred to you that if a law is really kept too quiet to be opposed, it may also be kept too quiet to be obeyed. It's not so easy to hush it up from a big politician without running the risk of hushing it up even from a common policeman."

"But surely that can't happen, by the nature of things?"

"Can't it, by God," said J. Leveson, appealing to a less pantheistic authority.

He unfolded a number of papers from his pocket, chiefly cheap local newspapers, but some of them letters and telegrams.

"Listen to this!" he said. "A curious incident occurred in the village of Poltwell in Surrey yesterday morning. The baker's shop of Mr. Whiteman was suddenly besieged by a knot of the looser types of the locality, who appear to have demanded beer instead of bread; basing their claim on some ornamental object erected outside the shop; which object they asserted to be a sign-board within the meaning of the act. There, you see, they haven't even heard of the new act! What do you think of this, from the *Clapton Conservator*. 'The contempt of Socialists for the law was well illustrated yesterday, when a crowd, collected round some wooden ensign of Socialism set up before Mr. Dugdale's Drapery Stores, refused to disperse, though told that their action was contrary to the law. Eventually the malcontents joined the procession following the wooden emblem.' And what do you say to this? 'Stop-press news. A chemist in Pimlico has been invaded by a huge crowd, demanding beer; and asserting the provision of it to be among his duties. The chemist is, of course, well acquainted with his immunities in the matter, especially under the new act; but the old notion of the importance of the sign seems still to possess the populace and even, to a certain extent, to paralyze the police.' What do you say to that? Isn't it as plain as Monday morning that this Flying Inn has flown a day in front of us, as all such lies do?" There was a diplomatic silence.

"Well," asked the still angry Leveson of the still dubious Hibbs, "what do you make of all that?"

One ill-acquainted with that relativity essential to all modern minds, might possibly have fancied that Mr. Hibbs could not make much of it. However that may be, his explanations or incapacity for explanations, were soon tested with a fairly positive test. For Lord Ivywood actually walked into the shop of Mr. Crooke.

"Good day, gentlemen," he said, looking at them with an expression which they both thought baffling and even a little disconcerting.

G.K. CHESTERTON

"Good morning, Mr. Crooke. I have a celebrated visitor for you." And he introduced the smiling Misysra. The Prophet had fallen back on a comparatively quiet costume this morning, a mere matter of purple and orange or what not; but his aged face was now perennially festive.

"The Cause progresses," he said. "Everywhere the Cause progresses. You heard his lordship's beau-uti-ful speech?"

"I have heard many," said Hibbs, gracefully, "that can be so described."

"The Prophet means what I was saying about the Ballot Paper Amendment Act," said Ivywood, casually. "It seems to be the alphabet of statesmanship to recognise now that the great oriental British Empire has become one corporate whole with the occidental one. Look at our universities, with their Mohammedan students; soon they may be a majority. Now are we," he went on, still more quietly, "are we to rule this country under the forms of representative government? I do not pretend to believe in democracy, as you know, but I think it would be extremely unsettling and incalculable to destroy representative government. If we are to give Moslem Britain representative government, we must not make the mistake we made about the Hindoos and military organization—which led to the Mutiny. We must not ask them to make a cross on their ballot papers; for though it seems a small thing, it may offend them. So I brought in a little bill to make it optional between the old-fashioned cross and an upward curved mark that might stand for a crescent—and as it's rather easier to make, I believe it will be generally adopted."

"And so," said the radiant old Turk, "the little, light, easily made, curly mark is substituted for the hard, difficult, double-made, cutting both ways mark. It is the more good for hygi-e-ene. For you must know, and indeed our good and wise Chemist will tell you, that the Saracenic and the Arabian and the Turkish physicians were the first of all physicians; and taught all medicals to the barbarians of the Frankish territories. And many of the moost modern, the moost fashionable remedies, are thus of the oriental origin."

"Yes, that is quite true," said Crooke, in his rather cryptic and unsympathetic way, "the powder called Arenine, lately popularised by Mr. Boze, now Lord Helvellyn, who tried it first on birds, is made of plain desert sand. And what you see in prescriptions as *Cannabis Indiensis* is what our lively neighbours of Asia describe more energetically as bhang."

"And so-o—in the sa-ame way," said Misysra, making soothing passes with his brown hand like a mesmerist, "in the sa-ame way the making of the crescent is hy-gienic; the making of the cross is non-hygienic. The crescent was a little wave, as a leaf, as a little curling feather," and he waved his hand with real artistic enthusiasm toward the capering curves of the new Turkish decoration which Ivywood had made fashionable in many of the fashionable shops. "But when you make the cross you must make the one line *so-o*," and he swept the horizon with the brown hand, "and then you must go back and make the other line so-o," and he made an upward gesture suggestive of one constrained to lift a pine-tree. "And then you become very ill."

"As a matter of fact, Mr. Crooke," said Ivywood, in his polite manner, "I brought the Prophet here to consult you as the best authority on the very point you have just mentioned—the use of hashish or the hemp-plant. I have it on my conscience to decide whether these oriental stimulants or sedatives shall come under the general veto we are attempting to impose on the vulgar intoxicants. Of course one has heard of the horrible and voluptuous visions, and a kind of insanity attributed to the Assassins and the Old Man of the Mountain. But, on the one hand, we must clearly discount much for the illimitable pro-Christian bias with which the history of these eastern tribes is told in this country. Would you say the effect of hashish was extremely bad?" And he turned first to the Prophet.

"You will see mosques," said that seer with candour, "many mosques—more mosques—taller and taller mosques till they reach the moon and you hear a dreadful voice in the very high mosque calling the muezzin; and you will think it is Allah. Then you will see wives—many, many wives—more wives than you yet have. Then you will be rolled over and over in a great pink and purple sea—which is still wives. Then you will go to sleep. I have only done it once," he concluded mildly.

"And what do you think about hashish, Mr. Crooke?" asked Ivywood, thoughtfully.

"I think it's hemp at both ends," said the Chemist.

"I fear," said Lord Ivywood, "I don't quite understand you."

"A hempen drink, a murder, and a hempen rope. That's my experience in India," said Mr. Crooke.

"It is true," said Ivywood, yet more reflectively, "that the thing is not Moslem in any sense in its origin. There is that against the Assassins always. And, of course," he added, with a simplicity that had something noble about it, "their connection with St. Louis discredits them rather."

After a space of silence, he said suddenly, looking at Crooke, "So it isn't the sort of thing you chiefly sell?"

"No, my lord, it isn't what I chiefly sell," said the Chemist. He also looked steadily, and the wrinkles of his young-old face were like hieroglyphics.

"The Cause progress! Everywhere it progress!" cried Misysra, spreading his arms and relieving a momentary tension of which he was totally unaware. "The hygienic curve of the crescent will soon superimpose himself for your plus sign. You already use him for the short syllables in your dactyl; which is doubtless of oriental origin. You see the new game?"

He said this so suddenly that everyone turned round, to see him produce from his purple clothing a brightly coloured and highly polished apparatus from one of the grand toy-shops; which, on examination, seemed to consist of a kind of blue slate in a red and yellow frame; a number of divisions being already marked on the slate, about seventeen slate pencils with covers of different colours, and a vast number of printed instructions, stating that it was but recently introduced from the remote East, and was called Naughts and Crescents.

Strangely enough, Lord Ivywood, with all his enthusiasm, seemed almost annoyed at the emergence of this Asiatic discovery; more especially as he really wanted to look at Mr. Crooke, as hard as Mr. Crooke was looking at him.

Hibbs coughed considerately and said, "Of course all our things came from the East, and"—and he paused, being suddenly unable to remember anything but curry; to which he was very rightly attached. He then remembered Christianity, and mentioned that too. "Everything from the East is good, of course," he ended, with an air of light omniscience.

Those who in later ages and other fashions failed to understand how Misysra had ever got a mental hold on men like Lord Ivywood, left out two elements in the man, which are very attractive, especially to other men. One was that there was *no* subject on which the little Turk could not instantly produce a theory. The other was that though the theories were crowded, they were consistent. He was never known to accept an illogical compliment.

"You are in error," he said, solemnly, to Hibbs, "because you say all things from the East are good. There is the east wind. I do not like him. He is not good. And I think very much that all the warmth and all the wealthiness and the colours and the poems and the religiousness that the East was meant to give you have been much poisoned by this accident, this east wind. When you see the green flag of the Prophet, you do not think of a green field in Summer, you think of a green wave in your seas of Winter; for you think it blown by the east wind. When you read of the moon-faced houris you think not of our moons like oranges but of your moons like snowballs—"

Here a new voice contributed to the conversation. Its contribution, though imperfectly understood, appeared to be "Nar! Why sh'd I wite for a little Jew in 'is dressin' gown? Little Jews in their dressin' gowns 'as their drinks, and we 'as our drinks. Bitter, miss."

The speaker, who appeared to be a powerful person of the plastering occupation, looked round for the unmarried female he had ceremonially addressed; and seemed honestly abashed that she was not present.

Ivywood looked at the man with that expression of one turned to stone, which his physique made so effective in him. But J. Leveson, Secretary, could summon no such powers of self-petrification. Upon his soul the slaughter red of that unhallowed eve arose when first the Ship and he were foes; when he discovered that the poor are human beings, and therefore are polite and brutal within a comparatively short space of time. He saw that two other men were standing behind the plastering person, one of them apparently urging him to counsels of moderation; which was an ominous sign. And then he lifted his eyes and saw something worse than any omen.

All the glass frontage of the shop was a cloud of crowding faces. They could not be clearly seen, since night was closing in on the street; and the dazzling fires of ruby and amethyst which the lighted shop gave to its great globes of liquid, rather veiled than revealed them. But the foremost actually flattened and whitened their noses on the glass, and the most distant were nearer than Mr. Leveson wanted them. Also he saw a shape erect outside the shop; the shape of an upright staff and a square board. He could not see what was on the board. He did not need to see.

Those who saw Lord Ivywood at such moments understood why he stood out so strongly in the history of his time, in spite of his frozen face and his fanciful dogmas. He had all the negative nobility that is possible to man. Unlike Nelson and most of the great heroes, he knew not fear. Thus he was never conquered by a surprise, but was cold and collected when other men had lost their heads even if they had not lost their nerve.

"I will not conceal from you, gentlemen," said Lord Ivywood, "that I have been expecting this. I will not even conceal from you that

I have been occupying Mr. Crooke's time until it occurred. So far from excluding the crowd, I suggest it would be an excellent thing if Mr. Crooke could accommodate them all in this shop. I want to tell, as soon as possible, as large a crowd as possible that the law is altered and this folly about the Flying Inn has ceased. Come in, all of you! Come in and listen!"

"Thank yer," said a man connected in some way with motor buses, who lurched in behind the plasterer.

"Thanky, sir," said a bright little clock-mender from Croydon, who immediately followed him.

"Thanks," said a rather bewildered clerk from Camberwell, who came next in the rather bewildered procession.

"Thank you," said Mr. Dorian Wimpole, who entered, carrying a large round cheese.

"Thank you," said Captain Dalroy, who entered carrying a large cask of rum.

"Thank you very much," said Mr. Humphrey Pump, who entered the shop carrying the sign of "The Old Ship."

I fear it must be recorded that the crowd which followed them dispensed with all expressions of gratitude. But though the crowd filled the shop so that there was no standing room to spare, Leveson still lifted his gloomy eyes and beheld his gloomy omen. For, though there were very many more people standing in the shop, there seemed to be no less people looking in at the window.

"Gentlemen," said Ivywood, "all jokes come to an end. This one has gone so far as to be serious; and it might have become impossible to correct public opinion, and expound to law-abiding citizens the true state of the law, had I not been able to meet so representative an assembly in so central a place. It is not pertinent to my purpose to indicate what I think of the jest which Captain Dalroy and his friends have been playing upon you for the last few weeks. But I think Captain Dalroy will himself concede that I am not jesting."

"With all my heart," said Dalroy, in a manner that was unusually serious and even sad. Then he added with a sigh, "And as you truly say, my jest has come to an end."

"That wooden sign," said Ivywood, pointing at the queer blue ship, "can be cut up for firewood. It shall lead decent citizens a devil's dance no more. Understand it once and for all, before you learn it from policemen or prison warders. You are under a new law. That sign is the sign of nothing. You can no more buy and sell alcohol by having that outside your house, than if it were a lamp-post."

"D'you meanter say, guv'ner," said the plasterer, with a dawn of intelligence on his large face which was almost awful to watch, "that I ain't to 'ave a glass o' bitter?"

"Try a glass of rum," said Patrick.

"Captain Dalroy," said Lord Ivywood, "if you give one drop from that cask to that man, you are breaking the law and you shall sleep in jail."

"Are you quite sure?" asked Dalroy, with a strange sort of anxiety. "I might escape."

"I am quite sure," said Ivywood. "I have posted the police with full powers for the purpose, as you will find. I mean that this business shall end here tonight."

"If I find that pleeceman what told me I could 'ave a drink just now, I'll knock 'is 'elmet into a fancy necktie, I will," said the plasterer. "Why ain't people allowed to know the law?"

"They ain't got no right to alter the law in the dark like that," said the clock-mender. "Damn the new law."

"What is the new law?" asked the clerk.

"The words inserted by the recent Act," said Lord Ivywood, with the cold courtesy of the Conqueror, "are to the effect that alcohol cannot be sold, even under a lawful sign, unless alcoholic liquors have been kept for three days on the premises. Captain Dalroy, that cask of yours has not, I think, been three days on these premises. I command you to seal it up and take it away."

"Surely," said Patrick, with an innocent air, "the best remedy would be to wait till it *has been three days* on the premises. We might all get to know each other better." And he looked round at the ever-increasing multitude with hazy benevolence.

"You shall do nothing of the kind," said his lordship, with sudden fierceness.

"Well," answered Patrick, wearily, "now I come to think of it, perhaps I won't. I'll have one drink here and go home to bed like a good little boy."

"And the constables shall arrest you," thundered Ivywood.

"Why, nothing seems to suit you," said the surprised Dalroy. "Thank you, however, for explaining the new law so clearly—'unless alcoholic liquors have been three days on the premises' I shall remember it now. You always explain such things so clearly. You only made one legal slip. The constables will not arrest me."

"And why not?" demanded the nobleman, white with passion.

"Because," cried Patrick Dalroy; and his voice lifted itself like a lonely trumpet before the charge, "because I shall not have broken the law. Because alcoholic liquors *have* been three days on these premises. Three months more likely. Because this is a common grog-shop, Phillip Ivywood. Because that man behind the counter lives by selling spirits to all the cowards and hypocrites who are rich enough to bribe a bad doctor."

And he pointed suddenly at the small medicine glass on the counter by Hibbs and Leveson.

"What is that man drinking?" he demanded.

Hibbs put out his hand hastily for his glass, but the indignant clock-mender had snatched it first and drained it at a gulp.

"Scortch," he said, and dashed the glass to atoms on the floor. "Right you are too," roared the plasterer, seizing a big medicine bottle in each hand. "We're goin' to 'ave a little of the fun now, we are. What's in that big red bowl up there—I reckon it's port. Fetch it down, Bill."

Ivywood turned to Crooke and said, scarcely moving his lips of marble, "This is a lie."

"It is the truth," answered Crooke, looking back at him with equal steadiness. "Do you think you made the world, that you should make it over again so easily?"

"The world was made badly," said Phillip, with a terrible note in his voice, "and *I will make it over again.*"

Almost as he spoke the glass front of the shop fell inward, shattered, and there was wreckage among the moonlike, coloured bowls; almost as if spheres of celestial crystal cracked at his blasphemy. Through the broken windows came the roar of that confused tongue that is more terrible than the elements; the cry that the deaf kings have heard at last; the terrible voice of mankind. All the way down the long, fashionable street, lined with the Crooke plate-glass, that glass was crashing amid the cries of a crowd. Rivers of gold and purple wines sprawled about the pavement.

"Out in the open!" shouted Dalroy, rushing out of the shop, sign-board in hand, the dog Quoodle barking furiously at his heels, while Dorian with the cheese and Humphrey with the keg followed as rapidly as they could. "Goodnight, my lord.

"Perhaps our meeting next may fall,
At Tomworth in your castle hall.

Come along, friends, and form up. Don't waste time destroying property. We're all to start now."

"Where are we all going to?" asked the plasterer.

"We're all going into Parliament," answered the Captain, as he went to the head of the crowd.

The marching crowd turned two or three corners, and at the end of the next long street, Dorian Wimpole, who was toward the tail of the procession, saw again the grey Cyclops tower of St. Stephens, with its one great golden eye, as he had seen it against that pale green sunset that was at once quiet and volcanic on the night he was betrayed by sleep and by a friend. Almost as far off, at the head of the procession, he could see the sign with the ship and the cross going before them like an ensign, and hear a great voice singing—

> *"Men that are men again, Who goes home?*
> *Tocsin and trumpeter! Who goes home?*
> *The voice valedictory—who is for Victory?*
> *Who is for Liberty? Who goes home?"*

XXIII

THE MARCH ON IVYWOOD

That storm-spirit, or eagle of liberty, which is the sudden soul in a crowd, had descended upon London after a foreign tour of some centuries in which it had commonly alighted upon other capitals. It is always impossible to define the instant and the turn of mood which makes the whole difference between danger being worse than endurance and endurance being worse than danger. The actual outbreak generally has a symbolic or artistic, or, what some would call whimsical cause. Somebody fires off a pistol or appears in an unpopular uniform, or refers in a loud voice to a scandal that is never mentioned in the newspapers; somebody takes off his hat, or somebody doesn't take off his hat; and a city is sacked before midnight. When the ever-swelling army of revolt smashed a whole street full of the shops of Mr. Crooke, the chemist, and then went on to Parliament, the Tower of London and the road to the sea, the sociologists hiding in their coal-cellars could think (in that clarifying darkness) of many material and spiritual explanations of such a storm in human souls; but of none that explained it quite enough. Doubtless there was a great deal of sheer drunkenness when the urns and goblets of Æsculapius were reclaimed as belonging to Bacchus: and many who went roaring down that road were merely stored with rich wines and liqueurs which are more comfortably and quietly digested at a City banquet or a West End restaurant. But many of these had been blind drunk twenty times without a thought of rebellion; you could not stretch the material explanation to cover a corner of the case. Much more general was a savage sense of the meanness of Crooke's wealthy patrons, in keeping a door open for themselves which they had wantonly shut on less happy people. But no explanation can explain it; and no man can say when it will come.

Dorian Wimpole was at the tail of the procession, which grew more and more crowded every moment. For one space of the march he even had the misfortune to lose it altogether; owing to the startling activity which the rotund cheese when it escaped from his hands showed, in descending a somewhat steep road toward the river. But in recent days he had gained a pleasure in practical events which was like a second youth. He managed to find a stray taxi-cab; and had little difficulty in picking up again the trail of the extraordinary cortège. Inquiries addressed to a policeman with a black eye outside the House of Commons informed him sufficiently of the rebels' line of retreat or advance, or whatever it was; and in a very short time he beheld the unmistakable legion once more. It was unmistakable, because in front of it there walked a red-headed giant, apparently carrying with him a wooden portion of some public building; and also because so big a crowd had never followed any man in England for a long time past. But except for such things the unmistakable crowd might well have been mistaken for another one. Its aspect had been altered almost as much as if it had grown horns or tusks; for many of the company walked with outlandish weapons like iron teeth or horns, bills and pole axes, and spears with strangely shaped heads. What was stranger still, whole rows and rows of them had rifles, and even marched with a certain discipline; and yet again, others seemed to have snatched up household or workshop tools, meat axes, pick axes, hammers and even carving knives. Such things need be none the less deadly because they are domestic. They have figured in millions of private murders before they appeared in any public war.

Dorian was so fortunate as to meet the flame-haired Captain almost face to face, and easily fell into step with him at the head of the march. Humphrey Pump walked on the other side, with the celebrated cask suspended round his neck by something resembling braces, as if it were a drum. Mr. Wimpole had himself taken the opportunity of his brief estrangement to carry the cheese somewhat more easily in a very large, loose, waterproof knapsack on his shoulders. The effect in both cases was to suggest dreadful deformities in two persons who happened to be exceptionally cleanly built. The Captain, who seemed to be in tearing and towering spirits, gained great pleasure from this. But Dorian had his sources of amusement too.

"What have you been doing with yourselves since you lost my judicious guidance?" he asked, laughing, "and why are parts of you a dull review and parts of you a fancy dress ball? What have you been up to?"

"We've been shopping," said Mr. Patrick Dalroy, with some pride. "We are country cousins. I know all about shopping; let us see, what are the phrases about it? Look at those rifles now! We got them quite at a bargain. We went to all the best gunsmiths in London, and we didn't pay much. In fact, we didn't pay anything. That's what is called a bargain, isn't it? Surely, I've seen in those things they send to ladies something about 'giving them away.' Then we went to a remnant sale. At least, it was a remnant sale when we left. And we bought that piece of stuff we've tied round the sign. Surely, it must be what ladies called chiffon?"

Dorian lifted his eyes and perceived that a very coarse strip of red rag, possibly collected from a dustbin, had been tied round the wooden sign-post by way of a red flag of revolution.

"Not what ladies call chiffon?" inquired the Captain with anxiety. "Well, anyhow, it is what *chiffoniers* call it. But as I'm going to call on a lady shortly, I'll try to remember the distinction."

"Is your shopping over, may I ask?" asked Mr. Wimpole.

"All but one thing," answered the other. "I must find a music shop—you know what I mean. Place where they sell pianos and things of that sort."

"Look here," said Dorian, "this cheese is pretty heavy as it is. Have I got to carry a piano, too?"

"You misunderstand me," said the Captain, calmly. And as he had never thought of music shops until his eye had caught one an instant before, he darted into the doorway. Returning almost immediately with a long parcel under his arm, he resumed the conversation.

"Did you go anywhere else," asked Dorian, "except to shops?"

"Anywhere else!" cried Patrick, indignantly, "haven't you got any country cousins? Of course we went to all the right places. We went to the Houses of Parliament. But Parliament isn't sitting; so there are no eggs of the quality suitable for elections. We went to the Tower of London—you can't tire country cousins like us. We took away some curiosities of steel and iron. We even took away the halberds from the Beef-eaters. We pointed out that for the purpose of eating beef (their only avowed public object) knives and forks had always been found more convenient. To tell the truth, they seemed rather relieved to be relieved of them."

"And may I ask," said the other with a smile, "where you are off to now?"

"Another beauty spot!" cried the Captain, boisterously, "no tiring the country cousin! I am going to show my young friends from the provinces what is perhaps the finest old country house in England. We are going to Ivywood, not far from that big watering place they call Pebblewick."

"I see," said Dorian; and for the first time looked back with intelligent trouble on his face, on the marching ranks behind him.

"Captain Dalroy," said Dorian Wimpole, in a slightly altered tone, "there is one thing that puzzles me. Ivywood talked about having set the police to catch us; and though this is a pretty big crowd, I simply cannot believe that the police, as I knew them in my youth, could not catch us. But where are the police? You seem to have marched through half London with much (if you'll excuse me) of the appearance of carrying murderous weapons. Lord Ivywood threatened that the police would stop us. Well, why didn't they stop us?"

"Your subject," said Patrick, cheerfully, "divides itself into three heads."

"I hope not," said Dorian.

"There really are three reasons why the police should not be prominent in this business; as their worst enemy cannot say that they were."

He began ticking off the three on his own huge fingers; and seemed to be quite serious about it.

"First," he said, "you have been a long time away from town. Probably you do not know a policeman when you see him. They do not wear helmets, as our line regiments did after the Prussians had won. They wear fezzes, because the Turks have won. Shortly, I have little doubt, they will wear pigtails, because the Chinese have won. It is a very interesting branch of moral science. It is called Efficiency.

"Second," explained the Captain, "you have, perhaps, omitted to notice that a very considerable number of those wearing such fezzes are walking just behind us. Oh, yes, it's quite true. Don't you remember that the whole French Revolution really began because a sort of City Militia refused to fire on their own fathers and wives; and even showed some slight traces of a taste for firing on the other side? You'll see lots of them behind; and you can tell them by their revolver belts and their walking in step; but don't look back on them too much. It makes them nervous."

"And the third reason?" asked Dorian.

"For the real reason," answered Patrick, "I am not fighting a hopeless fight. People who have fought in real fights don't, as a rule. But I noticed something singular about the very point you mention. Why are there no more police? Why are there no more soldiers? I will tell you. There really are very few policemen or soldiers left in England today."

"Surely, that," said Wimpole, "is an unusual complaint."

"But very clear," said the Captain, gravely, "to anyone who has ever seen sailors or soldiers. I will tell you the truth. Our rulers have come to count on the bare bodily cowardice of a mass of Englishmen, as a sheep dog counts on the cowardice of a flock of sheep. Now, look here, Mr. Wimpole, wouldn't a shepherd be wise to limit the number of his dogs if he could make his sheep pay by it? At the end you might find millions of sheep managed by a solitary dog. But that is because they are sheep. Suppose the sheep were turned by a miracle into wolves. There are very few dogs they could not tear in pieces. But, what is my practical point, there are really very few dogs to tear."

"You don't mean," said Dorian, "that the British Army is practically disbanded?"

"There are the sentinels outside Whitehall," replied Patrick, in a low voice. "But, indeed, your question puts me in a difficulty. No; the army is not entirely disbanded, of course. But the *British* army—. Did you ever hear, Wimpole, of the great destiny of the Empire?"

"I seem to have heard the phrase," replied his companion.

"It is in four acts," said Dalroy. "Victory over barbarians. Employment of barbarians. Alliance with barbarians. Conquest by barbarians. That is the great destiny of Empire."

"I think I begin to see what you mean," returned Dorian Wimpole. "Of course Ivywood and the authorities do seem very prone to rely on the sepoy troops."

"And other troops as well," said Patrick. "I think you will be surprised when you see them."

He tramped on for a while in silence and then said, with some air of abruptness, which yet did not seem to be entirely a changing of the subject,

"Do you know the man who lives now on the estate next to Ivywood?"

"No," replied Dorian, "I am told he keeps himself very much to himself."

"And his estate, too," said Patrick, rather gloomily. "If you would climb his garden-wall, Wimpole, I think you would find an answer to a good many of your questions. Oh, yes, the right honourable gentlemen are making full provision for public order and national defence—in a way."

He fell into an almost sullen silence again; and several villages had been passed before he spoke again.

They tramped through the darkness; and dawn surprised them somewhere in the wilder and more wooded parts where the roads began to rise and roam. Dalroy gave an exclamation of pleasure and pointed ahead, drawing the attention of Dorian to the distance. Against the silver and scarlet bars of the daybreak could be seen afar a dark purple dome, with a crown of dark green leaves; the place they had called Roundabout.

Dalroy's spirit seemed to revive at the sight, with the customary accompaniment of the threat of vocalism.

"Been making any poems lately?" he asked of Wimpole.

"Nothing particular," replied the poet.

"Then," said the Captain, portentously, clearing his throat, "you shall listen to one of mine, whether you like it or not—nay, the more you dislike it the longer and longer it will be. I begin to understand why soldiers want to sing when on the march; and also why they put up with such rotten songs.

> *"The Druids waved their golden knives*
> *And danced around the Oak,*
> *When they had sacrificed a man;*
> *But though the learnèd search and scan*
> *No single modern person can*
> *Entirely see the joke;*
> *But though they cut the throats of men*
> *They cut not down the tree,*
> *And from the blood the saplings sprang*
> *Of oak-woods yet to be.*
> *But Ivywood, Lord Ivywood,*
> *He rots the tree as ivy would,*
> *He clings and crawls as ivy would*
> *About the sacred tree.*
>
> *"King Charles he fled from Worcester fight*
> *And hid him in an Oak;*
> *In convent schools no man of tact*
> *Would trace and praise his every act,*
> *Or argue that he was in fact*
> *A strict and sainted bloke;*
> *But not by him the sacred woods*
> *Have lost their fancies free,*
> *And though he was extremely big,*
> *He did not break the tree.*
> *But Ivywood, Lord Ivywood,*
> *He breaks the tree as ivy would*

And eats the woods as ivy would
Between us and the sea.

"Great Collingwood walked down the glade
And flung the acorns free,
That oaks might still be in the grove
As oaken as the beams above
When the great Lover sailors love
Was kissed by Death at sea.
But though for him the oak-trees fell
To build the oaken ships,
The woodman worshipped what he smote
And honoured even the chips.
But Ivywood, Lord Ivywood,
He hates the tree as ivy would,
As the dragon of the ivy would,
That has us in his grips."

They were ascending a sloping road, walled in on both sides by solemn woods, which somehow seemed as watchful as owls awake. Though daybreak was going over them with banners, scrolls of scarlet and gold, and with a wind like trumpets of triumph, the dark woods seemed to hold their secret like dark, cool cellars; nor was the strong sunlight seen in them, save in one or two brilliant shafts, that looked like splintered emeralds.

"I should not wonder," said Dorian, "if the ivy does not find the tree knows a thing or two also."

"The tree does," assented the Captain. "The trouble was that until a little while ago the tree did not know that it knew."

There was a silence; and as they went up the incline grew steeper and steeper, and the tall trees seemed more and more to be guarding something from sight, as with the grey shields of giants.

"Do you remember this road, Hump?" asked Dalroy of the innkeeper.

"Yes," answered Humphrey Pump, and said no more; but few have ever heard such fulness in an affirmative.

They marched on in silence and about two hours afterward, toward eleven o'clock, Dalroy called a halt in the forest, and said that everybody had better have a few hours' sleep. The impenetrable quality in the woods and the comparative softness of the carpet of beech-mast, made the spot as appropriate as the time was inappropriate. And if anyone thinks that common people, casually picked up in a street, could not follow a random leader on such a journey or sleep at his command in such a spot, given the state of the soul, then someone knows no history.

"I'm afraid," said Dalroy, "you'll have to have your supper for breakfast. I know an excellent place for having breakfast, but it's too exposed for sleep. And sleep you must have; so we won't unpack the stores just now. We'll lie down like Babes in the Wood, and any bird of an industrious disposition is free to start covering me with leaves. Really, there are things coming, before which you will want sleep."

When they resumed the march it was nearly the middle of the afternoon; and the meal which Dalroy insisted buoyantly on describing as breakfast was taken about that mysterious hour when ladies die without tea. The steep road had consistently grown steeper and steeper; and steeper; and at last, Dalroy said to Dorian Wimpole,

"Don't drop that cheese again just here, or it will roll right away down into the woods. I know it will. No scientific calculations of grades and angles are necessary; because I have seen it do so myself. In fact, I have run after it."

Wimpole realised they were mounting to the sharp edge of a ridge, and in a few moments he knew by the oddness in the shape of the trees what it had been that the trees were hiding.

They had been walking along a swelling, woodland path beside the sea. On a particular high plateau, projecting above the shore, stood some dwarfed and crippled apple-trees, of whose apples no man alive would have eaten, so sour and salt they must be. All the rest of the plateau was bald and featureless, but Pump looked at every inch of it, as if at an inhabited place.

"This is where we'll have breakfast," he said, pointing to the naked grassy waste. "It's the best inn in England."

Some of his audience began to laugh, but somehow suddenly ceased doing so, as Dalroy strode forward and planted the sign of "The Old Ship" on the desolate sea-shore.

"And now," he said, "you have charge of the stores we brought, Hump, and we will picnic. As it said in a song I once sang,

> *"The Saracen's Head out of Araby came,*
> *King Richard riding in arms like flame,*

And where he established his folk to be fed
He set up his spear, and the Saracen's Head."

It was nearly dusk before the mob, much swelled by the many discontented on the Ivywood estates, reached the gates of Ivywood House. Strategically, and for the purposes of a night surprise, this might have done credit to the Captain's military capacity. But the use to which he put it actually was what some might call eccentric. When he had disposed his forces, with strict injunctions of silence for the first few minutes, he turned to Pump, and said,

"And now, before we do anything else, I'm going to make a noise."

And he produced from under brown paper what appeared to be a musical instrument.

"A summons to parley?" inquired Dorian, with interest, "a trumpet of defiance, or something of that kind?"

"No," said Patrick, "a serenade."

XXIV

The Enigmas of Lady Joan

On an evening when the sky was clear and only its fringes embroidered with the purple arabesques of the sunset, Joan Brett was walking on the upper lawn of the terraced garden at Ivywood, where the peacocks trail themselves about. She was not unlike one of the peacocks herself in beauty, and some might have said, in inutility; she had the proud head and the sweeping train; nor was she, in these days, devoid of the occasional disposition to scream. For, indeed, for some time past she had felt her existence closing round her with an incomprehensible quietude; and that is harder for the patience than an incomprehensible noise. Whenever she looked at the old yew hedges of the garden they seemed to be higher than when she saw them last; as if those living walls could still grow to shut her in. Whenever from the turret windows she had a sight of the sea, it seemed to be farther away. Indeed, the whole closing of the end of the turret wing with the new wall of eastern woodwork seemed to symbolise all her shapeless sensations. In her childhood the wing had ended with a broken-down door and a disused staircase. They led to an uncultivated copse and an abandoned railway tunnel, to which neither she nor anyone else ever wanted to go. Still, she knew what they led to. Now it seemed that this scrap of land had been sold and added to the adjoining estate; and about the adjoining estate nobody seemed to know anything in particular. The sense of things closing in increased upon her. All sorts of silly little details magnified the sensation. She could discover nothing about this new landlord next door, so to speak, since he was, it seemed, an elderly man who preferred to live in the greatest privacy. Miss Browning, Lord Ivywood's secretary, could give her no further information than that he was a gentleman from the Mediterranean coast; which singular form of words seemed to have been put into her mouth. As a Mediterranean gentleman might mean anything from an American gentleman living in Venice to a black African on the edge of the Atlas, the description did not illuminate; and probably was not intended to do so. She occasionally saw his liveried servants going about; and their liveries were not like English liveries. She was also, in her somewhat morbid state, annoyed by the fact that the uniforms of the old Pebblewick militia had been changed, under the influence of the Turkish *prestige* in the recent war. They wore fezzes like the French Zouaves, which were certainly much more practical than the heavy helmets they used to wear. It was a small matter, but it annoyed Lady Joan, who was, like so many clever women, at once subtle and conservative. It made her feel as if the whole world was being altered outside, and she was not allowed to know about it.

But she had deeper spiritual troubles also, while, under the pathetic entreaties of old Lady Ivywood and her own sick mother, she stayed on week after week at Ivywood House. If the matter be stated cynically (as she herself was quite capable of stating it) she was engaged in the established feminine occupation of trying to like a man. But the cynicism would have been false; as cynicism nearly always is; for during the most crucial days of that period, she had really liked the man.

She had liked him when he was brought in with Pump's bullet in his leg; and was still the strongest and calmest man in the room. She had liked him when the hurt took a dangerous turn, and when he bore pain to admiration. She had liked him when he showed no malice against the angry Dorian; she had liked him with something like enthusiasm on the night he rose rigid on his rude crutch, and, crushing all remonstrance, made his rash and swift rush to London. But, despite the queer closing-in-sensations of which we have spoken, she never liked him better than that evening when he lifted himself laboriously on his crutch up the terraces of the old garden and came to speak to her as she stood among the peacocks. He even tried to pat a peacock in a hazy way, as if it were a dog. He told her that these beautiful birds were, of course, imported from the East—by the semi-eastern empire of Macedonia. But, all the same, Joan had a dim suspicion that he had never noticed before that there were any peacocks at Ivywood. His greatest fault was a pride in the faultlessness of his mental and moral strength; but, if he had only known, something faintly comic in the unconscious side of him did him more good with the woman than all the rest.

"They were said to be the birds of Juno," he said, "but I have little doubt that Juno, like so much else of the Homeric mythology, has also an Asiatic origin."

"I always thought," said Joan, "that Juno was rather too stately for the seraglio."

"You ought to know," replied Ivywood, with a courteous gesture, "for I *never* saw anyone who looked so like Juno as you do. But, indeed, there is a great deal of misunderstanding about the Arabian or Indian view of women. It is, somehow, too simple and solid for our paradoxical Christendom to comprehend. Even the vulgar joke against the Turks, that they like their brides fat, has in it a sort of distorted shadow of what I mean. They do not look so much at the individual, as at Womanhood and the power of Nature."

"I sometimes think," said Joan, "that these fascinating theories are a little strained. Your friend Misysra told me the other day that women had the highest freedom in Turkey; as they were allowed to wear trousers."

Ivywood smiled his rare and dry smile. "The Prophet has something of a simplicity often found with genius," he answered. "I will not deny that some of the arguments he has employed have seemed to me crude and even fanciful. But he is right at the root. There is a kind of freedom that consists in never rebelling against Nature; and I think they understand it in the Orient better than we do in the West. You see, Joan, it is all very well to talk about love in our narrow, personal, romantic way; but there is something higher than the love of a lover or the love of love."

"What is that?" asked Joan, looking down.

"The love of Fate," said Lord Ivywood, with something like spiritual passion in his eyes. "Doesn't Nietzsche say somewhere that the delight in destiny is the mark of the hero? We are mistaken if we think that the heroes and saints of Islam say 'Kismet' with bowed heads and in sorrow. They say 'Kismet' with a shout of joy. That which is fitting—that is what they really mean. In the Arabian tales, the most perfect prince is wedded to the most perfect princess—because it is fitting. The spiritual giants, the Genii, achieve it—that is, the purposes of Nature. In the selfish, sentimental European novels, the loveliest princess on earth might have run away with her middle-aged drawing-master. These things are not in the Path. The Turk rides out to wed the fairest queen of the earth; he conquers empires to do it; and he is not ashamed of his laurels."

The crumpled violet clouds around the edge of the silver evening looked to Lady Joan more and more like vivid violet embroideries hemming some silver curtain in the closed corridor at Ivywood. The peacocks looked more lustrous and beautiful than they ever had before; but for the first time she really felt they came out of the land of the Arabian Nights.

"Joan," said Phillip Ivywood, very softly, in the twilight, "I am not ashamed of my laurels. I see no meaning in what these Christians call humility. I will be the greatest man in the world if I can; and I think I can. Therefore, something that is higher than love itself, Fate and what is fitting, make it right that I should wed the most beautiful woman in the world. And she stands among the peacocks and is more beautiful and more proud than they."

Joan's troubled eyes were on the violet horizon and her troubled lips could utter nothing but something like "don't."

"Joan," said Phillip, again, "I have told you, you are the woman one of the great heroes could have desired. Let me now tell you something I could have told no one to whom I had not thus spoken of love and betrothal. When I was twenty years old in a town in Germany, pursuing my education, I did what the West calls falling in love. She was a fisher-girl from the coast; for this town was near the sea. My story might have ended there. I could not have entered diplomacy with such a wife, but I should not have minded then. But a little while after, I wandered into the edges of Flanders, and found myself standing above some of the last grand reaches of the Rhine. And things came over me but for which I might be crying stinking fish to this day. I thought how many holy or lovely nooks that river had left behind, and gone on. It might anywhere in Switzerland have spent its weak youth in a spirit over a high crag, or anywhere in the Rhinelands lost itself in a marsh covered with flowers. But it went on to the perfect sea, which is the fulfilment of a river."

Again, Joan could not speak; and again it was Phillip who went on.

"Here is yet another thing that could not be said, till the hand of the prince had been offered to the princess. It may be that in the East they carry too far this matter of infant marriages. But look round on the mad young marriages that go to pieces everywhere! And ask yourself whether you don't wish they had been infant marriages! People talk in the newspapers of the heartlessness of royal marriages. But you and I do not believe the newspapers, I suppose. We know there is no King in England; nor has been since his head fell before Whitehall. You know that you and I and the families are the Kings of England; and our marriages are royal marriages. Let the suburbs call them heartless. Let us say they need the brave heart that is the only badge of aristocracy. Joan," he said, very gently, "perhaps you have been near a crag in Switzerland, or a marsh covered with flowers. Perhaps you have known—a fisher-girl. But there is something greater and simpler than all that; something you find in the great epics of the East—the beautiful woman, and the great man, and Fate."

"My lord," said Joan, using the formal phrase by an unfathomable instinct, "will you allow me a little more time to think of this? And let there be no notion of disloyalty, if my decision is one way or the other?"

"Why, of course," said Ivywood, bowing over his crutch; and he limped off, picking his way among the peacocks.

For days afterward Joan tried to build the foundations of her earthly destiny. She was still quite young, but she felt as if she had lived thousands of years, worrying over the same question. She told herself again and again, and truly, that many a better woman than she had taken a second-best which was not so first-class a second-best. But there was something complicated in the very atmosphere. She liked listening to Phillip Ivywood at his best, as anyone likes listening to a man who can really play the violin; but the great trouble always is that at certain awful moments you cannot be certain whether it is the violin or the man.

Moreover, there was a curious tone and spirit in the Ivywood household, especially after the wound and convalescence of Ivywood, about which she could say nothing except that it annoyed her somehow. There was something in it glorious—but also languorous. By an impulse by no means uncommon among intelligent, fashionable people, she felt a desire to talk to a sensible woman of the middle or lower classes; and almost threw herself on the bosom of Miss Browning for sympathy.

But Miss Browning, with her curling, reddish hair and white, very clever face, struck the same indescribable note. Lord Ivywood was assumed as a first principle; as if he were Father Time, or the Clerk of the Weather. He was called "He." The fifth time he was called "He," Joan could not understand why she seemed to smell the plants in the hot conservatory.

"You see," said Miss Browning, "we mustn't interfere with his career; that is the important thing. And, really, I think the quieter we keep about everything the better. I am sure he is maturing very big plans. You heard what the Prophet said the other night?"

"The last thing the Prophet said to me," said the darker lady, in a dogged manner, "was that when we English see the English youth, we cry out 'He is crescent!' But when we see the English aged man, we cry out 'He is cross!'"

A lady with so clever a face could not but laugh faintly; but she continued on a determined theme, "The Prophet said, you know, that all real love had in it an element of fate. And I am sure that is his view, too. People cluster round a centre as little stars do round a star; because a star is a magnet. You are never wrong when destiny blows behind you like a great big wind; and I think many things have been judged unfairly that way. It's all very well to talk about the infant marriages in India."

"Miss Browning," said Joan, "are you interested in the infant marriages in India?"

"Well—" said Miss Browning.

"Is your sister interested in them? I'll run and ask her," cried Joan, plunging across the room to where Mrs. Mackintosh was sitting at a table scribbling secretarial notes.

"Well," said Mrs. Mackintosh, turning up a rich-haired, resolute head, more handsome than her sister's, "I believe the Indian way is the best. When people are left to themselves in early youth, any of them might marry anything. We might have married a nigger or a fish-wife or—a criminal."

"Now, Mrs. Mackintosh," said Joan, with black-browed severity, "you well know you would never have married a fish-wife. Where is Enid?" she ended suddenly.

"Lady Enid," said Miss Browning, "is looking out music in the music room, I think."

Joan walked swiftly through several long salons, and found her fair-haired and pallid relative actually at the piano.

"Enid," cried Joan, "you know I've always been fond of you. For God's sake tell me what is the matter with this house? I admire Phillip as everybody does. But what is the matter with the house? Why do all these rooms and gardens seem to be shutting me in and in and in? Why does everything look more and more the same? Why does everybody say the same thing? Oh, I don't often talk metaphysics; but there is a purpose in this. That's the only way of putting it; there is a purpose. And I don't know what it is."

Lady Enid Wimpole played a preliminary bar or two on the piano. Then she said,

"Nor do I, Joan. I don't indeed. I know exactly what you mean. But it's just because there is a purpose that I have faith in him and trust him." She began softly to play a ballad tune of the Rhineland; and perhaps the music suggested her next remark. "Suppose you were looking at some of the last reaches of the Rhine, where it flows—"

"Enid!" cried Joan, "if you say 'into the North Sea,' I shall scream. Scream, do you hear, louder than all the peacocks together."

"Well," expostulated Lady Enid, looking up rather wildly, "The Rhine *does* flow into the North Sea, doesn't it?"

"I dare say," said Joan, recklessly, "but the Rhine might have flowed into the Round Pond, before you would have known or cared, until—"

"Until what?" asked Enid; and her music suddenly ceased. "Until something happened that I cannot understand," said Joan, moving away.

"*You* are something I cannot understand," said Enid Wimpole. "But I will play something else, if this annoys you." And she fingered the music again with an eye to choice.

Joan walked back through the corridor of the music room, and restlessly resumed her seat in the room with the two lady secretaries.

"Well," asked the red-haired and good-humoured Mrs. Mackintosh, without looking up from her work of scribbling, "have you discovered anything?"

For some moments Joan appeared to be in a blacker state of brooding than usual; then she said, in a candid and friendly tone, which somehow contrasted with her knit and swarthy brows—

"No, really. At least I think I've only found out two things; and they are only things about myself. I've discovered that I do like heroism, but I don't like hero worship."

"Surely," said Miss Browning, in the Girton manner, "the one always flows from the other."

"I hope not," said Joan.

"But what else can you do with the hero?" asked Mrs. Mackintosh, still without looking up from her writing, "except worship him?"

"You might crucify him," said Joan, with a sudden return of savage restlessness, as she rose from her chair. "Things seem to happen then."

"Aren't you tired?" asked the Miss Browning who had the clever face.

"Yes," said Joan, "and the worst sort of tiredness; when you don't even know what you're tired of. To tell the honest truth, I think I'm tired of this house."

"It's very old, of course, and parts of it are still dismal," said Miss Browning, "but he has enormously improved it. The decoration, with the moon and stars, down in the wing with the turret is really—"

Away in the distant music room, Lady Enid, having found the music she preferred, was fingering its prelude on the piano. At the first few notes of it, Joan Brett stood up, like a tigress.

"Thanks—" she said, with a hoarse softness, "that's it, of course! and that's just what we all are! She's found the right tune now."

"What tune is it?" asked the wondering secretary.

"The tune of harp, sackbut, psaltery, dulcimer and all kinds of music," said Joan, softly and fiercely, "when we shall bow down and worship the Golden Image that Nebuchadnezzar the King has set up. Girls! Women! Do you know what this place is? Do you know why it is all doors within doors and lattice behind lattice; and everything is curtained and cushioned; and why the flowers that are so fragrant here are not the flowers of our hills?"

From the distant and slowly darkening music room, Enid Wimpole's song came thin and clear:

> *"Less than the dust beneath thy chariot wheel,*
> *Less than the rust that never stained thy sword—"*

"Do you know what we are?" demanded Joan Brett, again. "We are a Harem."

"Why, what can you mean?" cried the younger girl, in great agitation. "Why, Lord Ivywood has never—"

"I know he has never. I am not sure," said Joan, "even whether he would ever. I shall never understand that man, nor will anybody else. But I tell you that is the spirit. That is what we *are*. And this room stinks of polygamy as certainly as it smells of tube-roses."

"Why, Joan," cried Lady Enid, entering the room like a well-bred ghost, "what on earth is the matter with you. You all look as white as sheets."

Joan took no heed of her but went on with her own obstinate argument.

"And, besides," she said, "if there's one thing we do know about him it is that he believes on principle in doing things slowly. He calls it evolution and relativity and the expanding of an idea into larger ideas. How do we know he isn't doing that slowly; getting us accustomed to living like this, so that it may be the less shock when he goes further—steeping us in the atmosphere before he actually introduces," and she shuddered, "the institution. Is it any more calmly outrageous a scheme than any other of Ivywood's schemes; than a sepoy commander-in-chief, or Misysra preaching in Westminster Abbey, or the destruction of all the inns in England? I will not wait and expand. I will not be evolved. I will not develop into something that is not me. My feet shall be outside these walls if I walk the roads for it afterward; or I will scream as I would scream trapped in any den by the Docks."

She swept down the rooms toward the turret, with a sudden passion for solitude; but as she passed the astronomical wood-carving that had closed up the end of the old wing, Enid saw her strike it with her clinched hand.

It was in the turret that she had a strange experience. She was again, later on, using its isolation to worry out the best way of having it out with Phillip, when he should return from his visit to London; for to tell old Lady Ivywood what was on her mind would be about as kind and useful as describing Chinese tortures to a baby. The evening was very quiet, of the pale grey sort, and all that side of Ivywood lay before her eyes, undisturbed. She was the more surprised when her dreaming took note of a sort of stirring in the grey-purple dusk of the bushes; of whisperings; and of many footsteps. Then the silence settled down again; and then it was startlingly broken by a big voice singing in the dark distance. It was accompanied by faint sounds that might have been from the fingering of some lute or viol:

> "Lady, the light is dying in the skies,
> Lady, and let us die when honour dies,
> Your dear, dropped glove was like a gauntlet flung,
> When you and I were young.
> For something more than splendour stood; and ease was not the only good
> About the woods in Ivywood when you and I were young.

> "Lady, the stars are falling pale and small,
> Lady, we will not live if life be all
> Forgetting those good stars in heaven hung
> When all the world was young,
> For more than gold was in a ring, and love was not a little thing
> Between the trees in Ivywood when all the world was young."

The singing ceased; and the bustle in the bushes could hardly be called more than a whisper. But sounds of the same sort and somewhat louder seemed wafted round corners from other sides of the house; and the whole night seemed full of something that was alive, but was more than a single man.

She heard a cry behind her, and Enid rushed into the room as white as one of the lilies.

"What awful thing is happening?" she cried. "The courtyard is full of men shouting, and there are torches everywhere and—"

Joan heard a tramp of men marching and heard, afar off, another song, sung on a more derisive note, something like—

> "But Ivywood, Lord Ivywood,
> He rots the tree as ivy would."

"I think," said Joan, thoughtfully, "it is the End of the World."

"But where are the police?" wailed her cousin. "They don't seem to be anywhere about since they wore those fezzes. We shall be murdered or—"

Three thundering and measured blows shook the decorative wood panelling at the end of the wing; as if admittance were demanded with the club of a giant. Enid remembered that she had thought Joan's little blow energetic, and shuddered. Both the girls stared at the stars and moons and suns blazoned on that sacred wall that leapt and shuddered under the strokes of the doom.

Then the sun fell from Heaven, and the moon and stars dropped down and were scattered about the Persian carpet; and by the opening of the end of the world, Patrick Dalroy came in, carrying a mandolin.

XXV

The Finding of the Superman

I've brought you a little dog," said Mr. Dalroy, introducing the rampant Quoodle. "I had him brought down here in a large hamper labelled 'Explosives,' a title which appears to have been well selected."

He had bowed to Lady Enid on entering and taken Joan's hand with the least suggestion that he wanted to do something else with it; but he resolutely resumed his conversation, which was on the subject of dogs.

"People who bring back dogs," he said, "are always under a cloud of suspicion. Sometimes it is hideously hinted that the citizen who brings the dog back with him is identical with the citizen who took the dog away with him. In my case, of course, such conduct is inconceivable. But the returners of dogs, that prosperous and increasing class, are also accused," he went on, looking straight at Joan, with blank blue eyes, "of coming back for a Reward. There is more truth in this charge."

Then, with a change of manner more extraordinary than any revolution, even the revolution that was roaring round the house, he took her hand again and kissed it, saying, with a confounding seriousness,

"I know at least that you will pray for my soul."

"You had better pray for mine, if I have one," answered Joan, "but why now?"

"Because," said Patrick, "you will hear from outside, you may even see from that turret window something which in brute fact has never been seen in England since Poor Monmouth's army went down. In spirit and in truth it has not happened since Saladin and Cœur de Lion crashed together. I only add one thing, and that you know already. I have lived loving you and I shall die loving you. It is the only dimension of the Universe in which I have not wandered and gone astray. I leave the dog to guard you;" and he disappeared down the old broken staircase.

Lady Enid was much mystified that no popular pursuit assailed this stair or invaded the house. But Lady Joan knew better. She had gone, on the suggestion she most cared about, into the turret room and looked out of its many windows on to the abandoned copse and tunnel, which were now fenced off with high walls, the boundary of the mysterious property next door. Across that high barrier she could not even see the tunnel, and barely the tops of the tallest trees which hid its entrance from sight. But in an instant she knew that Dalroy was not hurling his forces on Ivywood at all, but on the house and estate beyond it.

And then followed a sight that was not an experience but rather a revolving vision. She could never describe it afterward, nor could any of those involved in so violent and mystical a wheel. She had seen a huge wall of a breaker wash all over the parade at Pebblewick; and wondered that so huge a hammer could be made merely of water. She had never had a notion of what it is like when it is made of men.

The palisade, put up by the new landlord in front of the old tangled ground by the tunnel, she had long regarded as something as settled and ordinary as one of the walls of the drawing room. It swung and split and sprang into a thousand pieces under the mere blow of human bodies bursting with rage; and the great wave crested the obstacle more clearly than she had ever seen any great wave crest the parade. Only, when the fence was broken, she saw behind it something that robbed her of reason; so that she seemed to be living in all ages and all lands at once. She never could describe the vision afterward; but she always denied it was a dream. She said it was worse; it was something more real than reality. It was a line of real soldiers, which is always a magnificent sight. But they might have been the soldiers of Hannibal or of Attila, they might have been dug up from the cemeteries of Sidon and Babylon, for all Joan had to do with them. There, encamped in English meadows, with a hawthorn-tree in front of them and three beeches behind, was something that has never been in camp nearer than some leagues south of Paris, since that Carolus called The Hammer broke it backward at Tours.

There flew the green standard of that great faith and strong civilization which has so often almost entered the great cities of the West; which long encircled Vienna, which was barely barred from Paris; but which had never before been seen in arms on the soil of England. At one end of the line stood Phillip Ivywood, in a uniform of his own special creation, a compromise between the Sepoy and the Turkish uniform. The compromise worked more and more wildly in Joan's mind. If any impression remained it was merely that England had conquered India and Turkey had conquered England. Then she saw that Ivywood, for all his uniform, was not the Commander of these forces, for an old man, with a great scar on his face, which was not a European face, set himself in the front of the battle, as if it had been a battle in the old epics, and crossed swords with Patrick Dalroy. He had come to return the scar upon his forehead; and he returned it with many wounds, though at last it was he who sank under the sword thrust. He fell on his face; and Dalroy looked at him with something that is much more great than pity. Blood was flowing from Patrick's wrist and forehead, but he made a salute with his sword. As he was doing so, the corpse, as it appeared, laboriously lifted a face, with feeble eyelids. And, seeming to understand the quarters of the sky by instinct, Oman Pasha dragged himself a foot or so to the left; and fell with his face toward Mecca.

After that the turret turned round and round about Joan and she knew not whether the things she saw were history or prophecy. Something in that last fact of being crushed by the weapons of brown men and yellow, secretly entrenched in English meadows, had made the English what they had not been for centuries. The hawthorn-tree was twisted and broken, as it was at the Battle of Ashdown, when Alfred led his first charge against the Danes. The beech-trees were splashed up to their lowest branches with the mingling of brave heathen and brave Christian blood. She knew no more than that when a column of the Christian rebels, led by Humphrey of the Sign of the Ship, burst through the choked and forgotten tunnel and took the Turkish regiment in the rear, it was the end.

That violent and revolving vision became something beyond the human voice or human ear. She could not intelligently hear even the shots and shouts round the last magnificent rally of the Turks. It was natural, therefore, that she should not hear the words Lord Ivywood addressed to his next-door neighbour, a Turkish officer, or rather to himself. But his words were:

"I have gone where God has never dared to go. I am above the silly supermen as they are above mere men. Where I walk in the Heavens, no man has walked before me; and I am alone in a garden. All this passing about me is like the lonely plucking of garden flowers. I will have this blossom, I will have that."

The sentence ended so suddenly that the officer looked at him, as if expecting him to speak. But he did not speak.

But Patrick and Joan, wandering together in a world made warm and fresh again, as it can be for few in a world that calls courage frenzy and love superstition, feeling every branching tree as a friend with arms open for the man, or every sweeping slope as a great train trailing behind the woman, did one day climb up to the little white cottage that was now the home of the Superman.

He sat playing with a pale, reposeful face, with scraps of flower and weed put before him on a wooden table. He did not notice them, nor anything else around him; scarcely even Enid Wimpole, who attended to all his wants.

"He is perfectly happy," she said quietly.

Joan, with the glow on her dark face, could not prevent herself from replying, "And we are so happy."

"Yes," said Enid, "but his happiness will last," and she wept.

"I understand," said Joan, and kissed her cousin, not without tears of her own.

A Note About the Author

G.K. Chesterton (1874–1936) was an English writer, philosopher and critic known for his creative wordplay. Born in London, Chesterton attended St. Paul's School before enrolling in the Slade School of Fine Art at University College. His professional writing career began as a freelance critic where he focused on art and literature. He then ventured into fiction with his novels *The Napoleon of Notting Hill* and *The Man Who Was Thursday* as well as a series of stories featuring Father Brown.

A Note from the Publisher

Spanning many genres, from non-fiction essays to literature classics to children's books and lyric poetry, Mint Edition books showcase the master works of our time in a modern new package. The text is freshly typeset, is clean and easy to read, and features a new note about the author in each volume. Many books also include exclusive new introductory material. Every book boasts a striking new cover, which makes it as appropriate for collecting as it is for gift giving. Mint Edition books are only printed when a reader orders them, so natural resources are not wasted. We're proud that our books are never manufactured in excess and exist only in the exact quantity they need to be read and enjoyed.

Discover more of your favorite classics with Bookfinity™.

- Track your reading with custom book lists.
- Get great book recommendations for your personalized Reader Type.
- Add reviews for your favorite books.
- AND MUCH MORE!

Visit **bookfinity.com** and take the fun Reader Type quiz to get started.

Enjoy our classic and modern companion pairings!

9 781513 280530